"Get down!" Stacy's s⟨...⟩
and she braced hersel⟨...⟩
wheel to get them off ⟨...⟩
on the brake and throwing the truck in
Park, then ducked.

Stacy, her head between the seat and metal frame of the truck, kept her view on the paloverde tree. She'd seen a telltale glint.

The kind that came from the front end of a gun when the sun hit it. Almost blinding.

She'd been up against them enough to know.

As soon as she had the shot, she pushed the button to lower her window and pulled her trigger.

Mac, who'd positioned himself with dash protection without losing visibility, said, "No body fell."

"Or jumped down," she told him. She'd aimed for the trunk. There'd been no shots fired in their direction. And no way to verify if a loaded gun was pointed at them.

Could have been a hunter, out for illegal game.

She knew it wasn't.

Dear Reader,

Welcome back to Sierra's Web, where a firm of best friends, all experts in their fields, help solve crimes! *Deadly Mountain Rescue* is particularly close to me, literally! It's set in a fictitious town fashioned after the small town I live in, situated in the far east of Phoenix valley!

I sit and look at the mountains as I write, and finally, I'm up in them, too, while in this story! I've climbed to the top of the highest peak of the great Superstition Mountains, spent a lot of time in them and can promise you that everything you read here, in terms of mountain description and challenges, comes straight from those experiences. I've driven on the road mentioned in the first chapter. And have seen a car go over the side of the mountain, too.

But wait, I don't want to give too much away! Just one more little tidbit. Stacy's last name, Waltz. She's named after a famous German from these parts, Jacob Waltz. He mined in these mountains, brought out a lot of gold, but never told anyone where his mine was. People still come to our little town every year to go up in the mountains and hunt for the Lost Dutchman Mine!

As for the rest of the story...I fell in love with Jesse "Mac" MacDonald from page one. And would love to grow up to be Stacy. They have a very special bond, beyond just romantic, but it sizzles, too. I hope you enjoy spending time with them as much as I have. Happy reading!

Tara Taylor

DEADLY MOUNTAIN RESCUE

TARA TAYLOR QUINN

HARLEQUIN®
ROMANTIC SUSPENSE™

Recycling programs
for this product may
not exist in your area.

ISBN-13: 978-1-335-59399-3

Deadly Mountain Rescue

Copyright © 2024 by TTQ Books LLC

For questions and comments about the quality of this book, please contact us
at CustomerService@Harlequin.com.

TM and ® are trademarks of Harlequin Enterprises ULC.

Harlequin Enterprises ULC
22 Adelaide St. West, 41st Floor
Toronto, Ontario M5H 4E3, Canada
www.Harlequin.com

Printed in Lithuania

MIX
Paper | Supporting
responsible forestry
FSC® C021394

A *USA TODAY* bestselling author of over one hundred novels in twenty languages, **Tara Taylor Quinn** has sold more than seven million copies. Known for her intense emotional fiction, Ms. Quinn's novels have received critical acclaim in the UK and most recently from Harvard. She is the recipient of the Readers' Choice Award and has appeared often on local and national TV, including *CBS Sunday Morning*.

For TTQ offers, news and contests, visit tarataylorquinn.com!

Books by Tara Taylor Quinn

Harlequin Romantic Suspense

Sierra's Web

Tracking His Secret Child
Cold Case Sheriff
The Bounty Hunter's Baby Search
On the Run with His Bodyguard
Not Without Her Child
A Firefighter's Hidden Truth
Last Chance Investigation
Danger on the River
Deadly Mountain Rescue

The Coltons of Owl Creek

Colton Threat Unleashed

The Coltons of New York

Protecting Colton's Baby

Visit the Author Profile page
at Harlequin.com for more titles.

For Timothy Lee Barney, the man who challenged me
to climb to the top of the mountain. And who
holds my hand through every challenge we face.
I love you. Then, now and forever.

Chapter 1

"How is it possible that we grew up in the same town and I feel like I've been breathing lore and stories since I was born, and you are only half aware of a few of them?"

Saguaro Bend police corporal Jesse Macdonald listened to his partner of five years through his truck's sound system as he headed toward the gated community he called home. "I guess by the time you came up, they'd run out of interesting things to teach," he said, with a tired grin. They'd had a long night on duty—responding to three shooting calls, all unrelated, two resulting in victims being hospitalized.

But no matter how tough the shifts were, these respective drives home, the way he and Stacy always stayed on the line until they were both on their own properties, put him in a better mindset to get some rest.

"There's no way you didn't know that Geronimo ruled our mountains until the late 1880s…"

"I didn't," he admitted truthfully, while knowing full well he'd have denied knowing just to hear her exasperated reaction.

"Jesse Macdonald, you don't even try to learn!" she said, right on cue, bringing on his full smile.

"And you, Stace, need to join us here in the twenty-first century," he drawled. Words he told her often enough, but not ones he meant. Not only was Stacy the finest cop he'd ever worked with, she was also very much present in her daily life.

Aware of those around her. Aware of the world's struggles.

And deeply caring about both.

"It was a rough one tonight, huh?" Her soft tones came over the speakers, hitting him straight in the gut.

"Yeah. But, hey, we won two out of three." They'd apprehended two of the three shooters. Nothing beat that feeling. Which was why, at thirty-eight, he was still on the street. And planned to turn down the offer he'd heard was coming his way from the county sheriff's office. Just as he'd chosen not to take the lieutenant's position within the Saguaro police department.

He and Stacy had brought in more bad guys than any other duo in the state during their five years together. The invitations they received from other Arizona police departments to help with particular situations was a testament to that.

"I heard you have an offer coming in." Her words were upbeat.

He'd wondered if someone had said something to her. "You ready to take on a young pup? Bring him up?" He had to ask. At thirty, she'd proven herself. Should be moving up in the ranks, even if he chose not to do so.

"No."

He was alone in his truck. The satisfied nod, his hint of a grin, wasn't hurting anyone.

But holding her back would.

"You know, whenever you're ready, I'll support you completely."

Turning onto the short drive leading into his community, he slowed as he approached the gate, waited for the sensor to read the chip in his windshield and allow him access.

He'd drive around the neighborhood. Do a quick check. And by then Stacy would be home as well. Just outside city limits, on the desert property willed to her by her grandfather.

The smart, athletic brunette had been living there alone since her husband's death seven years before.

When she didn't respond, his gut sank. She *was* ready. And he would do everything in his power to make the transition easy for her. "Stace?" The present was as good a time as any to take the first step of the breakup. Admitting that it was time for her.

Helping her feel good about moving on. Joining in her anticipation of a new phase in her career—her life.

When she still didn't answer, he pushed again. "Stacy, it's okay…"

"What? Oh… Sorry, Mac. For a minute there, I thought someone was following me. But when I turned to take the long way home, just to be sure, they sped right on by…" Her tone was off.

Senses honed, Mac sat up straight. "Following you? For how long? What kind of vehicle?"

"Headlights higher than mine. Could still be an SUV. Maybe a truck. Dark. I couldn't really tell. Brights were on."

Driving in the desert in the dark, the high beam lights were a must. It needed to happen for safe driving. Javelina, coyotes, other animals hunted at night. But coming up behind someone?

"Head back to town," he said. "I'll meet you at Rich's."

An all-night diner they frequented not far from the station.

"No need." Stacy's voice came over the system, sounding more like herself. "I'm a big girl, Mac. And I'm fine."

He heard the warning tone. She was a damned good cop. Didn't need looking after.

And he didn't blame her. With her big brown eyes and long dark hair, she gained some attention. And there were still those who thought of women as needing protection.

Because some did.

Which made it hard for Stacy to hold her own sometimes.

"I know how to lose a tail," she said then, and he heard the irritation in her tone.

"No one's completely immune," he replied. Still not liking those bright lights. "We're human."

"And if I was worried, I'd be the first one to ask for help."

He knew that, too. One of the reasons they were such a good team was because they each brought something different to the page. And they talked things through, always.

"I don't like the brights on, coming up on your tail."

"Yeah, that's what triggered me to begin with. But the vehicle backed off. I made my turns, watched the response. I'm guessing the dude just forgot he had them on."

It happened.

"Whoa!" A hiss followed the exclamation.

"Stacy!" Foot immediately on the brake, Mac met his seat belt with some force as he made a U-turn on a street not made for one.

"Yeah, wow. I need some sleep. I almost clipped a van. Had to swerve to miss it."

"I'm on my way."

"Don't be ridiculous," she said then. "I'm serious, Mac. I'm half a mile from home. I'm going in and going to bed and if you show up, I'm not only not opening my door, I'll be royally pissed."

"Just tell me this…is there any possibility that the van is the same vehicle that was behind you earlier?"

"No. A van's skinnier than a truck or full-size SUV,

lower to the ground. Now quit demeaning me and go to bed."

"I'd hope you'd do the same for me, if your radar was on alert." He wasn't in a joking mood all of a sudden.

"Of course I would. You trust me with your life, right?"

"Implicitly."

"Then trust me with mine."

Right. "Point taken." They were both tired. And had seen more than the usual amount of abhorrent behavior that night.

"I'm turning into my place now," she told him. "And Mac?"

"Yeah?"

"Whenever I'm ready to move on, you'll be the first to know."

Hanging up from her partner as she waited for her automatic garage door to open, Stacy Waltz couldn't imagine a life that would be better than being Mac's partner. Which was why, every time she heard about an offer coming his way, she panicked a little bit.

That's what had caused her little bout of paranoia on the drive home—the pending promotion she'd heard about before their shift started the previous night. She'd waited all night for him to mention it. And when he hadn't, she'd had to bring it up.

A truck with headlights didn't scare her.

Losing Mac as a partner did.

Maybe not a healthy realization, overall. But understandable. They were great together.

Garage door up, she slowly moved her red SUV inside. In some ways, her years with Mac were the best of her life.

Hard to believe they'd been born and raised in the same

town, but she hadn't met him until after the worst days of her life. Joining the force after she'd lost Brett had been the only thing that kept her going. The first person she'd met, on her first official day of duty, had been Jesse Macdonald.

Shaking off the night, and the drive home, Stacy pushed the button to close her garage door and unlocked her glove box, grabbed her small clutch purse, and opened her driver's door with a promise to herself to branch out and spend off duty time with some of the other officers who were always inviting her to do things with them. She went occasionally. It was time to go more.

Just so she'd be prepared when Mac did get an offer he couldn't refuse.

As she well knew, nothing lasted forever…

What was that?

A shuffle on the pavement behind her vehicle?

Desert roof rats again? She hadn't checked the live trap before work.

Shaking her head, she was debating whether to do so before getting some rest. She made a move toward the door into the house and heard the garage door start to go up again.

Startled, she spun around.

A strong arm wrapped around both of hers.

Pulling her back against a much bigger body.

Even as she was shoving her elbows into abs of steel, she felt the prick. Saw a gloved hand pulling a syringe away from her arm, removing a long needle that had pierced her uniform sleeve.

She threw a heel back and straight up. Caught him right in the crotch.

A wave of sickness spread over her.

She had to puke.

Was dizzy.

Couldn't let herself lose consciousness.

Arms snaked beneath her knees, around her back. Lifting her.

She had to fight it. To be aware.

She kicked out. Hard. With both feet. Flailed her arms.

Her captor didn't let go.

Take note of every clue.

The cowboy boots on her garage floor.

No voices.

Her head swam more with every step.

The back of her SUV, open.

She was dropped to the carpet. Her time to escape. Legs…wouldn't move. She had to kick. Nothing happened.

Ropes wrapped around ankles. Pulled tight.

Arms jerked behind her, shoulders on fire.

Mac home in bed.

And then…nothing.

Chapter 2

Mac didn't go to bed. Those bright headlights were bothering him. He'd learned long ago to trust the tingling in his spine. Someone forgetting to turn off their high beams would surely have noticed when the blinding brightness reflected back at them from Stacy's shiny steel bumper. They'd have been nearly blinded.

Unless the driver had planned to follow a cop...hadn't wanted to be identified.

Still in his truck, he was backing out of his garage, and headed to Stacy's without a second thought.

She'd never have to know.

He'd drive by, see the lights on in her house and go home to bed.

One thing he knew about Stacy, at least the Stacy who'd come out of her husband's tragic death and joined the Saguaro police force, was that she was a creature of habit. She never went right to bed after a shift. She got changed, and then sat up and watched at least one episode of a sitcom.

There'd still be lights on at her house.

He just had to see the lights.

He repeated the words to himself all the way out of town, while he paid attention to every inch of ground he covered.

He just had to see the lights.

There were no lights.

Struck with panic, Mac quickly shut it down as he pulled into Stacy's drive. Grabbed his gun and went around the side of the house. To the back, the other side, and then, gun still in hand, watching his back, he strode toward the keypad outside her garage door.

Punched in the code.

Heard the hum of the garage motor, waited for it to rise enough for him to bend down and see inside.

And had his radio out before he'd straightened up.

"Possible officer in danger," he bit out. "Repeat, possible officer in danger." He quickly rattled off Stacy's address. And his phone rang.

It wasn't Stacy. Declining the call from their lieutenant without picking up, he dialed Stacy instead. The phone rang. Six times. And went to voice mail.

"Stacy, it's Mac. Call me, dammit."

She could be out. Might have had a hot date for the morning. Their sex lives, dating lives, were the one thing they didn't talk about.

What if she'd hooked up with a psycho?

They were going to amend their "no date" talk policy the second they were back together.

Jim Stahl, their lieutenant, was calling in a second time as Mac left his message.

Needing all the hands on deck he could get, Mac picked up.

In and out of consciousness, Stacy twisted her head, pulled her arms as far as she could to the side behind her and glanced at her watch. The lighted digital readout gave her a focal point. Half an hour had passed. She was pretty sure they'd been driving the entire time.

Driving in circles?

There'd been turns.

But not full ones. That she was aware of.

No streetlights at all.

Driving up the mountain was more like it. The crude road known as The Trail—which led from Saguaro Bend to a mining town on the other side of the mountain sixty miles away—was only half a mile from Stacy's property.

Judging by the bumps and the less than stellar condition of the road, they weren't on the newer highway just south of the trail that also went east, to the other side of the Clairvoyant Mountain range.

Keeping her fingers busy, she alternated between working the ropes binding her and pinching herself the only places she could reach. Her butt. Her hips. She had to keep herself awake. Aware.

Active at all times.

And quiet.

Only one door had opened before they'd pulled out of her garage. The car had dipped with the weight of one entry, and the door had immediately slammed shut. One captor.

Her key fob was in her front breast pocket.

Wasn't it?

Rolling, she tried to feel the push of plastic against her breast.

It wasn't there.

Staring at her breast, waiting for another turn, flashes of moon to illuminate her jail, she saw the unbuttoned shirt pocket and her stomach sank.

He'd taken her fob without her knowing. Had touched her breast.

What else was she unaware of?

What other clues had she missed?

And what was he planning to do with her when he reached his destination?

* * *

While he was still on the phone with Jim, relaying what he knew about the bright lights behind Stacy on her way home and the van that she'd nearly hit, Mac let himself into Stacy's house. Went from room to room, smelling her scent, trying not to notice the personal things that they didn't share with each other. Like...all of it.

They were work partners. They knew where each other lived. Knew how to access each other's houses in case of emergency.

But they'd never actually been inside each other's homes.

Her comforter was untouched. Gold and maroon.

She made her bed. There were throw pillows on it.

As he walked through, noting everything he could, he tried her cell again, his jaw tightening as it went straight to voice mail.

Stahl was already having someone put a trace on her number.

The entire place—two spare bedrooms, one set up as an office, both bathrooms, living room, kitchen, dining area—all spotless. Not a single sign that she'd been in it since she left that morning.

Sirens sounded, and he ran outside to meet his work mates. Fourteen out of the twenty Saguaro officers and detectives were either there or arriving—some in uniform, many still in plain clothes—with weapons on. Along with both lieutenants, all three sergeants and Chief Benson. One of their own was in trouble.

The sight relieved him. They'd find her.

And tightened every nerve in his body with fear. All of them there. A fact that indicated that she was in serious trouble.

As he was heading out to the team meeting he knew

would be forthcoming in seconds, Mac stopped, his gut sinking. "Chief," he called, knowing everyone else would follow. He couldn't take his gaze off the indentation in the hard desert earth just to the side of the end of Stacy's drive. "Someone was here and left in a hurry," he said. Tire marks wouldn't show. Someone burning rubber did. "The tire width is too large to be hers," he said, stating the facts he knew.

He'd been with Stacy when she'd bought the new tires on her SUV. He'd picked her up when she'd dropped off her vehicle.

"So are we thinking she was forced to drive her own car someplace?" Stahl asked.

It looked that way. But forced how? And why hadn't she called him?

Unless someone had been in the car with her, holding a gun on her—

"It's too early to know what we're thinking," the chief interrupted Mac's thoughts before they spiraled in a direction that was not going to help. "Let's split up. In twos. I want eight of you on foot, on her land, and surrounding acres as well. The rest get out there. Let's find her and bring her home safe."

Mac didn't have his "two" to jump in the passenger seat of his truck as he ran toward it. No one mentioned the lack. Or offered to drive with him. "Macdonald!" Chief Benson's voice came from not far behind him.

He stopped. If the chief thought he was going to keep Mac back…

"Her phone's not pinging," the older man said, his face looking more concerned than Mac had ever seen it. Which put another rock in Mac's gut. He'd known the man his entire life. Benson was a friend of Mac's father. Had sided with his dad during his parents' rancorous divorce.

"It rang the first time I called it," he said, his voice, his look, urgent. *Do better.* He wanted to bite out the command.

The man nodded. "And pinged off a local tower. Now it's not."

He stopped breathing. Stared. "You think she's close."

"You know her best since Brett was killed. What do you think?"

"I think if she's nearby, she'll be okay." He said the first thing that came to mind. But wasn't sure if he was talking like the respected, decorated cop he was, or just a desperate man trying to reassure himself.

Almost an hour had passed since she'd pulled into her garage. Dawn was breaking fast. She could see rock walls whizzing past.

Wherever he was taking her, it was remote.

Would make it harder for anyone to find her. The Clairvoyant Mountain range encompassed nearly two hundred thousand acres. Had she just dreamed that?

She was drifting in and out.

Anxiety, thank God, had left her.

She had to think.

To plan.

There were flares.

She loved the mountains. Had climbed to the top of the highest peak in the Clairvoyants once. With Brett. Or Mac?

Flares.

Inner sidewall storage. Driver's side. Above back wheel.

Plastic embedded knob to turn.

She was playing tag in the street with the neighbor kids. Brett ran fast. Caught her. She squealed.

He laughed.

Her shoulders screamed with pain. Bumps in the road.

Had to use her foot to turn knob. Get flares.

Couldn't let it show in the rearview mirror.

Shoes up. No good. Use rope.

Sweat. In eyes. Burning.

Couldn't close. Couldn't sleep.

Flares.

Flares.

Rope. Use rope. Angle foot.

Rope hooked. Push.

She didn't have a momma like the other kids. Her momma died. But she had the best daddy.

Your mom and I...we loved each other so much. And that love made you little belle of mine.

The flare. The rope had worked. She could see the flare.

Couldn't she?

Brett, can I see?

Our love was so strong because we grew up together. Knew each other our whole lives. We knew the good and the bad, too. Shared all the important memories. There were no ugly surprises, just more love, every single day.

The toes of her shoes. They had to be grabbers. Like tongs.

She liked that. Toes as tongs.

Alliteration.

And home. Tongs on the stove.

She put her shoes on at home.

Home. Mac.

No, Brett. No Brett.

Blood everywhere. Right in front of her.

No! A whimper? Hers?

Waking her up. Wake up!

The flare.

A plan.

Toes together. More sweat. She got it!

Rolled to her belly, bent her legs back, dropped the flare. Rolled to her side, her back to the flare.

Grabbed it.

Gotcha!

Abigail. Best puppy. Daddy brought her home. Called it gotcha day!

Puppy licks on her nose in the morning.

Wake up!

Flare, be ready. Flare in one hand. Other hand on cap.

The sun was shining through the car's window. Too hot.

She and Brett. Water. The sand. Honeymoon.

Slowing down.

Wake up!

Sleep felt so good.

Bumpity bump bump.

Wake up!

Stopping! Roll on back! Hide flare!

Feet toward hatch. Open.

Kick!

Body slam.

None of it mattered. He was bigger than her. Giant-sized. He took her hits. Overpowered her.

He was pulling her. Her hair caught.

She tried to fight. Was thrown over a shoulder. Hung there.

She might die.

Mac would never forgive himself.

Mac. She unscrewed the cap. Tossed the flare.

Saw a vehicle up ahead. In front of hers. Mountain car. There to rescue her?

Or was she just imagining it? Did she see it with her eyes opened or closed?

Her captor, facing forward, walking…did he know?

He plopped her down.

Oh! She was sitting in her own driver's seat. Was he going to…

With eyes barely able to focus, she tried to assess her dash. Was there enough gas?

His hand brushed her breast.

Oh God, no.

The seat belt came over her chest. Hand at her thigh.

Click. Belt locked in place.

She had to keep her eyes open.

Ropes.

No way to put her hands on the wheel.

Or push the pedals.

Open your eyes! Was that Mac telling her? No, Mac was home. She'd said she was fine.

She wasn't fine.

As she felt the car start to move, Stacy opened her eyes.

Saw the vast openness of space in front of her. Felt like she was floating.

Some part of her vaguely realized that she was going over the side of a mountain.

And pretended Mac was going to catch her.

Just like her daddy had always done when she was little.

Chapter 3

He'd made a mistake. Listening to Stacy's personal need to take care of herself, to protect herself, rather than his own instincts. He was a cop. Her professional partner. Not a personal one.

As Mac ran to his truck, got in and started driving, he prayed to whatever fates might hear him that his own lapse hadn't cost Stacy her life.

Shift fatigue gone with the sunrise, he scoured every inch of roadway between town and Stacy's place, and then past her place. Running cases through his head the entire time with one thought in mind. Who, of all the people they'd taken down, had run-ins with or generally made enemies of, would want Stacy, but not him?

Why just her?

Who would know what shift she was working? And where she lived?

If he could find the kidnapper, assuming there was one, he'd find her. It was basic cop work.

Tuning the police radio in his truck to the private channel the chief had designated, listening to every one of his fellow offercer's reports of places searched and found empty, he grew more and more focused.

Focused like a crazed being with only one goal.

He would not rest, would not stop until she was found.

And if she was hurt, God help whoever had harmed her.

When he'd exhausted the miles around Stacy's acreage, including knocking on doors and getting neighboring property owners out of bed, or talking to the early risers as the case was, he turned to what locals called The Trail. A sometimes one lane, partially paved road over the mountain.

Without any idea of who'd taken her, or why, he had to think like a kidnapper. He'd want all traces of evidence gone forever. Three hundred twelve miles of rugged, desert-covered mountain with cliffs that dropped off more than a mile down sheer rock face to boulders below. The minimal chance of covering all that inaccessible ground made the area a great dumping area for something one didn't want found.

Ever.

And something else was bothering him. Those tire marks at the end of Stacy's driveway. They'd been wide, but that didn't mean high. Maybe it wasn't Bright Lights who'd gotten to her. Maybe, like she'd said, the driver of that vehicle had been lax in turning off his brights. Not a danger to her. She had finely honed cop instincts, too. Her captor could have been someone lying in wait for her to get home. Not on the road, where she, a trained cop, would notice. But an off-road vehicle sitting in the dark in the desert…

Radioing in to have everyone on the lookout for a four-wheeler, he let those who'd been assigned up the mountain know that he was joining them and took the miles up the trail an inch at a time, looking for anything that might speak Stacy to him.

Where am I? Stacy came to with a sense of unreality. As though she'd been transported to a new dimension. One where people lived in clouds made of cotton.

When she tried to move, to ease the burning pain in her shoulders by bringing her hands around, nothing moved. Her muscles were clenching, but nothing more. Bands on her hands. Band on her body.

What universe was she in? Did she need to fight?

Lifting her feet to kick out, she felt her entire world rock precariously. The seat beneath her. The pillow upon which her face had been lying.

And knew she had to rest some more.

No one had found Stacy's SUV. Her clutch purse. Her phone. Anything to give any hint as to where she might be.

An hour into the search for her, then two, Mac was beginning to hope that she was off somewhere on some clandestine date—maybe in Phoenix, in a snazzy hotel room. He'd happily pay out of his own pocket for all the overtime being spent to search for her if he knew she was safe.

She hadn't been in her home. Hadn't changed out of her uniform. There hadn't been a dirty one in the washer or in the laundry basket he'd seen in her bedroom.

Maybe the guy had a thing for women dressed in cop uniforms and she'd gone straight from work, only telling Mac that she was on her way home. That she'd arrived there.

But then, why tell him about Bright Lights?

Or the van she'd nearly hit?

On the radio again, he asked the chief to have someone check vehicle ownership of every one of Stacy's neighbors, looking for a van. Just to be sure that Stacy's near miss had really been just that.

He asked for a check on all local businesses open to the public at six in the morning, too. Surveillance tapes at the grocery store, all gas stations, Rich's…just in case she'd decided, after she'd hung up with him, after she'd reached home, that she wanted something she didn't have.

The granola bars with chocolate on top that she loved.

Or something else with milk chocolate.

It would be just like her to turn around, go back to town and take care of her craving. That was Stacy, self-sufficient and willing to do whatever worked, put forth whatever effort necessary to take care of any issue in front of her. Rather than let it hang there, in the background, unresolved.

But she'd never have gone without her phone.

Or turned off her phone.

It *could* have run out of battery.

But only if the battery was failing. Something she'd have noticed and taken care of immediately.

He also called in a list of names—the ones that were most prominent in his mind—of past cases to look into. Benson and Stahl already had detectives and their two tech people looking into all his and Stacy's cases. Checking them against jail and prison release records.

Looking for any evidence that someone who might have moved out of state had come back.

And they were looking into her credit card usage, too. Had gained access to account information from the office in her home.

She'd hate that.

"Have you notified her father?" he asked the chief on a private channel. Benson and Mac's father had been in high school when Stacy's father was in grade school, but pretty much everyone in town knew the man. An Army Ranger, one who'd made the news for his heroism, had lost his wife, a Waltz, in childbirth—the day Stacy was born. He'd given up his career to stay home and raise his baby girl.

And when Stacy was grown and married, settling down

on her grandfather's property, Adam Sorenson had joined the Peace Corps and had been stationed overseas ever since.

"Not yet," the chief said. That was it, nothing more.

But Mac heard the rest, with lead in his gut. They didn't know if they were giving a missing person report or preparing a death notice.

As he drove, Mac passed parked police vehicles in the various pull-offs along the trail. And he heard reports come in after searches of areas were complete. He wasn't focusing on those areas. He was looking along the parts of the road where most people would not stop. Areas where, if he stopped, no one would be able to pass him. As the morning wore on, there was traffic on the road, making his check points more difficult to maneuver. But he still made them.

Finding absolutely nothing.

Growing tenser by the minute, he wondered if he was in the wrong place. Benson had put a call into the Phoenix police, and they were sending a helicopter up to search the area. An expense, with no evidence that Stacy was even in the vicinity.

Or officially missing.

She'd been gone four hours. An eternity to Mac.

But not even enough to report to the police in normal circumstances. If Stacy was a civilian who simply hadn't returned home as expected, her family would either need evidence of bizarre behavior, or wait another twenty hours before police would even put out a report.

For good reason.

Some people didn't return home on purpose. And couldn't be hunted because of it.

But Stacy wasn't people.

She was a cop who'd arrested two shooters that night alone.

A woman who put her life in danger every single day she went to work.

She was predictable. Dependable. Set in her ways. Not one who'd just disappear without telling someone or keeping her phone on.

She was also his partner.

They had to find her.

Why in the hell am I sleeping sitting up?

Stacy came to, thinking her upper arms and shoulders hurt so badly because she'd fallen asleep in a chair in her living room.

She didn't ever sit in that chair.

Her spot was the right end recliner on the couch.

And her pillow stunk.

Opening her eyes, she was still kind of floating in a sense of 'everything was going to be okay'. Until she noticed that her pillow didn't have a case. That it wasn't a pillow at all.

Her head was resting on an airbag.

Fear shot through her.

She'd been in an accident? Her fault?

Was anyone else hurt?

Raising her head slowly, not sure how badly she was hurt, she felt her SUV rock. Forward and back. Fear shot through her.

And bits of a nightmare surfaced. She'd been in the back of her vehicle. Bound.

She'd hit her head. Had a nightmare.

Was she still having it? Was she asleep dreaming that she was awake?

Pulling her arms, feeling the band cut into her wrists as she did so, she glanced around the airbag to see where she was.

Felt another rock. A bit of a slip with every little movement.

Saw the vast sea of nothingness in front of her.

And started to scream.

Climbing up a steep hill, slowing his truck as the road veered right to the edge of the mountain, Mac approached the curve up ahead with caution, not allowing himself to imagine the terror that could take place in the location. Just like he'd been doing all morning.

As he scanned the landscape his gut tensed, and he breathed a sigh of relief as he saw nothing. No sign that anyone had been out of a vehicle. No sign of a skirmish or trouble.

But then, if a crime had taken place on the pavement, how would he know?

A flash of red caught his eye just as he was about to turn into the curve. A dot of color in a bushel of sagebrush.

He stopped. Put on his flashers. Pulled out his police bubble and as he quickly exited, put the flashing light on the top of his truck. Stopping at that point, a one-lane road around a curve, was ludicrous. Anyone could come barreling around the bend and...

He ran to the color. Two seconds was all he needed.

Probably just a piece of desert flower blown and caught by the heartier plant...

It wasn't a flower.

It was a flare. The kind Stacy kept in her vehicle.

Reaching in, he pulled out the abandoned warning symbol.

And he knew.

Grew instantly cold.

And analytical.

The cap had been turned, but not far enough. As though someone had tried but couldn't complete the job.

Stacy.

On his radio, he put out the call. He needed another vehicle up on the road as soon as possible. They had to block the curve from both sides, where drivers would have a chance to pull off and stop safely. On one side, they could even turn around.

Backing his truck down, he blocked the road coming up the trail from Saguaro. Heard Miguel, a seasoned officer who had also grown up in Saguaro Bend, say he'd turned around and was five minutes out from blocking on the other side.

Miguel had gone to school with Stacy. One year ahead. He'd attended Stacy and Brett's wedding.

Thoughts surfaced. Facts only.

Nothing else.

Mac walked the area, his entire being a state of rock-hard ice, no feeling, thinking only about his next step as a cop on a case. Down to where Miguel would park.

Tire tracks.

He spotted them right as he heard his fellow officer, accompanied by Martha Mitchell, one of the oldest cops on the force, approach in their cruiser.

Pulled up against the mountainside on the opposite side of the road was a track identical to the one he'd seen in Stacy's yard. Snapping a photo, he opened it in his image and photo compare app, pulled up the one he'd taken early that morning, and confirmed what his gut already knew.

Standing straight, tall, he walked toward the curve, specifically to the place where something would go straight out and over the mile drop-off had it missed the turn.

He heard Miguel and Martha call out to him. Knew they were approaching.

He didn't respond. Just kept walking.

He would be the one. He'd do it.

For her.

Reaching the edge of the mountain drop-off, Mac forced himself to look over.

"Oh God, NOOOOO!" The sound tore out of him. Burned his throat. As, hands to forehead, burying his face in his arms, he dropped to his knees.

Chapter 4

*T*hink, man.

The second his knees hit hard ground, Mac's mind went into high gear. So high up that there was no feeling.

Just numb determination. There was no mistaking Stacy's red SUV.

He had to get to the vehicle.

There was a chance it had gone over empty.

That someone had pushed it off the cliff to make them think that Stacy was gone.

That someone had her for information. Or other things that it didn't behoove him to think about.

That she still needed rescuing.

"It's wedged between two rocks," he heard Miguel say, and turned to see his fellow officer on the radio he wore on his belt.

"Fifty yards down," Mac said. "Sheer rock face." Clarity came as he worked, and he grabbed the radio. "Chief Benson, it's Mac," he said, waiting to hear the man acknowledge that he was on the channel.

"I'm here."

"We need Luke Dennison from Sierra's Web if we're going to save her, sir."

"That hotshot firefighter case we helped on?"

"Yes. He's an expert in mountain rescue. Tell him the vehicle is wedged, but only from just in front of the back tires. A move from the inside, in the wrong direction, will have it rolling down the mountain, front end first."

"I'm making the call now."

Mac handed the radio back to his fellow officer. Felt both of his peers watching him. And didn't make eye contact with either one of them.

"I'm going down," he said.

"Mac! No!" Martha spoke first.

"No way, man, you said it yourself, one tip of that SUV and…"

"I'm not going to touch the vehicle," he gritted out between clenched teeth. "If she's in there. And alive, she needs to know what she's up against. Not to move. To know that we're on it. And just to hold on."

She might not be in the SUV. He wanted to hope that she wasn't.

But why trash her vehicle if, ultimately, she wasn't going to die as well? Why destroy a vehicle if you didn't want people to think the person driving it was dead?

He *knew*.

There was no stopping him.

If there was any chance his partner was alive, he was going to keep her that way.

Or die trying.

Clarity returned slowly. And with it, came a stab of fear.

Feeling groggy—like the time she'd woken up in the dentist's chair after having her wisdom teeth pulled, only worse—Stacy tried to figure out what to do.

She had no phone.

Was afraid to move again. Scared about what could happen if the car rocked another time.

Looking out the windows on either side of her, she saw nothing but a lot of space between her and surrounding mountainside even on the farthest horizon. Same as she'd seen in the brief glimpse out front.

The rearview mirror was her only source of hope. Showing her she had solid rock at her back. Not just air. Keeping her gaze there as much as she could, she took comfort from the airbag she'd purposely left in place. Letting it cushion her chest, as though guarding her spirit, come what may.

And the odd calm came over her again. She was powerless. Had no more control. Whatever was going to happen was going to happen.

Mac wouldn't be missing her until shift time. He'd be heading to bed. Unlike her, when they worked night shifts, he liked to have his off time after work and before bed, getting up to go to work, where she went to bed shortly after shift, and took care of her personal life before heading in to work. His day was from six in the morning until sometime early afternoon. Hers was from early afternoon until nine when she had to get ready for work. Only when they were on night shift.

He came to work freshly showered. Always smelling like pine. She came to work hours after she'd showered, done her hair and makeup. No reason to have a fresh face to take on criminals. And her hair had to be pulled back when she worked.

The thought brought her back to a sense of self. Oh God. Was she going to die? She wasn't ready. Had too much to live for. She had to do something. *Think, woman, think!* Panic flared so sharply she felt dizzy with it.

And then just felt dizzy.

She had to face the fact that she was probably going to die. Her father would be devastated.

Mac would blame himself, though the fault was in no way his. She was the one who'd practically shamed him for being concerned.

And her? She sat there, the same woman she'd been when she'd pulled into her garage. Weirdly calm again. Shouldn't she be seeing angels or something?

Had Brett known, before he went, that it was coming? In that split second before the deadly right hook had caught him in the temple?

She'd have thought there'd be a connection with her deceased husband. Feel him reaching out for her. Coming to get her.

Comforting her at the very least.

All she felt was the hard thump of her heart pounding against her chest, a head that felt twice its size and full of pressure, and—as tears filled her eyes, slowly trickling down her cheeks—a longing for one more look at Mac's face.

He could slide down the rock face. It would be the quickest way. With the least chance of success. He wasn't going to do Stacy any good if he was dead.

To the left, on the driver's side of her vehicle, was a patch of rock and boulders, with some growth interspersed among them. A strip of land not washed smooth through the years—a strip the water didn't stream down when the snow melted.

Sitting on the edge of the cliff, with the two officers at his back—Martha asking him to reconsider, to at least wait until they could get a harness on him—he pushed off with his hands and lowered himself until his foot touched rock.

Steadied. Tested his weight. Finding the rock solid enough to hold him, he let go of the ledge.

"Radio for a harness for me," he called up. No point in being reckless. He could use the help climbing back to the surface. Most particularly if he had something to carry.

Any belongings Stacy might want from her car before it crashed into oblivion.

Unless the SUV was teetering, ready to go over, he wasn't going near it. Luke Dennison was the expert. If there was a chance of getting Stacy out safely, the hotshot firefighter would do it. And if there wasn't a chance—knowing Luke, he'd make one.

As he slowly lowered himself down, Mac kept the SUV in his peripheral vision, focusing on his own safety, and corralling his fears for Stacy's life so he could do his job effectively. He thought about the families Luke had saved from a small mountain town surrounded by fire a while back. Dennison had been the only one who'd been able to get into the town and had managed to have everyone lifted out safely.

Mac took another successful step. Rock to rock, testing every surface before putting any weight on it. Every stone, every boulder, could roll at any second. All he had to do was look down to see how many of them had already met that fate. Signs on the road above warned about falling rock.

As he had the thought, his right foot slid out from underneath him. Almost like he'd fated it to happen. He heard the rain of stones plunging down the hill even as he wrapped his arms around a boulder and held on.

"Come on, man," Miguel's voice called from above. "Wait for help."

He couldn't wait. If Stacy was hurt, on the brink of death… he had to be there. To let her know that help was coming.

To let her know she wasn't alone.

How he was going to get her attention if she was lying in the back of her vehicle, maybe even unconscious, was what he needed to be thinking about.

Not death.

Assuming she was even in the car. The hope that she wasn't presented again.

And if she wasn't down there, he was wasting time not finding out where she was.

It was possible that whoever had kidnapped her was still in the car with her. That the SUV over the cliff had been the result of traveling too fast to get away and missing the turn.

It was the tire tracks up above—like the ones in her yard—that told him otherwise. There'd been a getaway vehicle.

He slid again. Scraped his entire left forearm. Saw the raw skin, the bits of blood. Couldn't care less.

His gut knew what he was facing.

That SUV wedged on two boulders had not been the intent. Stacy was supposed to have hurtled, in her vehicle, more than a mile down to crash against the dry rock bed of what used to be a creek. Or maybe even a river, centuries before.

Someone had wanted her death assured.

But to have it look like an accident.

He had to save her first.

And to that end, started calling her name with every forward movement he made.

If she moved, the SUV was going to tumble down the mountain.

If she didn't, she'd starve to death. If she didn't die of dehydration, first.

She had a choice. Go quickly.

Or take it slow.

She could yell until she had no voice. No one would hear her.

And she didn't want to rock the unsteady vehicle.

Which meant she'd made her choice.

The last one available to her.

She wasn't going to go quickly.

Laying her head back against the headrest, she closed her eyes. Accepted that she was powerless to move, but that didn't mean she had to give up.

Or waste her last hours.

She could spend them reliving every good moment she'd had. Remembering all the good stuff.

With no earthly barriers left, no years ahead to protect, she could go imagining what it would be like to have sex with Jesse Macdonald.

Over and over and over again.

She could, so she did. And got so good at it, she even started to hear his voice, calling her name out every time they climaxed together.

He'd made it down as far as he could. A good ten yards to the left of the back of the vehicle, which was where he'd figured Stacy to be. Had radioed up that he was fine. Had heard back that Dennison was on his way. As were a couple of rescue helicopters.

As soon as Dennison got Stacy out of the vehicle, they'd be able to get her safely extracted from the mountain range and winging off to full medical care.

The plan was working.

If she was in the vehicle.

Made the most sense. Tie her up. Shove the car over the cliff.

Hands cupping his mouth, he'd given every ounce of himself into his repeated calls. "Stacy!"

Just her name. His voice.

Over and over.

"Stacy!" he called again, same urgency in his tone, uncaring of the rawness in his throat. He'd been hollering to her for more than half an hour.

There'd been no answer. He'd expected that. He just needed her to hear him. And to pay attention. It had to be enough to keep her hanging on.

So he stood there. Aching in every part of his being. Calling out to her.

And continued to do so, somewhat to keep his heart out of his throat, after Luke Dennison arrived, rappelled down, assessed and started calling up orders.

Stopping only when the man made his way over to Mac.

Because fear constricted his airway. He didn't want to know.

Wasn't ready to let go.

He had to keep hanging on to her.

"She's in there," the man said straight off. "Front seat."

Mac nodded. Appreciating the other man's no-nonsense approach. Luke had a reputation for being a man of few pleasantries. He was all about getting the job done.

Which was all Mac needed from him.

Front seat.

Whoever had taken her wanted it to look like an accident.

Or worse, a suicide.

"Airbag deployed."

And it hit him. "If she's still in the seat, she was belted."

"Right. Boulders holding her are solid, but the SUV is only slightly caught up."

Meaning it could go with any breeze. *Would* go soon. Mac had already figured that much. He nodded.

Was she breathing?

He didn't ask. It couldn't matter at the moment. They had to get her out of there before the vehicle went over.

"She's head back, eyes closed."

Jaw tight, swallowing with difficulty, he nodded again.

"I didn't detect blood."

Good. Good news. He kept staring at the SUV, was thankful for the sun glinting off the metal, even as he considered heat exhaustion.

January temperatures wouldn't reach more than seventy, but in a dark car, with no air, and Arizona sun, it could still happen.

They'd have her out before then.

One way or the other.

Dennison continued to talk to him in staccato bits and pieces, his eye on the scene in front of them at all times. The expert was waiting on equipment and manpower. He'd sent for members of his hotshot team. The plan was for a group of them to rappel down and do what they could to stabilize the SUV before lowering a claw to attach to the roof to pull the vehicle up and out.

Then suddenly, while they both watched, the red vehicle started to move. A forward slip. Just an inch or so, but Mac held his breath.

Steady. Steady. Steady.

Dennison rechecked the clasp on his harness. "I'm going over."

"I'm coming with you. You shore up one side, the other could give way." It didn't take an expert to see that much.

Pulling a second harness out of his backpack, Dennison tossed it to him, told him to put it on, while he unhitched a second rope coming down the mountain from his anchor system, separated it from his own and handed it to Mac.

"You ever rappel before?"

"A couple of times."

The man didn't look pleased. Mac didn't much care.

Following orders explicitly, he made it to the back left bumper of the vehicle, refusing to allow himself to glance toward the front. Seeing Stacy, in any form, would be a distraction he couldn't afford.

He continued to move as he was told, hold, lift, pull, settle, as he and Dennison got the SUV tires braced as well as they could until his team arrived.

After that, Mac stayed back, ready if his help was needed, but out of the way so that the trained professionals could do their jobs as quickly and efficiently as possible.

Jacks were produced, locked into the mountainside, and then up to the SUV, to steady it. And finally, after an agonizing hour, Dennison faced the mountain, his feet braced, leaned back into his harness and opened the car door.

Long seconds later, Mac heard, "She's alive."

And, staring at that open driver's door, swallowed as his eyes filled.

Chapter 5

Mac wasn't there.

"Stacy, can you hear me?" She heard the voice again but wasn't ready to answer. To open her eyes. She didn't want the dream to end.

"Officer Waltz."

She opened her eyes. Saw the concerned vivid blue eyes, short sandy blond hair and shoulders of an uber fit man leaning over her. "Luke Dennison?" Her throat hurt as she spoke. She couldn't cough.

The movement would kill her.

But why had the hotshot fireman she and Mac had helped the previous year suddenly appeared in her dreams?

She'd been happier hearing Mac's voice.

She blinked. And jerked upright. Or would have if not for the hand holding her upper chest gently in place. "We don't know what kind of injuries you've sustained," the man said.

"We?" Moving just her eyes, she glanced around her. Noticed harnessed bodies around the parts of her SUV she could see. "I'm being rescued?"

She couldn't comprehend…couldn't believe…until she heard the loud whirring of a helicopter moving closer and closer. A sound she recognized from car accident evacuations. Critical shooting victims. It was a care flight.

"I'm being rescued," she said then, tears filling her eyes. "Oh my God, I'm being rescued."

But Mac wasn't there.

He'd just been in her dreams.

Mac waited until the stretcher carrying Stacy was loaded into the helicopter. He heard it whirring away before getting himself back up the mountainside.

He had work to do.

"Make sure someone's there to meet the copter," speaking into his radio, he bit the words out. He paused, hanging off the mountainside, as another thought occurred to him. "Someone wants her dead. She needs round-the-clock protection."

"Chief's already on it, Mac." Martha's voice came over the radio. Followed by a chorus of others weaving in, one after another, congratulating him, as he finished the climb.

As though he'd had much of anything to do with the rescue.

He had been the one to find her, though.

He'd followed his gut and he'd found her.

Time to follow his gut and find her intended killer.

Several officers, most of them off duty, were at the top, waiting for him. Reaching to give him, and members of Dennison's team, a hand up.

He felt the pats on his back, heard the voices, but only had one real thought on his mind. Find the fiend, or fiends, and take them down.

He ended up at the closest hospital to Saguaro because the chief had insisted getting him checked out before he'd be cleared for duty.

And once there, he couldn't step away until he'd seen Stacy.

Just had to get a glimpse at the machines she'd be hooked up to, check out the steady heart rate, and be on his way.

Except that when he asked to see her and was shown into a cubicle much like the one he'd just come out of, she wasn't hooked up to any machines.

She was sitting up on the gurney, dressed in her uniform, minus the ponytail and gear, her phone in hand.

"Mac!" Was that joy he heard in her voice? He couldn't go there. He knew that. But deep down, he was glad.

"Way to go, Stace," he told her, assessing every inch of her, concentrating on the face that he'd grown to read better than his own. "Ruin a good night's sleep for me, why don't you?"

She grinned, the expression a little off. "Guess I shouldn't rub it in, then, that I managed to squeeze in a few hours."

She'd been drugged. He'd been filled in. Midazolam. It induced sleep. Lessened anxiety. And inhibited the ability to create new memories when one was fully under.

Also mild enough to be used in a dentist chair. And on animals.

A killer with a conscience?

He wanted to deliver a smart-ass remark and head out. When he looked at her, sitting there alone—as she'd been during the hours she'd been hanging on the brink of death— he just…kept looking.

"I heard that you were the one who found me, who asked for Luke Dennison to be called in," she said then.

He cocked his head. "Yeah, well, I knew you'd never let me live it down if I didn't."

Had she heard that he'd gone hoarse calling out to her, too? During the seemingly unending time he'd stood there, helpless, watching her teeter on the verge of death on those boulders? He didn't ask.

She didn't say, either.

"Yeah, well, I'm never going to let you live it down if you don't speak to the chief for me," she said. "He's telling me I have to take a mandatory week."

Mac had been hoping for longer than that. "Might not be a bad idea…"

She shook her head, and though those big brown eyes pierced him with the stare that criminals got when they were on the wrong side of the barrel of her gun, Mac stood his ground.

"Someone wants you dead, Stace. Until we know who… we can't let him get a second chance."

Chin raised, she slid off the gurney, came toward him. "Physically, I'm fine Mac. A little groggy still, but clear-headed in thought. My hands and ankles sting a bit from where I pulled at the ropes around them, and I've got some bruising around my rib cage from the airbag, but otherwise, I'm not hurt." She'd stopped moving. Was a few inches away, her face gazing up into his. "And who better to help you get him, but me?"

The challenge came through clearly. They'd long been deemed the partnership most likely to succeed. Which was why they were on call to police departments all over the state. It was why they'd been asked to help investigate when Luke Dennison had been left for dead in an arson case in the desert.

"I'm the one with the most details," she said then, not backing down an inch. "And while my memory of the incident is a bit sketchy, due to the drugs, you know as well as I do that as we get further into this, things could come back to me. Critical things that I might not otherwise ever remember."

She was good. One of the best. No argument there. And

she'd been at the scene of the crime. The entire time the kidnapping had taken place.

"I'm not going into hiding, Mac. I've already made up my mind on that one. It wouldn't be emotionally or mentally healthy for me to do so."

He nodded then. Not in agreement with any plan she'd come up with. But in acknowledgment of the truth in her words. Stacy didn't run. She fought. It was part of what made her who she was.

"He thinks you're dead. You're safe as long as he continues believing that."

"And you have a much more difficult time finding him without me. Which means, what, I stay in hiding for... ever?" She glared at him. "Right now, what do you have that's actually going to lead you to him?"

Tire marks, someone who hadn't wanted her to suffer unduly, a four-wheeler, a large male suspect from what he'd been told from her initial report...

"A large man with access to an off-road vehicle who likely has the capability to feel emotion, since he could have hurt you, made you suffer, and didn't. Maybe he thought sending you over the mountain would end things quickly without a lot of pain. And he's someone with some kind of connection to you."

"You've just described over half of the adult males in Saguaro Bend, and God knows how many everywhere else. With all the cases we've solved, the list gets longer. And if he's satisfied, goes away, we never find him. Like I just asked, you thinking I'd stay in hiding forever? Or even the months it could take to find him? We need him to know I'm alive, Mac. We have to draw this guy out."

He listened to every word. It was how they worked. Bounced thoughts of the case against each other. Pretty

much every thought they had. As long as they were per-
taining to the case.

And before he could think about what he was saying,
he gave her the solution that made sense to him. "You're
never alone," he told her. "My preference would be that I
stay with you." They'd shared space before, with adjoining rooms. Several times. Out of town, working cases. "If
I can clear it with the chief that we're assigned to this one
twenty-four seven—and that's a big if—then we stay at
your place, or mine, and if I have to be away, someone else
is with you, period."

She was nodding and he held up his hand. "If at any time,
for any reason, you fail to abide by this, I'm going straight
to the chief and having you removed from the case. From
the entire department if that's what it takes. I'll have your
badge and gun stripped..."

With his reputation, he could probably do it. "At the
very least, you and I never work together again," he said.

"You done?" she asked him, reaching for her clutch. Putting her phone inside it. Both things that had been retrieved
from her SUV when they'd brought it up.

The vehicle was being processed. If they got exceedingly
lucky, there'd be a fingerprint. A hair follicle. Something.

Stacy had said her abductor wore gloves, and she
couldn't remember him having hair...

"I need more than a nod, Stacy."

With her clutch under her arm, she folded her hands
in front of him, drawing his attention to the welts on her
wrists, and looked up at him.

The welts almost made him take back his offer. The look
in those eyes kept his mouth shut.

"I fully agree to your stipulations and more than that, I

thank you for them. For your concern on my behalf. And for working with me to catch this guy."

Her words were so different from what he'd expected, from anything she'd ever said to him before, that Mac stood there speechless as Stacy preceded him out of the room.

"Oh, and I think my place is best." Stacy continued talking to Mac as they walked through the emergency room out to the waiting area where she'd been told several officers, including their lieutenant, were waiting to see that she was fine. "That way he'll be sure to know I'm alive."

Thinking of being in her garage again made her shudder inside. But, as her grandfather had taught her, when you fell off a horse, you got right back on. She flashed back to her four-year-old self crying, not hurt just scared, being lifted back up on the new pony she'd slid off. She'd ended up riding rodeo in high school. Would still own a horse if she had the time to care for it.

She'd inherited her little home—and the bigger house as well as all the acreage—from her grandfather, her mother's dad. Bore his name, too, since her mother kept it when she married. Had spent many, many happy hours visiting with the man when she was growing up.

And had happy times on the property with Brett, too—both growing up and after they were married.

No way she was allowing some jerk to rob her of that joy. Of her home…

"Let me get the chief's approval and subsequent input first, before we start honing the plan," Mac was saying as they pushed through the doors—and conversation between them was halted by the crowd of cheering officers welcoming her back to the fold.

Which pleased her, but not as much as Mac's hand at

her back, his standing by her, and his reminder to everyone that she hadn't been to bed in nearly twenty-four hours.

The crowd of dark blue parted to allow her and Mac to duck out to the waiting police van.

As of that moment, no one was supposed to know she was alive.

The officers had all been waiting in a private room by a back exit. No one else but the hospital staff who'd cared for her knew she was there.

That was going to change, whether Chief Benson approved or not.

She'd waited at the hospital long enough for the effects of the sedative to wear off. As long as anyone would wait after coming out of surgery. She'd already talked to a mental health professional and would do so again. She'd suffered an incredible trauma. She wasn't ignoring that.

She just wasn't giving in to it. She wasn't going to let it beat her. Or define her.

She was going to take it on, deal with it and continue living life, albeit with a new appreciation for every minute, every day, she had.

Inside the van, strapped in a seat in the back with Mac where there were no windows, Stacy started to sweat. She'd been trapped in long enough. Unbuckled herself. Stood up.

And...maybe she was going to have some anxiety to work through.

"Stacy!" Mac's call was little more than a whisper, but she sat back down immediately. Buckled herself in.

And swarmed with a different kind of warmth. That voice. Saying her name. It had been in her dreams there at the end. Inappropriate and completely out of the blue—ha ha, literally—in her sexy dreams about her work partner, he'd been out of his work blues. Those dreams. They'd saved her sanity.

And now she had to wipe them out as if they'd never been.

"The chief arranged for us to have a cabin out on West-dale ranch for the night," Mac was saying, as though she hadn't just exhibited signs of being somewhat off the wall. "He's having toiletries and some clothes brought in for you. Mind you, he's still under the assumption that we're keeping you dead."

"So why are you going to be there?" she asked him, still reeling from the mental sexual replay with a man who'd run a dozen miles if he knew what she was imagining. Forcing herself to picture, instead, the popular tourist dude ranch half an hour from Saguaro.

"Because I was first on the scene," Mac said, "which means that, until I'm not, I'm the officer in charge and I have questions for you."

Right. Because, "It's not like you have any more conflicts of interest than anyone else on the force." And it wasn't like she didn't have her own very personal association with the case. Conflict of interest just didn't carry weight in light of getting the work done.

It was just that…she had to get them, in her mind, back on the professional ground that helped make them one of the best cop teams in the state. Had to make sure that he wasn't there because he'd been personally upset by her abduction, like she'd been personally comforted by thoughts of him throughout it.

Jesse Macdonald was just a cop on a case.

A case she'd be working with him. As his partner. Nothing else. They were after a killer. Not protecting a victim.

Regardless of what anyone else thought.

* * *

Saguaro PD was a small police force. Mac used that fact when he went to bat for his partner, set on getting her the positive response to her request that she needed.

He didn't kid himself, though. He needed the response just as badly.

"She's not going to stay in hiding, sir. You can fire her, but you can't cage her up." He didn't mention how clearly Stacy had made that point—her not being caged—in the van an hour before, when beads of sweat had appeared on her upper lip and she'd thrown off her seat belt.

"As long as you are in full agreement with this," the chief said, referring to Stacy's plan that Mac had just outlined for him, "you have my approval. Like you, I know full well she's going to be out there working on this anyway. She deserves our protection while she's doing so. And the two of you are who'd I'd call in if it was anyone else among us."

He'd been prepared for a battle when he'd met the chief on the lawn outside the cabin he and Stacy and Martha would be sharing for the night. Martha hadn't arrived yet— she was home sleeping so she'd be ready to take night duty while he and Stacy slept—and Mac was eager to get inside to Stacy.

Maybe because he needed time with them together more than she did. Something he was taking note of, keeping firmly to himself, and would deal with accordingly.

"Because this was such a blatant, destructive act against one of our own, I'm using private funds that the department has been given over the years for the benefit of the Saguaro PD, to hire Sierra's Web to assist with the investigation," Benson was saying. "Their tech and science experts will get you answers far more quickly than we'll be able to do here. Use them as much as you need."

Mac nodded. Feeling the load on his chest lighten some. "I appreciate that, sir," he said, itching to make his first call to them immediately. Some things couldn't wait until morning. Couldn't wait for sleep.

"You know they recommended, on the Dennison case, that Luke and the woman in danger with him go into hiding," Chief Benson said, with a raised brow.

"Yes, and I also know that they both agreed to do so."

Stacy wasn't going to agree. "And in the end—"

Benson's nod cut him off. "I know."

Being in hiding hadn't been the best thing on the Dennison case, after all.

"She's in danger. We know that now," he said. "We can take measures to protect against it, while we go get this guy." He believed every word.

And hoped to all the fates that be that he wasn't going to be made to regret the decision to go with Stacy on this one.

She was alive. But it was only by a miracle of SUV meeting rock that she'd been saved the first time. Round two didn't sound at all palatable.

He just knew, without doubt, that he couldn't let her go fight her demons on her own.

Chapter 6

Stacy would have preferred her own stretch jeans and soft sweaters to the jeans and sweatshirt that came from the donated stash at the department, but she wasn't ungrateful for all the ways people were bending over backward to help her. She just desperately needed to regain her sense of self.

The unfamiliar clothes, along with the cabin and twin bed in a room much smaller than her own, just made her feel further away from achieving that goal.

She and Mac had agreed to stay up until a normal day shift bedtime—eleven for both of them—in order to get themselves back on track to hit the ground running in the morning. Or rather, Mac had said he was going to do so, encouraging Stacy to head to bed early—at which time she'd reminded him that she'd had some sleep during the ensuing hours after the abduction. He had not.

He'd made sloppy joes for her, and she'd almost teared up as she'd come out of the shower to find them on the table.

"I didn't know you knew how to make these," she said, pulling out her chair. Rich's diner made them. And she ordered them every time they went in together. Because anytime she and Mac were dining together, they were either on shift, or coming off one.

They didn't eat together otherwise. Work partners. Nothing else. The lines had been very clearly drawn, without words, from day one, by both of them.

"I learned to cook for myself when I was in elementary school," he told her, taking a seat perpendicular from her.

That was news. Taking a bite of her sandwich, finding it, amazingly, even better than Rich's, she said, "Your mother taught you?" The idea was interesting to her, especially since she'd been raised by a single dad and ate out a lot.

"*I* taught me," he told her. "My parents were going through an unfriendly divorce. Both of them had other love interests, and I found it more peaceful just to fend for myself. I'd offer, they'd be grateful, and it worked out all the way around."

He didn't sound bitter. Or even resentful. More like he was pleased he'd found a solution to a problem.

Stacy wanted him to know that he'd deserved so much more. But kept her mouth shut around the delicious food in it.

She was too busy searching for the woman she'd been on shift the night before. The one who'd known his parents were divorced—kind of a general piece of information since they each lived with their new spouses and had grown kids in town—but hadn't known that it had been an ugly one. Or that Mac had been caught in the middle of it.

Kind of explained why he didn't do Christmas morning with any of them, though. She'd always thought, when she'd upped herself for the shift every single year and he'd put himself on with her, that he'd just been feeling sorry for her. She'd explained that with her father overseas full-time, and then Brett dying, working on the holiday had just seemed logical to her. Leaving those with families to be with them. She hadn't wanted, or needed, pity.

Turned out he'd just been doing what she had. Being logical.

And to that point, "I didn't see the guy's face," she said. It was in her initial report. He'd have read it. But when they shared a meal on shift, they talked about work.

"What can you tell me about him?"

Also in the report, but she understood his question. Welcomed it. Something new could emerge. Most particularly with how comfortable she was talking to Mac.

"He wore cowboy boots," she told him. "At least an eleven. Brown. Worn. Nothing fancy, but not cheap. Real leather."

One glance had given her that? Mac had turned on his phone's recorder. Didn't seem to doubt her testimony. And thinking about her garage floor early that morning… "They were the same brand my grandfather used to wear. There's an engraved symbol on the toe."

She named the brand. Mac, holding up a hand, tapped his phone and lifted it to his ear. "Hudson? I've got a brand of cowboy boot." He relayed the information, hung up, and that's when he told her that Sierra's Web was on the case.

"That was Hudson Warner?" she asked, having heard the name a lot during the Dennison case.

At Mac's nod, she had to physically prevent herself from tearing up again. The department was going all out for her. Mac believed in her enough to be sitting there, risking his life, and bothering a partner in an elite, nationally renowned firm of experts, after hours.

What day was it?

Tuesday. They'd come off a Monday night shift Tuesday morning. Middle of January.

She didn't like that she'd had to think about it.

And wondered again about the cowboy boots. Was she

remembering right? Or had she only transposed her grand-father's boots on that same floor to the kidnappers?

Like she'd imagined Mac's voice calling her name during lovemaking?

Shaking her head, Stacy took another bite of the sandwich Mac had made. Wondering what else she didn't know about him.

Telling herself she didn't want to know.

But fearing that, deep inside, maybe she did.

She knew her captor was white. She'd seen a bit of wrist when he'd belted her into the driver's seat of her vehicle before pushing the SUV off the cliff.

"And there was a four-wheeler." Mac froze when he heard Stacy's words. Dinner had come and gone. Dishes done. And they were still sitting at the table, awaiting Martha's arrival before they turned in. He'd asked Stacy to close her eyes and just start talking. Any thoughts she'd had, pertinent to catching the would-be killer or not, could lead him to a clue that would.

But… "Have you read the case file?" he asked, his tone harsh, even to his own ears. "I apologize," he said before she had a chance to reply. "You weren't supposed to read the file until I finished interviewing you, and this isn't going to work if I can't trust you to follow the set protocol. You got what you wanted here…" He stopped when he saw what looked like real fear flit across Stacy's face.

"What?" he asked.

"You don't trust me?" The emotion in her tone…he'd have thought he'd been an unfaithful husband, hearing accusations from his wife. Or what he imagined it would be like, had he ever been married, or been unfaithful. The latter would never happen. He'd leave first. And the former wasn't an option he gave himself.

None of which had any bearing at all on Stacy's reaction.

He gave himself time to choose his response carefully. Then opened his mouth and heard the heartfelt truth come out. "Of course I trust you, Stace. I also know that you were abducted this morning and spent hours suspended over certain death with little to no hope of survival. No one could blame you, *I* don't blame you, if you're a little off. To the contrary, I'd worry if you weren't. But at the same time, your life is clearly in the balance here. We managed to get lucky once. I'm not relying on luck a second time."

Her gaze never left his. When he finished, those big brown eyes had cleared, and she nodded. "Fair enough."

She bit her lip. Straightened her shoulders. And he prepared himself to hear that she'd gone behind his back, understanding, just as he'd told her, that she wasn't herself.

"And to answer your question, no, of course I didn't look at the file. I'm struggling a bit here with finding my emotional equilibrium, but my brain is in full working order. I'm not eager to ever have a repeat of this morning. For myself. You. Or anyone else, for that matter."

Sitting forward, blood racing, he asked, "You saw a four-wheeler?"

"Yes, why?" Her frown comforted him. She really didn't know. He pushed back against the second of shame that hit him for doubting her, not once, but twice.

"Because I saw a tire track at the end of your driveway that indicated an off-road vehicle. And I found another track up on the mountain, just yards ahead of where your SUV went off."

"Did you run the images through your photo compare app?"

It wasn't an official departmental tool, but the two of them both believed in it because it had proven them right on several occasions. "Yes," he told her. "And they matched. But the tires could have been on any number of vehicles..."

"...and off-road vehicles are so prevalent in the area," she said, finishing his statement.

He waited for more. When nothing came, he said, "Close your eyes and just talk to me, Stace."

She nodded again. "Sorry, I'd forgotten about the four-wheeler, but now that I remember it, I'm trying to think if I know anyone who might own one like it."

Yes. Mac smiled. That was his partner. Jumping ahead to get the job done.

It was good to have her back.

And even better to know that they were still clicking.

By the time Martha arrived, and Stacy headed to bed, Stacy and Mac had made a list of items and winged them over to Hudson Warner's team. Techies would be working through the night to find out whatever they could about owners or renters of gray four-wheelers with extended chassis that had full windshields and black removable tops. The team was also running cowboy boot searches. Sierra's Web had also been given all surveillance camera coverage available to Saguaro PD, as well as a list of the cases Stacy and Mac had handled over the past five years, with emphasis on any situations where Stacy had made the actual arrests. Saguaro PD had already determined which of those cases corresponded with early jail releases and had been on the street since dinnertime, tracking down every single released inmate. So far, all they'd found had verifiable alibis.

It was a weeding out process to lead them to the one guy they couldn't find. Or who couldn't produce an alibi.

"It could all be over by morning," Mac said as Martha went outside to familiarize herself with the perimeter of their cabin—one of twenty set in a semicircle around a multiacre desert park area.

Stacy turned at her doorway, hardly thinking of the case. Instead, the sight of Mac's shoulders, so strong and real, distracted her, sending her tired mind back to noncase-related images from earlier that day. Ones that seemed so real to her she wanted to tell him about them.

Wanted to say, *I heard your voice saying my name.*

But knew she never could. If Mac knew she'd had sexual fantasies about him during her brush with death, they'd never be able to work together again.

Her job gave her life value and purpose. Her partnership with the eight years older cop made her happy.

"Get some rest," Mac said when she just stood there, not responding to his hopeful comment.

With a nod she went into her room, shut the door and stood there. It could all be over by morning in a bad way, too. Her killer could find her. Get the job done second time around. And she'd never know what it felt like, in real life, to be held by Jesse Macdonald.

Did she want to die that way?

Not knowing?

No! She couldn't think like that. Erotic thoughts involving Mac had never happened before that day, before she'd been perched on the verge of death. They were a result of the kidnapping. And she couldn't let that man, whoever he was, get away with stealing her from herself.

A killer had already robbed her of one life, the one she'd built with Brett. And while marriage to her husband hadn't turned out to be the paradise she'd thought it would be, she'd been happy enough. Content and secure. Ready to start a family and raise her children in Saguaro.

But then, she had no way of knowing if paradise even existed. Her father had spun such wonderful stories about the love he'd shared with her mother. Making love songs seem real. He'd certainly remembered himself deeply in love. To the point of never dating again after her mother died. He'd had his love, he'd always said, when she'd encouraged him to find companionship. No one was going to ever be to him what her mother had been. Not only did he not want to settle for second best, he'd never do that to another woman—never ask a woman to live as second best.

Stacy got ready for bed, slipping out to use the cabin's one bathroom, and then back to her room without even glancing in the direction of Mac's door. She saw a light on in the living area down the hall. And Martha's shadow as the veteran officer sat on the couch. But wouldn't let herself even check to see if a light still shone under Mac's door.

Whether the man was in there in the dark, was lying in bed, maybe without pants and shirt, was none of her business.

And she'd damn well make sure that she didn't make it her business. By thinking about Brett.

Lying in bed, she closed her eyes and forcibly ran through memories of her husband, one after another. The time Brett had hit a home run in the multicity baseball league he'd competed in. He'd been fourteen at the time and after touching his foot to home plate had run over to the stands to kiss her.

She'd been bowled over by the romantic move. As had everyone around them. It had been their first kiss. Her first kiss, ever. And she'd never looked at another boy after that.

Not even after they'd started sleeping together and she

never again felt the spark she'd felt that first day. She'd figured people overestimated the ecstasy of physical copulation. It was nice. Just nothing that reminded her of fireworks. Or mind-numbing pleasure.

And yet, in her moment of facing death, she was flying to the stars in a sexual dream? Involving a man she'd never even been on a date with? A man she'd never considered in a sexual way, at least, not consciously?

It must be the drug she'd been injected with. Nothing else made sense.

So thinking, she turned over, told herself to sleep.

And started thinking about the case, instead. Because it was a normal thing for her, because it felt good to be normal, she allowed the thoughts. Soon found them mingling with others she'd had that evening and sat straight up in bed.

Texting Mac, she asked him if he was still awake.

His response came immediately. Followed by a phone call.

"I have a suspect," she told him as soon as she connected to the call. "I can't believe I didn't think of it sooner…"

"Hold on…" Mac's voice came over the line, and then from outside her door, too. She heard the knock. Scrambled for the shirt she'd pulled off, to get her bra off, before lying down. Pulled it back on. "Come in," she said, sitting up in bed, the covers up over her breasts.

Since he'd had no time to dress, she had the answer to her earlier wondering about what he'd be wearing in bed in the room right next door to her that night. Jeans.

With the zipper closed, but the top button undone. And a tank style T-shirt. Thin. Ribbed.

She blinked. Told herself she hadn't been staring. And, too late, saw Mac's glance at the only chair in her room.

Where he might have taken a seat if not for the telling pair of jeans thrown across the arms.

"Just give me a name," he said, standing in the open doorway. Martha appeared then, gun out, surveying the room.

"We're good," Mac told the woman as Stacy hastened to say, "Landon Manning."

Both the other officers stared at her and then at each other and she blurted, "It fits." But she understood their skepticism. Even as she wondered how long it would be before the people in her world quit doubting her. She'd never given any of them any cause not to trust her. To the contrary, she worked hard to maintain that trust.

And now some fiend, in the space of a morning, had somehow lost it for her?

"The *rodeo* star?" Martha asked incredulously, standing in the doorway as Mac came farther into her room.

She nodded, suddenly dry mouthed, wishing so badly she had on those jeans taking up the one chair, not only so Mac would sit and quit towering over her, but also so she could get out of bed and take the conversation into the other room. Stacy realized she had every right to do just that. "Can we take this up out there?" she asked, pointing toward the door.

And seconds later was staring at her closed door. It was going to come out. Not even Chief Benson knew. She'd made a bargain with a killer, and she was about to break it.

But he'd broken it, first.

By coming after her.

Problem was, she hadn't made the deal for him. For him, she'd have turned it down. She'd made it for herself. Because she needed to come home and live a normal life.

Which she'd done.

Until that morning when the monster had come back into her life to ruin it a second time.

Pulling on her jeans, Stacy made one promise to herself. When they found the guy, she was going to do everything in her power to make certain that he never got his life back again.

Chapter 7

Mac was breathing again—out in the living room. Seeing Stacy in that bed...with those jeans where they were...on top of having almost lost her that day...he clearly needed some sleep.

And maybe a date, too. It had been a while, before the holidays, since he'd been out with anyone.

"You have any idea what she's talking about?" Martha asked, sitting in the room's only armchair. Leaving either end of the couch for him and Stacy.

"I do not," he said. Succinctly. He was not going to talk about his partner behind her back. Even if the concern he was reading in Martha's eyes mirrored some of his own thoughts.

He'd known it was too early for Stacy to be back at work. But in her defense, had he been in her position, physically unharmed, he'd have been just as adamant about finding whoever had tried to kill him. Department sanctioned or not.

Before Martha could say anything else, Stacy appeared, her hair pulled back into a ponytail instead of cascading down around her shoulders and over the covers as they'd been moments before.

An image he feared he'd be trying to forget for a long while.

There was a reason he and Stacy never saw each other outside of work, never even met for a meal on days off, or over holidays. As partners who faced life and death situations at work, they couldn't afford to be anything but 100 percent on the job. Couldn't allow anything to interfere with the determination to get the bad guy.

"I'm going to ask you both to consider, strongly, keeping what I'm about to say to yourselves." His heart sank further as Stacy started in. Drama was not her way. Ever. She wasn't meeting his gaze. Or even looking in his direction at all.

She always looked him in the eye when she was talking to him. He wanted to stop her—had they been alone he probably would have. But with Martha there, he knew he had to let the scene play out.

"You both know, I'm assuming, that Brett rode rodeo for a living." She glanced at him at that, then at Martha, gaining nods from both of them. And then just sat there. She rubbed at her wrist, and Mac couldn't look away. Hated the welts there.

Hated what the abduction was doing to her.

"He died riding." Martha's soft tone broke the tense silence. "At a rodeo in Colorado."

"No." Mac's gaze shot straight to Stacy's face when she uttered the word. He was shocked to find her staring right at him. She'd told him herself. Brett Bennet had been thrown from a bull, suffered blunt force trauma to the head. He was pretty sure the news had been in the local paper.

"Brett was killed behind a barn at that rodeo, breaking up an alcohol induced fight between a man and his wife. The woman had been talking to Brett about something—I suspect it was the way her husband was abusing her, but I have no proof of that. The man had seen the two of them together behind the barn and assumed the worst. He pulled them apart, though they weren't even touching, slapped his wife, and Brett intervened, to pull the guy off from her. I came around the corner in time to see the slap…and to see the guy throw the right hook that killed my husband."

She held his gaze the entire time. Showed no emotion. As if caught in the middle of some horror flick, Mac couldn't look away. Couldn't believe what he was hearing. Couldn't speak.

"I don't get it." Martha's tone was still soft. Caring.

Because she thought Stacy was remembering incorrectly? Mac knew better. Stacy was there. Just…changed.

And maybe, still under some effect from the drugs she'd been given? Was remembering something she'd dreamed?

"Why would everyone think that Brett died in the ring?"

"Because that's what I told my father, and what he told the local paper." She was looking straight at Mac again. As though trying to tell him something. If so, he wasn't getting it.

Any of it.

"Why would you lie to your father? If what you say is true, your husband died a hero. He grew up in this town. I know his folks were gone by then, but there are others here who've known him all his life, friends…they deserve to know the truth."

Sucking her lower lip—a move Mac recognized as meaning she was holding back emotion—Stacy nodded, and said, "I actually went to my in-laws' graves when I returned to town," she said. "I told them the truth."

As well as Mac could recall, Brett Bennet had been an only child, born to a man in his fifties and a woman in her late forties. The couple had been killed in a small plane accident shortly after Brett and Stacy were married.

He'd looked up the article about their deaths when he'd first heard that Stacy was being assigned to him in her second year as an officer, after her training and start with the Phoenix PD. A guy had to know who he was dealing with.

Yet there he was, five years into the partnership, finding out he hadn't known her at all?

"Why would you lie?" Martha asked, not seeming as appalled as Mac was.

No way the past five years had been a lie. Or did he need to get her to the hospital? They'd gotten the drug wrong. She was suffering aftereffects of a hallucinogen.

But when Stacy glanced down again, her chin to her chest, he had a flash of the first time she'd told him about her husband's death. They'd just finished telling a young wife her husband had died and Stacy had told the woman she'd been there and understood. She'd given the woman her card. Had told her to call, anytime day or night, if she needed help.

In their squad car afterward, he'd asked about Brett's death. It had seemed the human thing to do. And, her chin to her chest, she'd told him about the bull ride gone tragic.

She hadn't been looking him in the eye then.

But she was at that moment. Staring at him hard.

And he got it. She needed him to pay attention. To listen. To know. To trust their partnership.

"Landon Manning is the man who killed Brett."

Mac heard Martha's gasp even as a strange calm came over him. He waited.

"No way! The man just returned to the circuit six months ago after thinking he'd never get to ride again. That groin injury almost ruined his career."

"I wouldn't say almost." Stacy's tone was the same one Mac had heard her use when she knew a confession was imminent. She rattled off facts. "He's not winning. Not even coming close. He's too old. The riders are all younger than he is. Have been training full time for years. While he hasn't even been on a horse in more than five years."

Out of the corner of his eye, Mac saw Martha sit back in her chair. "Tell us," he said, and then added, "And I'll do everything I can to see that this goes no further than it needs to go."

He glanced at Martha and saw her nod.

Taking a noticeable deep breath, Stacy held his gaze steadily and started pouring out words as though she'd rehearsed them. "I held Manning, pinning him to the ground with his hands behind his back until police got to the scene. Everyone, including me, were frantic about Brett. He'd only been hit once, should have been fine. I'd expected him to roll over and get up and come after Manning again. Anyway, by the time anyone was questioned, Manning had had a good five minutes with his wife, holding her, talking quietly to her. Everyone just thought it was a simple fight between overcharged rodeo guys. Mrs. Manning testified that Brett had picked the fight. That Manning was only defending himself. I didn't know that, of course, and in my separate interview I said what I saw. In detail. Detectives went back to check Manning's wife for signs of his abuse, and while they did find it, including a fresh bruise right where I'd seen him slap her, she claimed that she'd fallen. I couldn't let it go. Wasn't going to let it go. Brett was dead for trying to save a woman from abuse. Detectives found a few more people to testify that they'd witnessed Manning get angry when he drank. Manning tested above the legal limit. Brett had only had one beer. It was still going to be a 'he said, she said' thing, but detectives determined they had enough to at least press charges. And when, the next day, the prosecutor's office agreed, Manning's attorney came forth with a proposed plea agreement. We'd all been under gag order until that point, because of the investigation still being open, and Manning being who he was. The agreement was that Manning would plead guilty to drunken disturbance, prosecutors would ask for a light sentence and Manning would go into counseling. We were looking at second degree murder at best. Maybe even manslaughter. And since so much of the evidence was either circumstantial or 'he said, she said,' we could have lost in court. The one caveat to the agreement was that the details of Brett's death had to be sealed. Manning didn't want to lose his reputation, and the future earnings it could bring him. I think that's why Manning didn't chance going to trial and winning. The details of Brett's death would have been all over the papers, and Manning's reputation would have died right along with my husband. So the story was drunk and disorderly charges with mitigators due to the fact that Brett died of blunt force trauma from a fall that was pursuant to the argument in the charges. And the judge, who had the right to impose a lengthier sentence than the plea agreement suggested, sentenced Manning to fifteen years in prison."

Her voice broke then. Maybe with a small hint of leftover victory, but not much. It had only been six or seven years. Manning had been back on the circuit, failing but there, for six months.

"Fast forward to today," Mac said then, pulling her out of the telling and back to the life she'd built. The one she thought this Manning guy was trying to steal from her.

She shook her head, shrugged. "Manning got out on a technicality. Something about the way the plea agreement was presented. He's lost his touch. Can't ride well enough to even place. And because he was egotistical enough to try, he's lost his reputation after all. If he'd just come out, gone with the groin injury story that hit the papers, retired, he still could have made a ton of money. Even if the criminal charges hit the papers, along with his prison term, a lot of his fans would have understood, explaining it away as a one-time thing due to frustration from the injury. At his heyday, he was the best of the best."

"He's lost everything, and you think he blames you," Martha said then, sounding completely cop-like.

Stacy looked at Mac. "Look and see what brand cowboy boots he wears. Look at the emblem on them."

He didn't have to look. He'd already placed it. They were Mannings. Named for Landon's father, who'd been a rodeo star before him.

"I can't believe I didn't get it this morning," she said then. "Or figure it out before now..."

"You were drugged." Martha's words, filled with anger now, said a lot.

But not enough. Not nearly enough.

Enough wouldn't happen until Landon Manning was back behind bars.

Mac got on the phone with Sierra's Web, and then, getting Heath Benson out of bed, Mac put an APB out on the fallen rodeo rider.

And strongly resisted his sudden urge to hug his partner.

Stacy was up and dressed in the uncomfortable clothes by six, undeterred by the blackness outside. She'd slept on and off, and the rest of the time had lain in bed fighting demons of one kind or another. Reliving her kidnapping and near death the day before. Looking for clues she might have missed. And trying to reason herself out of any sexual awareness she might have imagined for her partner as she sat at death's door.

Concocting the fantasy, she totally understood. Though she'd have thought she'd have imagined Brett in the male role. But having a body experiencing actual physical reactions now that she was back in her life—that was not cool. Or in any way acceptable.

Moving quietly, she tiptoed out to wave to Martha, who was sitting in the chair reading, and then went back down the hall to the bathroom.

A disposable razor and travel-sized can of shaving cream, and toothbrush and paste sat in one corner of the vanity. She'd carried her small toiletry bag in with her. Decided to wait until she got home to shower, not to get naked in a shower Mac could be using, and then, smelling bacon, headed out to help Martha with breakfast. Only to find that Mac was already there, fully dressed in police uniform, frying eggs.

"I've checked the perimeter, and the vehicles left for us outside," he said as he dished up plates of food. "As soon as we're done here, we can head out."

She should have put on her uniform—death stench or not.

Ignoring the sight of her partner in the kitchen, she sat across from Martha and ate. Was glad to have the other officer there. Made it like sitting in the break room at work. Except for Mac's cooking. The uniform helped put her back on track, though.

And once there, she intended to stay put. No more nonsense. She and Mac were going to be residing in the same place until her would be killer was caught. If the fates were on her side, it would be yet that day. And if not, she had to be able to stay on the job and off fantasies concocted on a death bed.

She could do it.

Her life was at stake. What better incentive could there be?

The thought straightened her backbone right up. A call to her father, as their little caravan drove away from the dude ranch, put the starch back in it. He'd been insisting on flying home until she told him that by the time he got a flight out and arrived home, they'd have her potential killer behind bars. And if not, no point in giving the kidnapper more chance to hurt her by kidnapping her father, too. She wanted him safely across the world until the danger was contained.

Martha and Mac both accompanied her home long enough for her to get a shower and into uniform. And to let anyone who might be watching her place see life there. With Mac patrolling outside and Martha in the house, she allowed herself to enjoy the warm water. Was actually starting to relax. And suddenly smelled a gaseous, rotten egg scent coming up in force from the drain.

Partially dried, dressed and out in the front room in less than a minute, she had her shoes, socks and gun in hand and already packed go-duffel with the rest of her gear over her shoulder, as she ordered Martha out of the house, telling her what was going on as they ran.

"Go!" she hollered to Mac outside, heading toward his truck. "I smelled gas." She told him what she'd relayed to Martha. The veteran officer was already in her patrol car, radioing for a bomb squad and Sierra Web's hazardous material response team.

Stacy didn't realize, until she was dripping all over Mac's front seat, that her hair was sopping wet. And other than what the water might be doing to his leather interior, she didn't much care.

"Did you get the soap out?" he asked, as she opened the window and tried to wring out the long strands, leaving them in the forty-degree winds to try to dry.

"Yeah. And I'm thinking that whatever he put in my pipes was backup in case he didn't get me in the garage," she continued, her mind racing. "I'm assuming the perimeter was all clear?"

"It was." Mac's expression flattened, as it generally did when focused deeply. His gaze was broad, taking in the road in front of him, the mirror views, and out the side windows, too, as he did when they were on patrol. The familiarity settled her. A lot.

"I hope the house doesn't explode." All her stuff…every piece of memorabilia from thirty years of life…

"At least you aren't in it." Mac's response, typically unemotional, came right back at her. Grounding her more.

"There's no reason for the guy to have gone to my house after pushing me over the side of a mountain," she said. "That has to have been from before."

"I agree, but I still want to check it out as soon as we get the all clear."

She nodded. In complete agreement. Tamping down her immediate need to buy a load of boxes to pack up all her stuff and hide it where no one would ever find it.

Or her.

Chapter 8

Stacy wasn't going to let her abductor get to her. He would not rob her of her mental and emotional stability.

"I just got off the phone with Hudson Warner before you and Martha ran out," Mac said, speeding down the two-lane road that led out of open desert land. "Manning isn't at his place in Colorado. His wife hasn't seen or heard from him since day before yesterday. Claims that he said he needed some solitude and time to think. That he's planning to retire from the rodeo. She also said that he dried out in prison and hasn't had so much as a sip of beer since he got out. She begged the investigator to just leave them alone."

Her gut tightened. "Do you believe that?"

He glanced at her. "You didn't say anything about smelling alcohol on your abductor's breath."

She shook her head. "He never spoke. For all I know, he never opened his mouth at all, but he didn't reek."

The stiff set of Mac's jaw told her he was worried. Which strengthened her resolve to stay focused and get the job done. She'd insisted she was capable of working the case. He'd given her the chance. She wasn't going to let him—or herself—down.

"His phone is off," her partner continued as he headed toward town. "Benson already got a warrant for a trace on his credit cards and bank accounts. Sierra's Web is tracking surveillance cameras, and his internet accounts. We'll find the murderer, Stace, but we have to keep you safe until we do."

She frowned, tensing. "Why would he still be on the run if he thinks I'm dead? And who was driving the four-wheeler that followed us up the trail to drive him back down?" The only theory that made sense.

"His wife says he's been spending time with the younger brother of a guy he met in prison. Says the guy helped him out on the inside and now he's trying to give the kid a hand up whenever he can. Guy's name is Troy Duncan. He's twenty-two and currently employed at a horse farm north of Denver…"

"Let me guess, he didn't show up for work yesterday."

"And probably won't be there today, either," Mac told her. Turning onto Main Street. "You all right with stopping in at the station?" he asked, per usual.

He never just drove them someplace without actively obtaining her consent. Something she'd taken for granted until right then. And didn't like that she felt grateful for the consideration all of a sudden. "Yeah," she said slowly. Then, to save herself from further emotional turmoil that served no good purpose, jumped right back to the conversation that gave her a sense of control. "If I'm clearly dead, why are they on the run?" she asked.

The questions she and Mac asked each other provided answers. Every time. It was who they were. What they did.

"Could have had a falling out," he said, pulling up in front of the station, rather than heading to the officer parking lot around back.

"Or want to lay low until the dust settles," she offered, opening the door, looking all around, with her hand on her gun, before she left the protection of the metal frame. "He has to know that an officer gone missing, even if it's made to look like I might have just chucked it all and taken off on my own, is going to cause a fuss."

Mac was out of the vehicle, his body shielding her from the road, before she'd made it to the sidewalk. "He'd likely realize that we'd be watching your bank accounts to make sure you were okay."

"It's way too coincidental that he'd suddenly tell his wife he needed solitude to make a major life decision at the exact time I'm abducted and sent to my death." She had to say the words, to keep thinking them, to take away their power. She'd faced death.

And she'd survived.

She was not a victim. She was a survivor.

"Excuse me, Stacy?" The female voice behind them triggered instant response. Mac spun, ramming his backside against hers, as they both pulled their guns.

"Um, sorry, Officer Macdonald, I just... Stacy?"

Recognizing the voice, slowing down enough to let her brain process, Stacy dropped her gun to her side and turned around to stand beside Mac. "Kaylee," she addressed the city clerk, a woman three years younger than her that she'd tutored in history during high school. "I'm sorry, we're just..."

"I know, I heard," the pretty redhead said, her smile as sweet as always. "That's why I'm here, actually. I saw you guys pull up." She motioned toward the three-story brick building across the street that housed city offices. "I was going to come over this morning, anyway," she continued. "I thought maybe you should know that someone accessed your property records last week."

"Who?" Mac's response was gunshot sharp.

Kaylee shook her head. "That's just it. I have no idea. It wasn't current records. I was helping in the assessor's office, and I noticed a light on in the public records room. It houses everything that isn't digitized. When I went to turn off the light, I saw this paper on the floor. It was an old tax notice for your address. I opened the drawer where the file should be…"

"…and it was gone?" Mac interrupted, clearly needing the woman to get to the point at a more rapid pace.

Sending him a glance, Stacy looked back at Kaylee as the clerk frowned. "No, it was right where it was supposed to be. But I could tell that it had been gone through pretty thoroughly. Nothing was in the order in which we file it. I would have said something, but it's not all that unusual to have someone looking at old records. Especially during snowbird season when the gold panners are here. And, you know, they're public, so…"

"Surveillance tapes," Mac said. "Are there cameras in the room?"

"No." Kaylee almost seemed afraid of Mac, which wasn't at all uncommon when the man was on a hunt, but it struck Stacy differently that morning. More deeply. Not to have someone afraid of him, but to have him so fiercely ready to protect and serve.

It was the first time he'd been protecting her.

"As far as I know, they're only on the first floor," Kaylee was saying. "And only at the public entrance area where everyone goes through the metal detector."

"We need those tapes," Mac said. Kaylee nodded, as though she could reach in her purse and produce them on the spot. "I'll send someone over," he said then, his face softening. "And…thank you. You might have just helped us get Stacy's would-be killer off the streets."

Kaylee smiled, nodded, seemed a bit shy all of a sudden, and for the first time since she'd been partnered with Mac, Stacy felt superfluous standing there next to him.

Was Kaylee flirting with Mac? He was eleven years older than her. Not that age mattered so much, but...the clerk *was* his type. Pretty and with a soft spirit that gave the sense that she needed protection. The only kind of woman Mac ever dated.

Which left Stacy completely out in the cold in that arena.

And that was exactly where she wanted to be.

So why on earth would she be feeling jealous of her younger classmate of more than a decade ago?

He should never have come on so strongly with the city clerk. Mac tried to make amends as best he could with the younger woman but chafed at his uncharacteristic behavior. If she'd been a suspect, then, hell yes, he'd go at her. But someone who was only trying to help?

He needed to reel it in.

And maybe admit to himself that almost losing Stacy—seeing her in that car teetering on boulders that were going to let go with a good wind—had taken a toll on him. More than any other officer-down incident he'd encountered during his eighteen-year career.

Benson had designated the largest conference room in the building the Waltz case room, and Mac and Stacy set up there for the rest of the morning. They'd been through every case they'd handled together that coincided with a recent jail release. Had agreed on a couple of names for Sierra's Web to pay particular attention to.

Midmorning, they got word that her SUV had turned up nothing. Stacy's prints were the only ones present. The only hair they'd found had been hers. Both on the driver's seat and in the back.

Mac watched Stacy's face as the chief told her that the vehicle was totaled. She'd nodded. Hadn't flinched. But he knew how much she'd liked that vehicle. It had been the first one she'd purchased, on her own, with cash.

"Looks like we're going vehicle shopping, huh?" he asked, just to try to ease the pain she wouldn't show.

And was rewarded with a surprised smile sent in his direction as she said, "When this is over, you're on."

He'd been no part of the earlier purchase. Had no reason to be a part of the next one. And no acceptable explanation to himself as to why he'd offered.

The fact that she'd accepted didn't sit well, either.

What in the hell were they doing?

Shortly after that, Hudson Warner called in his morning report. While midazolam could be purchased at any drugstore with a prescription—and anyone could have easily used a portion of their own or someone else's prescription—it was also commonly used by veterinarians and others treating animals. That didn't even consider any illegal markets. Many prescription medications in the US were also legally available without prescriptions just over the border in Mexico and legally brought into the States after purchase. The firm wasn't going to give up on tracing down the substance used to drug Stacy. They were also looking at syringe purchases. It just wasn't going to be a quick task.

Hudson's team had found a couple of social media accounts that appeared to belong to Manning, in addition to the rodeo star's official accounts. One included a tirade against police and the entire legal system, stating that they ruin lives without ever considering circumstances. Ending with a statement that it had to change. It was posted after Manning's first rodeo humiliation coming out of prison.

Nothing had been posted since, but they were keeping an eye on both accounts, and still looking for others. That, too, could take days or even weeks, considering not only the plethora of internet social sites, but all the sites on the dark web.

Landon Manning's credit cards and bank accounts had still not been accessed.

Troy Duncan, the younger man Manning had been looking out for, didn't have credit in his name. Only a bank account with a small balance, set up with an address that led to a local grocery store. The account also hadn't been accessed.

After the Sierra's Web investigator had talked to Manning's wife, she'd headed to talk to the owner of horse farm where Duncan worked. The young man was a hard worker. Loved horses. Got paid in cash.

And had never before missed a day of work. No one knew where he lived. A couple of guys on the ranch thought he was renting a place. A few others thought he stayed with a friend but didn't know who. Duncan didn't own a vehicle. No one seemed to know for sure how he got to and from work.

A fact that brought dread to Mac's gut. They were looking for a somewhat famous man…and a ghost.

Hudson told him their investigator was looking for friends and associates of Wendall Duncan, Troy's older brother and Manning's eventual cellmate and friend, thinking they'd be looking out for the little brother, just as Manning had been doing.

Lots of leads, no arrests. Mac saw Stacy's shoulders droop as the call ended, and he felt her disappointment as though it was his own. Was reaching out a hand to squeeze her shoulder, when she stood and started pacing around the table. "I need to be out there, Mac, looking for this guy. Not sitting around waiting while everyone else does the work. I took him down before. I can do it again."

She had the best of the best working for her. And he didn't doubt her, either.

He also heard the desperation in her voice. "As soon as we hear that we're clear to head back to your place, we need to go over every inch of the property. You're the only one who will know if anything has been disturbed." He'd already told her he'd intended to do so. Had been picturing her safely in the house, but when he talked to her cop to cop, he knew that having her along made sense.

Just as her standing up to prevent him touching her did. Not that he was at all sure she'd stood when she had on purpose, or that she'd seen his hand coming toward her. But the messages were clear. Warnings being sent to him, by his psyche or some weird twist of fate, that they were on shaky ground at the moment, coming off from her near death.

They couldn't let a few moments out of time rattle who they were or the great work they did together.

"It sounds like Manning could be out for revenge, just as you thought. He lost years of his life, and potentially his career because a judge gave him a harsher sentence then he'd expected when he pled guilty." He told her what he'd been thinking. All strengthened by Hudson's report. "He might also be on a drinking binge, in spite of what his wife thinks. Unfortunately, as we've seen more than once, the wife is sometimes the last to know. He could also be on whatever substance he gave you, or something else entirely. He had a drinking problem. The addiction could have turned into some other substance during his time in prison."

"Both of which make him unpredictable," Stacy said, re-joining him at the table. "And more apt to make a mistake. Which is all the more reason to get me out there, Mac. To put me in his face, so to speak. We don't want him going into hiding."

"It also makes him that much more dangerous." The words came out. He knew she didn't need his reminder.

"That's right, it does," she said, meeting his gaze full on for the first time in a while. "We have to be smart about this, use backup everywhere we can, but if anyone can get this guy, it's you and me."

Meeting her eyes, seeing the strength in their depths, and the truth, Mac nodded.

And felt gutted, too.

She was just his work life.

But work was pretty much all he had.

What he was best at.

She knew that.

Was counting on him to help her bring this one home.

And, remembering how he'd felt, standing on that mountain, watching her vehicle rock and being unable to save her, he wasn't positive he could.

The one thing he was sure about, though, was that if he lost her on the job, he'd never forgive himself.

Stacy was energized by Mac's agreement to let her get out and show herself. To have her back, to be right by her side as she did so. It was risky.

But so was going to work every single day. They'd faced two shooters head-on the other night. Their work wasn't a walk in the park.

What bothered her was the strange look on his face. Like he'd just seen a dog get hit by a car or something. While

Mac wouldn't get a dog for himself, no matter how many times she'd told him he should, the man had a way with animals like no one else she'd ever known. He was sensitive to their pain in a way that touched her. He handled dead bodies with professionalism. The time they'd walked in on an illegal dogfighting ring at the end of a night of fighting, he'd had to turn around and walk out.

He'd made the arrest. But he'd called for another team to clear away the bodies.

"Property records in Arizona are public record," she said then, reminding herself that her job was to focus solely on the case. To work for her freedom from imminent personal danger. "In this county everything is on the internet. You just go to the assessor's office, click on parcel search and type in a name." Pulling the laptop they'd been using all morning toward her, she typed, clicked and typed, and turned the screen to him.

Her property address, acreage and tax information were all right there.

"So Manning does the current search, finds your address. Why risk coming to town, entering a public building, and getting caught looking at the records?"

She'd been wondering about that on and off all morning. "Because the property has two homes on it," she said. "Before my mom died having me, she and dad lived in what is considered the main house. It's a quarter mile down the road, around the curve. I actually go to that box to collect my mail—though anything of importance comes electronically now…" She stood again. Circled the table, feeding off her own energy, glad to have it back. "When my mom and dad got engaged, my grandfather had them move into the main house and built the house I'm living in now. Technically, it's a guesthouse on the property, not the single-family residence. He had the garage added later. After my mother died, Grandpa and Dad and I stayed in the house. Some of my dad's things are still there, though he moved into his parents' place in town when they passed. I didn't find out until my grandfather died that he'd willed the entire property to me." She stopped. Threw him a grin. "I live in my own guesthouse."

Mac didn't seem to find any humor in the statement. His gaze was sharp again. "We need to get to that main house. He might have hit that earlier, found it vacant…" He held her gaze. "He went to the city records office to physically look you up, to see any other properties that might come up…"

"He looks up property, finds out that it's more than the main house…"

Stacy sat back down. "And finds me."

"We need to get out to the house you don't live in."

They were no closer to finding Manning's current whereabouts. But they were doing their jobs. Putting pieces into place.

To find a killer.

Together.

Chapter 9

Being in the station, surrounded by memories of her own personal strength, working, Stacy felt more and more like herself as the morning wore on.

She and Mac were going to bounce back. They'd be just fine.

Or so she thought, until she came back from the restroom to see him out in a far corner of the squad room, speaking with the sheriff of Canal County.

The man who'd offered Jesse Macdonald a well-deserved, much higher paying position within the sheriff's department.

She'd forgotten all about the conversation they'd had just before she was kidnapped. They'd been on the phone after shift. Martha had told her just before they'd gone on shift that night that she'd heard Mac had been offered the position. She'd thought he'd told Stacy. That Stacy would know whether he was planning to take the job.

The phone conversation on the way home that night… she'd been distracted by the bright headlights in her mirror. And then the van she'd almost hit.

But… Mac had never said he wasn't leaving the Saguaro Police Department.

She'd asked.

And he'd turned the conversation on her. Asking her if *she* was ready to move on. As in, take on a new partnership. A younger officer she could help bring up.

Just like Mac had with her.

She remembered making it quite clear she'd let him know when she was ready. Thinking to herself that it would be never.

Had he been hoping for a different response?

Wanting her to be at a turning point because he was?

Taking one last glance at the two men conversing quietly in the corner, Stacy went back to the conference room in which she'd spent her morning. Stood in front of the whiteboard where most of the pertinent information was listed so that anyone working on aspects of the case could see where they were at.

She studied details as though Stacy Waltz was just a citizen she was serving.

If Mac wasn't planning to take the position the sheriff's office had put forth, or if he wasn't at least interested in discussing the possibility, he'd have sent an email. She knew from previous offers.

Instead, he was in conversation with the man who could potentially be his new boss.

Which was no business of hers unless he wanted to make it so. Not until she came to work one day to find herself partnered with someone else...

The idea had never been a pleasant one. But it was always a possibility. It wasn't like police partners were under any legally binding partnership. They didn't have to go through a divorce to separate. They just...moved on.

Those had been his words to her the other night.

He'd wanted to know if she was ready to move on.

Dread filled her, and a quiet fear that didn't strike out at her so much as it permeated her mood. Taking her down at a time when she was struggling to get up.

"Stace!" The sound of Mac's voice, saying her name in that urgent tone, rent through her, and for a second she wasn't sure if she was back in her dream or if he'd just come in the room. Until her eyes shot toward the door and saw the serious look on his face. "The sheriff just gave me an update on your place," he told her, grabbing his keys and holding out her clutch.

"Your address is Saguaro Bend, but the property is outside city limits. The sheriff's office insisted on being involved," he said as he led the way out of the station, forgoing his truck for their patrol car.

She'd liked being in his personal vehicle.

So the patrol car was definitely best.

She wasn't asking what the sheriff found. Wasn't sure she was ready to know how she might have died had she not been kidnappable two nights before.

She took a deep breath and thought about the fact that Mac had a legitimate reason to have been in conversation with the sheriff. But that didn't rule out job talk. Especially since whatever they had to say about the case, should have been said to her at the same time. Stacy mentally pulled on a pair of big girl panties and set her mind to work.

"Tell me," she said, as soon as they were buckled in and Mac had called their destination coordinates over the radio.

"Punctured canisters of methane had been dropped inside your septic tank," he told her. Natural gas had no odor. But when being produced for commercial distribution, something was added to produce a rotten egg smell, so consumers could be alerted to a leak.

"He knew how to kill me in a very insidious, and yet

painless, way. But he didn't know about the rotten egg smell?"

"Methane produces naturally in septic tanks. If you didn't get it cleaned out regularly, you'd end up with the smell anyway. I'm guessing he was banking on you thinking you needed the tank emptied."

"I just had it done a few months ago." But there was no way a man in Colorado would know that.

"There was enough gas being emitted to kill you overnight," Mac said. She appreciated his candor. Looked over at him, and so badly wanted to ask if he was taking the job with the sheriff's office but knew she couldn't.

She'd brought it up once. He'd prevaricated. If he wanted her to know, he'd tell her.

And as his work partner, she had to accept his right to handle things how he saw fit. She'd be fine. If not him, she'd be given another partner.

It was all part of the job, she reminded herself for what seemed the umpteenth time in the past fifteen minutes.

Maybe because she didn't want to think about going to sleep in her home, feeling safe and secure, only to never wake up again.

"Going to the cabin last night saved my life," she said then. "Good call."

"The tank has been emptied," Mac said, ignoring her praise, at least verbally. "Your house is being aerated. And yes—" he glanced her direction "—if you'd gone home last night, it would have been like someone who'd turned on a gas stove to commit suicide. You'd have probably started to feel slightly drunk. Might have worried what was happening to you as you drifted off to sleep."

She'd already seen that vision. Didn't need to dwell there anymore. "What's with this guy?" she asked then, filled with fear and frustration and a resurging sense of power-lessness that she absolutely abhorred. She was not a weak person. "He wants me dead, but doesn't want me in massive physical pain first? He should do his research. A well-aimed gunshot would be the least fearful way…"

Even as she said the words, she knew. "He wants me to suffer emotionally," she said the words aloud. "He's inflicting mental anguish at the time of my death, just like he's suffering now at the death of his career."

"And probably as he suffered during the years he saw his rodeo life wasting away in prison." Mac's words came softly. But they were there.

Telling her that he was doing exactly as she'd asked. Treating her as he would on any other case. Any thoughts left unsaid could prevent them from finding the whole truth.

And without that, even if they were on the right path, they could be ambushed.

Or, after the arrest, the perpetrator could end up getting off.

Without a conviction, an arrest meant nothing.

"I'm assuming they checked the main house?" she asked Mac as he turned out of town toward the desert. "For gas, and other toxic materials, yes. I asked that they leave the physical inspection to us. I didn't want anything moved by one of our team until you had a chance to see if anything looked at all different from the way you remembered it."

As they'd discussed. He was doing just what he'd said he'd do. Because that was Mac. He might be leaving the Saguaro PD, but he was still Mac.

Exactly who he'd always been to her.

As long as he was her partner, she could trust him with her life, just as he could trust her.

And nothing else was on their table.

* * *

Mac parked in the drive of the house Stacy had grown up in, recognizing the home he'd passed hundreds of times. He'd just never known it was part of the same property on which she currently lived.

Five years they'd been together, and he'd never known that. The fact didn't bother him. They didn't share personal stuff unless it was pertinent to a job. But it felt odd, not knowing that she owned so much property. Or that she chose to live in a small home on the other side of that property, rather than in the one she'd shared with her father and, he was assuming, her husband.

"I was just here a few days ago," Stacy said, as they slowly made it through the mostly empty rooms of the sturdy two-story home. "I come in and flush toilets and run water in all the faucets at least once a month," she continued.

And he got another glimpse he'd never seen. A woman keeping up two homes, on several acres of desert property, all on her own. He wasn't surprised that Stacy could do it. Not in the least.

Just…the woman was changing before his eyes. Becoming more than he'd ever known before. That, on top of having just spent hours expecting to see her fall to her death, was messing with him. Making him want to grab her up, hold on and never let go.

He didn't ask, when they reached the upstairs, which of the empty bedrooms had been hers growing up. Or confirm whether she and her husband had shared what was clearly the master. The stuccoed home was old, yet had all the amenities, including a bath off the largest bedroom. Another bath between the other two bedrooms upstairs. And a full bath downstairs, as well as a fourth bedroom.

He didn't speak at all, needing her fully focused on every

inch of the interior of that home. Looking for any sign that someone had been there after her.

She opened every door and cupboard, checked corners, windowsills and behind every curtain, with him following right behind her.

Back in the living room, she turned to him. "Nothing's been tampered with," she said. "Even the dust bunnies are exactly as I noticed them when I was here. I made a mental note to get over here and clean..."

The two and a half car attached garage was completely empty. Swept clean. As impressive in its own way as the house.

And he just had to ask, "Why don't you live here?"

As soon as the question was out, the cop in him wanted to suck it back in. And slowly had to acknowledge that the man did not.

"After Brett died, it just didn't make sense for me to be wandering in all this space alone all the time..."

The words made perfect sense. And left a lot unsaid. Things he wanted to draw out of her.

But didn't. Couldn't.

"I keep thinking I'll rent it out," she answered one of his unspoken questions. "You know, next summer, or next fall, or next year." With a shrug she added, "Maybe I'll get on it as soon as we catch Manning."

Because she'd looked death in the eye and didn't want to keep putting off getting on with her life?

She was only thirty. Had lots of time to meet someone else, fall in love again, fill her big house with family. He didn't tell her so.

It wasn't his place.

Even if a part of him wanted it to be.

The greater part knew better.

* * *

Stacy was glad to be out of the big house. Every time she was over there, she struggled with the dreams she'd lost. All she'd wanted, growing up, was to find love as her parents had. To be with someone she'd known her whole life, who shared memories and values with her, so that they could be best friends and then forever partners, raising children in the house that had seemed so lonely her entire life.

First her grandfather, widowed young, living there alone as he'd raised Stacy's mother. And then her father, with her. She'd had such high hopes when she'd married Brett. Even after the sex hadn't turned out to be all that remarkable, and her heart had never lusted after him, she'd loved him. He'd truly been her best friend. And would have made a wonderful father...

"Stacy!" She heard her name called before she saw the older man heading up the front walk toward them as she locked up. "I saw ya over here and just wanted to say how glad I am that you're okay."

She'd known the tall man in jeans, a plaid flannel shirt, boots and cowboy hat her entire life.

"I'm fine, Tom, thank you," she said, trying not to sound as impatient as she felt. The last thing she needed at the moment was to have to smile and be polite. To be...normal.

Except in her relationship with Mac.

She wanted to feel in control like her normal self, but until her killer was found, her life was insular. Nothing mattered, not even neighborliness, until the man was caught.

"I couldn't believe it when I went into Rich's last night and heard what had happened..."

They'd wanted the word to get out that she'd survived. Confirmation that it had done so was welcome.

Introducing the neighboring miner to Mac, she continued slowly toward their car in the drive. Not so fast that she was turning her back on her visitor. He could walk along with them if he chose. She just hoped he wouldn't.

Which meant, of course, that he did.

"I…um…" He bit his lip. Not something she'd ever seen him do before. Or look the least bit unsure of himself. Which had her stopping in her tracks.

"What's up, Tom? Is everything okay with you and Mary?" The man's wife had been ill in the fall, but last Stacy had known she'd completely recovered.

"Mary's gone to stay with her sister for a while," Tom said. "She's fine, though. I came over to apologize to ya," he said then, glancing down, and meeting her gaze, his own eyes somewhat shaded by the wide brim of the hat she'd hardly seen him without. "The other night, I'd been in at the bar. Had my one beer and was headin' home…was on the phone with Mary, tryin' to get her to come home, and wasn't watchin' my speed. I came up on you a little too close, forgot I had my brights on and…"

"That was you?" she asked, feeling Mac stiffen and then relax beside her.

"Yeah." The man looked at Mac then. "My wife's not happy with my choice to continue workin'. Her illness last fall, she says it was a warnin' that it was time to get out and live life. She wants to travel. To cruise and spend time on the world's beaches like we always said we'd do. Problem is, I'm a miner. I run a business. It's all I've ever been or wanted to do. We went to the beach over the holiday and I 'bout lost my mind with nothin' to do and so much needin' doin' here. Still, I told her I'd give her one week every quarter, but it wasn't enough for her." Tom included Stacy in his glance as he said, "Anyway, after I heard what happened, and there I was, had to be just minutes beforehand, coming home myself. I probably scared ya, afraid I distracted ya. When I should have been noticin' whoever was out here, waitin' for ya."

Feeling oddly comforted, Stacy reached out to squeeze the older man's arm. "It's okay, Tom. As you can see, I'm fine."

Tom frowned then. "You got any idea who did this?" he asked. "Makes me kinda glad Mary's gone for now. And nervous, too, you know?" He looked back to Mac as he finished.

Like Stacy couldn't possibly know or understand. Tom was of the old regime, her father had always told her. Didn't mean Stacy had to like his chauvinistic way of talking "man to man" when she was standing right there, perfectly capable of understanding just as well as Mac did. Maybe even better, since she knew Tom and Mary.

"We have a lead," she told the man. Not just for his sake. Tom was a talker. And she should have cleared the move with Mac first.

Tom's eager nod showed his relief. "He from around here?"

"We don't think so." She answered quickly. If Manning got word they were on to him, all the better. She needed him desperate, making his move, or giving up and going home, where the Colorado police would arrest him on the out of state warrant that had already been issued to bring him in for questioning as a person of interest in an attempted murder investigation.

Straightening, Tom's relief was clear then. "Well, you just let me know if you need my help with anythin'," he said then. "I'm always here."

Telling the man she appreciated his offer, she made a beeline for their cruiser as Tom headed back toward the

SUV he'd left parked out by the road, headed toward his own drive.

What she appreciated far more than the offer was the reassurance that she hadn't called things wrong the other night.

She'd known the SUV wasn't following her. Or, rather, she'd been bothered at first, but had calmed down when the vehicle hadn't followed her turn.

But she'd let Mac's continued concern get to her.

Like she trusted him more than she trusted herself.

And that wasn't okay.

Chapter 10

Just as with the midazolam, the propane canisters pulled up out of Stacy's septic tank could have been purchased in hundreds of places all over the Phoenix valley alone, let alone anywhere between Colorado and Arizona. Sierra's Web was tracing serial numbers but had so far only narrowed a shipment down to a three-state radius.

Manning-endorsed cowboy boot sales were much harder to trace as no one knew how far back to look. Stacy had been certain the boots weren't new. They could be a decade or more old. Shops that sold them had come and gone. And thousands of pairs had been sold in that time. Beyond that, finding a pair that Landon Manning might have purchased wasn't likely. Since both he and his father before him endorsed the boots, he'd likely have whatever he wanted free of charge.

A team consisting of one city office employee and one Saguaro PD employee were going through the city building surveillance footage. So far, they had not turned up any likeness of Landon Manning. Or anyone else that they didn't recognize or couldn't trace to legitimate business in the building. There'd been one image, a tall person in a black hoodie whose face had never been visible to the camera, who'd been in the previous week. No one knew who it was. Or why he'd been there.

They'd sent the footage to Stacy via phone, and while she hadn't been able to identify Manning, she'd agreed that it could be him.

Mac and Stacy were just leaving her property, having found nothing suspicious, when he got another call from Hudson Warner. The firm of experts had found Manning on surveillance tape at a private airport in Denver the week before. There were no manifests with his name on them, but they were following other leads on the matter. When Manning's wife was asked about other absences, she admitted that her husband was gone a lot. For rodeos and just to work out his life, as she'd put it.

"If he's flying by private plane, he could be traveling between here and Denver daily," Stacy said, as she listened to the call over speakerphone as they sat in the cruiser outside her house.

"Exactly," Hudson's voice came over the wire. "We're checking flight manifests for Denver to Phoenix flights," he said. "We know his name isn't registered on any flights, but once we know which ones to track, we can get surveillance from the various airports, both private and commercial, in the valley, too."

"It's also possible that he drove," Mac pointed out. That would have been the more logical choice if the man was hoping to stay unnoticed. Almost an entire day had passed, Stacy had escaped death twice in the past thirty-six hours, and they still were no closer to an actual arrest.

To eliminating the imminent danger to his partner's life.

"We've got traffic cam footage between here and Denver," Hudson was saying, impressing Mac, if not easing his frustration any. "As many major and minor routes as we could find that had them, and we have people going through them one by one..."

"…but if he's not in his own vehicle, he'd be pretty impossible to trace." Stacy voiced what they all knew.

"We could also get lucky, get a glimpse of his face, and find out what he's driving," Hudson came back at once. "This isn't our first rodeo," the man said, adding, "No pun intended. We can do scans for facial likeness…"

"Have you had success with that before?" Mac had to ask. Had to know what they were up against.

"We have. Several times."

Good to know. He glanced at Stacy, who happened to be looking at him. Their eyes met. She was doing okay.

And his tension eased some.

Stacy wanted to be fine. She'd told Tom she was. If Mac or anyone else asked, she'd say the same. But having just spent two hours walking around her property, starting with the two houses and branching out from there, looking for anything out of place or that seemed unusual to her, she wasn't really fine.

Had she and Mac just been for a walk, then maybe. But canvassing her own property, her safe place, with guns out and covering each other's back, she felt…violated.

Not by Mac.

But by whoever had forced her to have to check her own land for criminal activity.

Landon Manning.

Again.

She'd thought, after testifying at his trial, that she could put the past to rest. Try to recover and move on.

Until the early hours of the morning before, she'd have sworn that she'd done so.

"I've been a bit on edge since I heard Manning was out of jail," she told Mac as they traveled back through town toward his gated community. The plan was for him to pack up some things and stay in her spare bedroom for the duration.

Or until the plan changed.

A couple of officers were being assigned to patrol her property, and the area around it, all night, every night, until Manning was caught.

"They had to notify me of his release, since I was the victim's family, and I've had this niggling feeling ever since. Like I had to be on constant watch."

"Why didn't you say something?" His question was probably natural, given the circumstances. She still felt affronted.

"Because there was no factual basis for it. It was just reaction from past personal trauma. And we agreed, Mac, from the very beginning. No personal talk. Look at us, a partnership known all over the state. Our boundaries work, Mac. We only let work occupy our working hours. And to do that we have to keep all personal life away from each other."

He nodded. Let it go.

When she'd wanted him to say something. To argue or discuss. Bring up another side to the story.

Instead of just confirming what, in her heart, she knew to be true. There were lines they couldn't cross, or they'd lose the best thing either of them had ever had.

She knew that to be the truth for her.

He'd said as much for himself in the past.

And she just couldn't stop herself from asking, "Are you taking the job?"

"What job?"

"With the sheriff's office. And don't prevaricate again, Mac. Not now. Don't try to put it off on me. I just need to know. After five years, if my work life is going to change…" She shrugged, and said, "I just need to know."

She'd almost said she had a right to know.

In reality, she didn't. Lieutenant Stahl could assign her to work with any other officer in the department at any time, without her prior consent or knowledge. When you signed on to serve, you turned those choices over to those who led.

"No."

He didn't elaborate.

And she didn't say any more either.

She was too busy fighting tears of relief.

And couldn't let that show.

Stacy had wanted to wait out in the cruiser while Mac ran in to collect his things, using his gated community as assurance that she'd be safe, but they both knew the fallacy of the remark. They'd worked cases where electronic gates had been compromised. He didn't call her on her weak argument, just looked at her and she'd followed him inside.

The incident in itself was a nonentity, except that it told Mac that Stacy hadn't wanted to enter his private abode.

Since he knew, by virtue of the fact that she'd strongly requested that he be the one to stay with her in her home, that she wasn't at all uncomfortable being alone in a private home with him. Which meant it had to be *his* home in particular that was getting to her.

And the guy in him took note of that with a small amount of pleasure.

Which, of course, couldn't please him.

She waited in the foyer. Had it been any other day, and them together for any other reason, he'd have teased her about it.

Had she been any other woman, he'd have taken pleasure in drawing out of her just why she didn't want to let herself get too far into his personal space, angling for an admission that he was having an effect on her.

Which would lead to a soft kiss.

And assurances that she was having an effect on him, too.

Well, any other woman who affected him as Stacy did. If there'd ever been another one who constantly challenged him. Keeping him on his toes all the time. Sparring with him. Making him think harder.

Just plain making him better.

At the job they shared.

With Stacy, it was always only at the job.

So thinking, he threw things in a duffel and got them both out of there in less than five minutes. They stopped for carryout chicken, to heat up and eat later, and then to exchange the cruiser for his truck. They were heading back to her place when her phone rang.

"It's Benson," she said, naming their chief, as she answered it on speakerphone.

"A couple of sheriff's deputies just found a white van matching your description, Stace. I'm sending you photos now…"

"Where?" Mac interrupted. He had to know location details. To have an idea of areas Manning had possibly been.

"Pushed over the side of a mountain off The Trail a mile east of Stacy's attempted murder. It's nose first, three-quarters of a mile down. Front end isn't visible in the photo. But we got a clear view of the back. It's been there less than a day. Helicopters flew over the area yesterday morning, looking for Stacy, and have footage of the area."

Too much of a coincidence not to see the connection.

"And the plates?" he asked, already knowing what was coming. Benson's tone of voice wasn't speaking victory.

"The vehicle was reported stolen a week ago."

"From?" he prompted, biting back impatience.

"Denver." Yep. That was the one.

"It's Manning," he declared. Appreciative of the confirmation. And uncomfortable with everyone's inability to find the fallen hero. They'd had the best of the best hunting him down for a full day, and they had nothing.

"Or his friend Troy," Stacy said.

Right. "He might be the easier of the two to find," Mac said, homing in again. "Find him, he'll lead us to Manning."

"Unless he's in that four-wheeler." Stacy's tone brought him straight back to her. He could almost hear the shudder within her. "The man had a pretty failproof plan. But it failed. We wanted to make him desperate. Maybe enough to not only get rid of the vehicle he used in the crime, but perhaps his driver, too. Like Mac just deduced, Troy would be the weak link. He's not going to leave that hanging around."

"This guy…he's making all attempts on your life look like accidents," Benson said, clearly to Stacy. "Late at night, after shift, you could have gone for a drive, missed that turn, gone over. The methane…a danger of septic tanks that haven't been cleaned out. If we hadn't been specifically aware, looking, we might not ever have found those tanks. They were small enough to sink if there'd been enough refuse down there. You were damned lucky you'd just had the tank cleaned. And now, with him trashing the van…we have to assume he's still here. We have to assume he's going to be escalating." Benson's tone had a definite warning to it.

One that Mac was already feeling to his core. He needed a different plan than hanging Stacy out as bait. A better one.

"Him escalating is exactly what we need." Stacy spoke strongly. Mac could feel her gaze boring into him. "I want this to end," she continued, "and end soon. We have to keep him worried."

"She told a neighbor, an older guy who dines at Rich's, that we have a suspect from out of town," Mac reported, feeling as though he was tattling on his partner, betraying her. Sent her an unapologetic look as he did so.

He was executing her plan with her. But he was going to cover all bases, everywhere he could. As long as she lived through the ordeal, she could hate him all she wanted.

"He should be getting the word around town right about now," she said, with a somewhat sheepish glance back at him.

Which meant what? She knew what she'd done. Had done it deliberately. Without talking to him first. He'd already known that much.

Had put it down to having spent hours trapped in a vehicle on the verge of death less than two full days before.

Had there been more to it than that?

What, she didn't trust him anymore? Not like she used to?

Shaking his head, he dismissed the thought immediately. Admonished himself for even having it. He wouldn't be there if she didn't trust him with her life.

And him not taking the promotion...that had mattered to her.

A lot.

The pleasure he took from that knowledge didn't bode well, however.

As he pulled into Stacy's drive, and then her garage, parking in her spot automatically, he made another very strong mental note to himself to put aside any over the top feelings that might be rolling around inside him where his partner was concerned. They had only emerged because he'd had to sit there waiting for help to come, knowing that any second he could be watching her plunge to her death.

That had to be it.

They'd been together too long, with no personal emotion issues between them, for there to be any other explanation.

A fact he reminded himself of once again as he entered her house.

Other than double-checking all possible entrance points, Mac didn't pay attention to the interior of Stacy's home as he dropped his bag in the room she'd indicated. He was glad to know he'd have his own bathroom—a hallway access, but fine—and as she warmed up the chicken and put a salad together, he got set up at the kitchen table for a night of work.

Hudson Warner had strongly recommended that Mac and Stacy go through Stacy's private life, talking through memories to see if anything stood out to either of them. To Mac, if not her. Just as Sierra's Web was still going through cases the two of them had handled, they wanted Mac and Stacy to do the same with her personal world. Looking for anything that could be a recent stressor for someone, case related or not, and all outside contacts that could point to Stacy in any way.

Because, as Hudson Warner had said, it was just plain foolish to only focus on one possibility. No matter how certain they were that they had their guy.

In the jobs Stacy and Mac did, assignments from detectives and higher-ups who ran investigations, they were always just on one trail.

Which was part of what made them so good at what they did. They were excellent investigators who followed one suspicion until it panned out or didn't.

And now they had to focus on all trails.

Mac had no doubt both of them were up to the task.

They'd both turned down multiple offers to move up to detective status. His discomfort lay in setting out to deliberately cross the line they'd swore they'd never cross. To break their cardinal rule. No personal life at work.

Manning had crossed the line when he'd tried to take Stacy's life. Both work and personal. One didn't exist without the other.

A fact that Mac was finding difficult coming to terms with.

Officers were already outside. Miguel, who was running the protection duty, was first up with his regular partner, Beth Parker. Another pair, deputies from the sheriff's office, would take over at midnight, and Martha and her partner would show up at six in the morning. All were volunteering for extra duty until Stacy's intended murderer was caught.

For everyone's sake, he had to get his instincts in full gear, be the cop he'd been born to be, and get the job done.

Once he was off duty, and away from Stacy Waltz, he could be a man with personal needs.

Chapter 11

She'd planted the seed with Tom on purpose. A move that, any other time, she and Mac would have discussed first. But she hadn't waited for him.

Because she'd thought Mac might be taking another job. Ending their partnership. Without even telling her.

He hadn't been.

She'd overreacted.

Responded personally, not professionally.

In five years as his partner, she'd never done that.

Which, in that moment, scared Stacy more than Landon Manning did.

But not quite as much as sitting down at her table with him, plates of food beside each of them, ready to go to work.

She'd stalled as long as she could. Had to look at her life as though she was just another person she and Mac were interviewing.

It wasn't personal.

Just like them delving into the intimate lives of their victims didn't mean any kind of relationship was starting between them. They were first responders doing their jobs.

Mac took a bite of food. She did as well. Searching her brain for a way to come out proving that she was in complete control and not the least bit emotionally involved in what was to come between them.

"Tell me about Tom Brandon." Mac seemed so relaxed, so ordinary. Like they were at Rich's sitting across from each other in a booth, rather than her kitchen table. He hadn't changed out of his uniform, which helped.

Neither had she.

She'd needed the barrier. For Mac.

And for herself. She was desperately searching for a return to the sense of safety the uniform had always given her. In uniform she was strong. Capable. Armed and ready.

She'd been abducted in her uniform. With all her gear on her. And hadn't been able to access any of it...

"What?" Mac's question brought her back to the table. He'd stopped eating, his fork halfway to his mouth.

Looking at her in that way he had of letting her know that he knew she'd gone somewhere, and he wasn't letting up until she'd told him where.

Because in the past, when she'd traveled off in her mind around him, it had always been case related.

Her personal fears were not so. And right then, when they were about to dive into her past to reassure themselves that there were no other possible murderers lurking there, she had to stay case related.

She blurted what came to mind. "My grandfather and Tom didn't see eye to eye," she told him. "Tom was younger, had all these ideas about making profits off the land, and my grandfather was this wickedly smart but extremely gentle man who cared about the land. And his animals."

"Brandon said he's a miner."

"Right. He owns the Layby mine. It butts up to his home property. He'd spent years up in the Clairs—" she used the term the locals did when referring to their mountains, the Clairvoyant Mountain Range "—searching for gold. He was the first person who ever told me the story about the

Superstition mine and spent his summers all through college trying to find it."

More than a century before, a German man had staked a claim and came out of the Clairvoyant Mountains with gold. Again and again. He mined alone, with a pickax and little else. And he died alone. Without ever telling anyone where the mine was located. People still flocked to Saguaro every year to head up into the mountains to try to find that gold.

"In later years, he made a lot of money hiring himself as a guide to visitors wanting to find the Superstition mine, or any other gold that hadn't been legally claimed yet."

"Layby mine?" Mac asked, frowning. "I thought that was a gold panning tourist trap for kids."

She shrugged. "In the front parking lot, it is. Like I said, Tom's all about using the land, and her legends, to make a buck, but he actually did find gold. Just not up in the Clairs. He found it not far from his property, bought the land, and staked the claim. He's got a crew. And they bring up enough gold to support them. Tom has always said that there's a main vein that his gold feeds off from and as soon as he gets to it, he'll be a millionaire. Mary's tired of waiting for him to strike it. And, frankly, I don't blame her. Still, she married him, knowing that his thirst for gold was as much a part of him as the blood in his veins. She used to tell me stories about some of his adventures in the mountains. He'd hit some coal and make enough money to support them for a year or two, and that just fed his lust."

As long as Mac would let her, she'd keep talking about her eccentric old neighbor.

"When he hit that small vein of gold, and started mining down here, that's when he and my grandfather started having problems. Until then, they'd share beers and stories on their porches. But once Tom started bringing in trucks and tearing up the land, once he built some of the processing operation, which my grandfather considered a huge eyesore, my grandfather started talking about moving. Instead, he gave the big house to Mom and Dad, and built this place. Since it's around the corner, and over the hill, the two of them were able to live compatibly enough…"

End of her story. And she still wasn't ready to begin.

"I'm not currently involved with anyone and have no exes, or exes of exes, no currents of exes…no one that we could look to as suspects," she finally told Mac, looking him right in the eye. There he had it. She wasn't drop dead gorgeous dating material. He wasn't the only one who didn't find her so. Yet, ironically, though she was pretty much invisible in the dating field, someone found her noteworthy enough to see that she dropped dead.

"Anyone who had a crush on you?" he asked, still holding her gaze.

"No." She shook her head. "Brett and I were inseparable from the time we were little. The segue between best friends and something more just kind of happened. Frankly later than I think everyone thought it had. Kids at school used to act like we were a couple, thinking we'd be attending junior high dances together as a couple, that sort of thing, long before we ever actually held hands. Or went on a date."

Because she'd already been getting everything she needed from him. His heart. His soul. And when he'd told her that he wanted more, that he'd fallen in love with her, that he wanted her to be his girlfriend, and eventually his wife, she'd been thrilled.

There'd never been anyone else who attracted her, either. Growing up an only child with only a father and grandfather to guide her, she'd been a bit of a tomboy. Not wanting to be a boy, just not knowing how to be girly, either.

Her relationship with Mac was a perfect example of the rest of her life, she could have told him. Great relationships with the opposite sex. Just…no sex.

"Miguel said once that if Brett hadn't already stolen you from the time you learned to walk, he'd have asked you out…"

"WHAT?" She stood as she hollered the word. Then, because she had to make it look like she'd meant to stand, started clearing their plates. "That makes no sense. When did he say that?"

Miguel Gomez was a happily married father of two adorable little girls.

"Years ago. When we first started working together. He'd wanted to make sure I knew that you'd lost your husband to violence…"

Mac didn't get up to help. Instead, he turned and glanced out the window behind him, as though checking the perimeter. In spite of the pitch-blackness.

And *Miguel?* She'd never known.

"My point is, if there's one Miguel, there could be more…"

"And out of the blue, a decade later, he decides I need to die because of it?" Just didn't make sense.

"Unless there's someone who's tried over the years." Mac's tone grew serious, and he was gazing at her again as, their plates in the dishwasher, she sat back down. "All I'm asking is that you think for a second, Stace. Open your mind to the possibility. Is there anyone who's been friendly with you over the years? Maybe off and on? Anyone who was even a little bit flirty? You'd probably have taken for granted that he was teasing. And maybe this someone just had a bad breakup. He might have told you about it. Could even be someone at work…"

Everything in her stilled as he said that. Not because she had anyone in mind. At all. But because he'd just taken away her last vestige of normalcy.

"We have to consider every possibility," Mac said then, his eyes looking solidly into hers. "This guy, he knew your schedule. Knew just how to time things to get in and get you out within a minute or two. If not for those boulders, his plan would have been near perfect. Even if we'd flown helicopters looking for a sign of you, there was every possibility that we'd never have seen your SUV if it had gone all the way down…"

He was scaring the hell out of her. And bringing her back to life, too. Keeping her sharp.

"Same with the methane. I'd have just gone to sleep and natural gas would have been the cause," she said then, nodding. Determined to do as Mac and Sierra's Web had asked. Look for any and all possibilities. Then look again. With a cop's view of her life.

They weren't taking any more chances.

Going back in her mind…grade school, a jump ahead to high school, college, police academy, her wedding, junior high, five years in the police department…just flashes. Faces. Moods. No real conversations. Just impressions.

And eventually, still looking at Mac, shook her head. "Other than Brett, I was pretty much an introvert. Lived in my own little world. I read a lot. And spent most of my free time with Brett and the horses. And after Brett… I joined the force. If there is someone else, I sure don't know it," she told him. Not sure if the pronouncement was all that great. Thirty years old and, other than Brett, she'd never raised any kind of intense passion in anyone.

Except the man she'd taken down, held down, after he'd killed her husband.

* * *

Relief flooded him. Sitting at Stacy's kitchen table, Mac couldn't stop the light flow of feeling, the lessening of tension in his muscles, as he listened to his partner talk.

He'd gone with Manning as their suspect—all clues led in that direction—but, like Hudson Warner, he'd needed to be sure he wasn't missing something right there in front of him.

He'd been dreading sitting there listening to a past filled with admirers. And others who'd been jealous of her. All potential suspects to rule out. Most particularly after he remembered Miguel mentioning once having had a crush on Stacy.

She hadn't known. Had been shocked.

All good stuff.

What wasn't good was an honest affirmation that a fair amount of his lightening mood had to do with the fact that Stacy wasn't romantically involved. And that there were no past loves she might still pine for.

There could be only one reason for that fact to bring him any pleasure at all.

Because he wanted her for himself.

Until the day before, when he'd been helplessly watching her teeter on the verge of death, he'd never even thought of Stacy in a personal sense.

Not because he didn't find her attractive. But because if he looked at her in that way, he couldn't work with her. And he valued his work life more than any other thing on earth.

Was it possible he valued Stacy more?

That she was part of the reason his work called to him, fulfilled him, as much as it did?

Or was he still just suffering the aftereffects of a traumatic experience?

Either way, he didn't doubt, for a second, his ability to give his life, and his full attention, to keeping his partner safe. No one cared more than he did, would give more than he would, to see her kidnapper caught.

But after that...

Unless he woke up to find his new awareness of the woman exorcized, he wasn't going to be able to continue partnering with her.

So he'd do whatever he had to do to exorcize the bizarre surge of inappropriate emotion.

"What about you?" Stacy, arms folded, pinned him with one of her "I'm not backing down" stares.

Had she read his damned mind?

In the second it took him to shake his head and get up to speed, she said, "We can only continue working together if we're on equal footing. We have a no personal information rule, which now has been revised in such a way that weights us unfairly."

"You want to know about my past relationships?"

"I want you to sit there and tell me who, in your past, could have it in for you. Or have unresolved issues that could result in some future shot across the bow."

Staring her down, determined to get her to look away first, Mac considered what she'd said. And what he'd just been thinking.

His partnership with her meant more to him than anything else.

Including his own privacy. Or pride.

Without looking away, not needing to lose that battle to give her what she required, he said, "I've never been in a serious relationship. I'm always exclusive when I date a woman, but it's clear, up front, that it's not going anywhere permanent. No moving in. No plans for the future. If, at any time, I get an inkling that she's starting to want more, I end things immediately. So, perhaps I have a woman or two out there who's not happy with me."

Stacy's chin jutted like it did when she was accepting information she hadn't yet processed. Information she intended to process.

He liked knowing that. Wanted to goad her about it. But wasn't sure if he should.

Which, in itself, was uncharacteristic of their relationship.

"Saguaro is all about family," she said then, surprising him. Her tone was conversational. Maybe a bit challenging, but only marginally so.

The Stacy he knew and loved working with.

"So." He shrugged, still looking her right in the eye.

They'd once eye wrestled, as she'd put it, for half an hour at Rich's diner. A more challenging form of arm wrestling, she'd told him. She'd won that round. But only because he'd allowed himself to get bothered by those coming and going, people they worked with, noticing them sitting there staring at each other like lovers.

At least, he'd been afraid others might see it that way.

"You grew up here." Her tone remained completely uninvolved. "More to the point, you stayed. How, then, could you not want the life?"

He blinked. Blinking was allowed. Closing out sights, otherwise known as a long blink, was not. Mac kept his gaze steady on hers. Fending off the near glitch.

"I have the life I grew up in," he told her, comfortable with his truth. With choices deliberately made years before. Ones that suited him. "The latter part, where I was happy. And no risk of the former, where I was not."

"You didn't grow up alone."

He hadn't dug deeper into her revelations. Was considering calling a foul on her. But, that hint of challenge in her tone, he didn't want her to think she was making him sweat.

"My early years were filled with arguing, then fighting, then tense silences, and finally bitterness and attempts to win at all costs. When my parents remarried and had children with their spouses, I had loving families. Two of them. Those years were spent living week by week, back and forth between two homes, two sets of rules, two sets of siblings. I loved. And was loved. But was never fully a part of either family. My experience with love and loyalty, with security, is living on the edges of it. Not all in. It's what I know. What I'm good with. I get the good without risking the arguing, then fighting, love turning to hate thing."

Stacy's gaze changed. Slowly. Challenge drained away, leaving…warmth.

Compassion.

And Mac looked away.

Chapter 12

They were living in a bizarre no-man's-land. Being full time on one case wasn't unusual for her and Mac. Even staying in the same lodgings with separate rooms, same.

Eating food that one or the other of them prepared, in a private kitchen—never.

Having no time off—just didn't happen. Police work was hard. All encompassing. They needed down time to keep themselves sharp.

But death wasn't going to wait around for any of them to get rested before it struck again. And since it was knocking at Stacy's door, she couldn't very well pass the job on to someone else while she took a moment to rejuvenate.

When she woke Thursday morning to find Mac already in full uniform in the kitchen, with coffee made, she tried to get him to at least take a breather. Just the day, if that's all he wanted, to return before dark.

"That's what you'd do if it was my life on the line?" he asked.

Hell no. She didn't speak the words aloud.

"And why not?" he asked anyway.

"Because living it every minute, you take in every detail as it happens, every piece of information as it comes in, and the accumulation is what often brings the break in the case." He'd taught her that.

"We retired to our rooms early last night," he said then. "Just like when we're on the road and have done all we can do for the day."

He was right, of course.

She just…needed more space from him. To get over the insidious dreams that continued to come even now that she was off the drug and out of the SUV casket.

Made worse by her new visions of a younger Mac, a kid Mac, being passed back and forth between families without ever belonging fully…anywhere.

She'd never had a mother. He'd had two.

She'd only had one father. He'd had two.

And yet, she'd always been wholly part of a solid family unit that drove her to want exactly that for her future. A husband, children.

The big house filled with squeals and laughter, with challenge and obstacles, too. But always with the security that set you free.

Things Mac not only didn't value, but things he didn't even understand.

Which was fine.

He wasn't the man in her mental scenario. He couldn't be.

She didn't even want him to be. No way she wanted to trade her days with Mac for days without him.

She just…needed some space.

She badly needed time apart from him to recover from her recent emotional trauma.

And just as much, she wanted him there. Doing what he did best. There was no one she trusted more to get the job done.

They'd just finished a working breakfast. Going over reports from the night officers watching her place, checking in with Martha. They were determining that they'd start the day back in the conference room at the department head-quarters when Hudson Warner called.

Thinking it would just be his morning report, updates with no immediately actionable news, Stacy tended to her tattering nerves by clearing the dishes from the table as Mac answered on speakerphone.

"We've got a lead," the expert tech boss said. "Manning flew into a small private airport about fifteen miles east of you last week. The runway is part of a gated community. Owners park their planes at their estates, some in hangars, some not. There's parking for a few nonresident planes as well, but you have to know someone who knows someone to get landing permission."

"Someone there knows him?" Stacy asked, dirty bowls—empty of the oatmeal and bananas that had been in them—in hand. "His name came up?"

"Not that much of a lead." Hudson's reply showed no emotional response at all. "We got him on a homeowner's security system. I'm sending the image to you, but not only is it pretty obviously him, we've run it through software as well. We can send someone out to the neighborhood to question people if you'd like."

"No." Mac spoke before Stacy could. "We'll go. This is the part we do best…"

And just like that, they were back to work. Their real work.

Stacy and Mac.

Police partners.

With an assignment.

Adrenaline surged through Stacy. Leaving the dishes in the sink, she grabbed her gear and followed Mac out the door.

Telling herself that by nightfall, life would be normal again.

And she and Mac would go back to being who they'd always been.

Mac opted to take his private vehicle to the south valley. Not only did he want to get right on the road, hoping to catch at least some of the homeowners before they left for the day—he also wanted to be free to go wherever the wind took them from there.

Like he and Stacy always did when they were on assignment outside Saguaro PD.

He didn't say so, but he also hoped that Stacy would be a little less conspicuous in a truck that looked like so many other vehicles on the road. While he understood the reason for making it known that she hadn't died as intended, potentially putting a target on her back, he wasn't going to dangle her in front of Manning with a light shining on her.

He'd driven about a mile or so up her road, approaching the area's largest gold mine that had been closed a century before due to flooding. It had since been turned into a ghost town tourist stop. Suddenly, Stacy yelled, "Stop!"

He pulled off into a dirt circle in front of a small gold panning venture and local ore and rock shop, which also had a restaurant known for its biscuits and gravy.

Hand on his gun, instincts on full alert, he was reaching with his other hand to push her head down out of shooting range, when she pointed. "That van, Mac. The white one…"

She was getting out, her hand on her gun. Stood behind the opened passenger door. "I recognize it," she told him, glancing into the truck. "That's the van I almost hit the other night. I don't know what's down the mountain, but that van right there was pulling out just as I came around the corner."

He slid over to her side of the vehicle, and then down, behind her.

The van was a full-size, seven passenger model, and from what he could tell it was American made, newer. And looked to him like any number of others they saw on the road every day. In the Arizona heat, white was one of the most popular vehicle colors.

But he didn't doubt his partner. Stacy, even on her worst days, wasn't prone to drama.

"That sticker on the windshield. It just hit me. It's what I saw when I swerved," she said. "My headlights caught it. It's fuchsia and yellow. They don't really go together..."

"That was right before you pulled into your drive," Mac said, all senses on alert. "Maybe he'd been waiting for you to pass so he could follow you, let his passenger out in the dark to duck into your garage as you pulled in..."

Adrenaline flowing, he assessed the situation.

"If at all possible, we need to wait until he comes out," Stacy said. "Least chance of civilians getting hurt."

Mac, having reached the same conclusion, said, "Get back in. I'll pull up and park nose to nose with the van." She did. And he did.

"It's a Parker Lake sticker," Stacy said without a hint of fear in her tone.

And Mac, glancing over at her, thankful that she was alive, replied, "Get down." And then, "Please. We're here. We've got him. There's no point in alerting him with your face shining right at him. Or giving him an easy chance to get you."

"If it doesn't go down quick and smooth, I'm coming out to help," she warned him.

"I know."

Which was why he had to focus and get it right.

He took in the parking lot, the people coming and going from the restaurant, the distance between the van and the cars parked next to it, a window in the distance behind the van. He figured his best chance to take Manning down without anyone else getting hurt was to wait until he was reaching for the door of his van.

If he wasn't alone, Mac was going to have to involve Stacy.

Either way, they'd have their doors for cover and show their guns before Manning had a chance to reach for his—assuming he was carrying.

He'd order the craphead to the ground, and enjoy putting a foot to the man's back as he cuffed him.

"If he's not alone…"

"…already on it, Stace. You'll take your door, I'll take mine."

She nodded. Glanced up at him. "I hate pink."

"I remember. The nightclub in Globe. Pink walls. Waiting for the coroner." They'd had three dead bodies.

"Yeah, that was a tough one."

But they got the shooter. Stopped him from taking another ten lives.

Two minutes of silence seemed like hours. "Maybe you should go inside. Make sure he doesn't go out the back…"

He'd been thinking the same. Didn't like it, though. He'd need her backup. Which could put her right in Manning's line of fire. If the guy was escalating—a ruined life, with no hope, set on revenge—he wouldn't likely care who he hurt in the process.

"There are a lot of kids in there," he said. He'd been watching three of them, elementary school age, sharing a doughnut as they walked behind their parents in the parking lot. Two of the three had chocolate on their faces, reminding him of his dad's kids when they were little. Innocent. Probably on vacation since they were getting along so well.

The closer they drew to his truck, the tenser he grew. He needed them in their car and gone before Manning appeared.

They didn't veer off. Instead, they just kept coming at him. Mom, Dad and three kids. Walking right into the path of potential danger.

Until…they stopped at the van.

And climbed inside.

"We know the van I almost hit visited Parker Lake at some point." Stacy told herself not to feel stupid for her overreaction, but she did anyway. Mac had called Sierra's Web, to have them get any surveillance cameras they could from the lake's public parking, and also to see if the van trashed down the mountain had the same sticker.

"Parker Lake's between here and Colorado," he said. "We know Manning flew into the valley once, prior to this week, but he could have driven this time. Or other times, too."

She'd been ready to tell him not to humor her—mostly because she was feeling a distinct rush of letdown—when his phone rang.

Hudson Warner again. Mac answered on his truck's audio system.

"I had one of my experts trace times on the east valley private plane neighborhood security footage and compare it to the footage from the city building. Same day. Manning isn't wearing the hoodie in the east valley tape, but he's got a duffel on his shoulder that obviously contained something."

"Why not a hoodie?" Mac asked, smiling over at Stacy.

She knew that smile. They were getting close, and he was eager to bring the guy down.

"We should have the Parker Lake footage within the hour," Hudson reported then. "I've got my team looking for Troy Duncan, too. Could be Manning flew but had the kid drive."

And just like that, Stacy felt validated again. Something that should have been happening from the very beginning. Mac didn't doubt her ability to do her job.

Hudson Warner certainly didn't appear to. Had she not recognized the sticker, had that flash of memory, they'd never have known to look at Parker Lake.

Or to check the van they found for the Parker Lake sticker. An actual identifier. Mac had already called the chief to have all patrol officers on the alert for any other white vans with Parker Lake stickers as well. Just in case.

The only one who was doubting her was her.

Just then on the job—and before that, with the bizarre dreams about Mac.

And that was just going to stop. Period.

Manning had already robbed her of one life—her life with Brett.

He was not going to take her ability to do police work, her life with Mac, away from her, too.

Manning had flown into town within an hour of the black hooded likeness of him appearing at the Saguaro city building. They were closing in on him, one step at a time.

Doing their jobs.

Getting closer.

And Stacy was still with him.

Doing hers.

As he pulled into the east valley gated community, stopping first at the house where the security cameras had caught images of Manning—the owners of which had given them the access code to enter—he and Stacy made their rounds all over the neighborhood. One house at a time. Walking door to door. Looking for anyone who knew Landon Manning personally.

Needing to find the one who'd given him permission to land on the private runway.

And in the end, found out that a private company leased a couple of small-plane parking lanes from the homeowners association to bring celebrities in and out of Phoenix anonymously.

Apparently, Manning still qualified as a celebrity in some circles.

Or knew someone who'd pulled strings for him.

The company was refusing to give any further information without a court order. Their entire business was built around the promise of confidentiality.

And as yet, there was no solid proof that Landon Manning was a kidnapper and attempted murderer.

He glanced at Stacy as they walked back to his truck. "Feel like some lun…" Mac's heart lurched, his gut turned to rock as he dove for his partner, tackling and rolling with her in the pebbled desert landscaping of the yard they'd been passing.

He'd moved on instinct. A sense of immediate danger, not conscious thought.

Keeping his body over hers, tucking his face in her hair, he put his hands over his head and felt her breathing beneath him. Felt her softness…

A boom rang out. Leaving his ears ringing, encased in

cotton. Still, he lay there. Waiting. His body pressing into Stacy's knee to knee, groin to butt, chest to back.

Seconds passed. He heard running. "You guys okay?" a voice called out.

"I've called 911," another said.

Nine-one-one. First responders. The police. He and Stacy, in full uniform, *were* the police.

And Mac didn't want to get up. He wanted to stay right where he was, feeling Stacy's body beneath him. Her body breathing.

Her head lifting brought him back to reality. Slowly rolling her, he waited for her to turn over, waiting to see her expression. And saw the blood on her wrists, instead.

Scrapes. And a spot on her sleeve that was wet with blood.

She was staring at the remains of an explosive on the sidewalk. "How...what..." Open-mouthed, she looked up at him as if they were the only two people there. Seemingly completely oblivious of the crowd that was gathering.

"It seemed like a bird," he said, looking up at the sky. Thanking the fates that some part of him had realized in time...

"Wow, man, I saw it from my window," a young man, maybe eighteen, said, coming up to them in jeans, a sweatshirt and flip-flops. "I'm into drones, but you know, with the airstrip, we have to be really careful. But this one, it came in quick, dropped its load and left just as quickly."

"A drone?" Stacy was staring from Mac to the kid, to the sky, and back to Mac. Paying no attention at all to the blood dripping down her forearm. A woman came up, pressing a tissue to the gash, and Stacy took the white substance from her, holding it as she walked with Mac to the explosive.

"It had one of those new hooks on it," the kid said, keeping up with them. "You can get 'em now for really small drones and with the cameras on good ones, you can hit your target within half an inch…"

With his ears still ringing Mac pulled out his phone. Called the chief.

And reported that there'd been another attempt on Stacy's life.

If Mac hadn't noticed the "bird" flying low above, the drone would have dropped its load right on Stacy's head.

Chapter 13

If Manning was trying to put her in mental hell, because he himself was in one, he was doing a fair job of it. Stacy wouldn't say she was paranoid as she and Mac headed back to their part of town, but she was most definitely jumpy.

Uncomfortable.

Constantly watching from all directions.

"It's not too late to get you to a safe house," Mac said, watching all his mirrors as he drove. His attention, like hers, was all around them. Guarding against what could come next from any direction.

When it must have become obvious she wasn't going to validate the comment with a response, he added, "Manning clearly knows you're still alive. We can make it harder for him to find you."

"And then what? He implodes on someone else? His wife, maybe? I'm a cop, Mac. Sworn to protect others. Not to run and protect myself. We need this guy off the streets. As soon as possible. Let me do my job."

Fear wasn't going to stop her. It was going to make her better. More aware.

Hudson Warner, who lived with his wife and newly discovered daughter in the east valley, had come to the scene to take the remainder of the explosive, and surveillance footage into custody. Glen Thomas, Sierra's Web science expert, had people in the lab waiting for the explosive, and Hudson's team would put the morning's footage on priority status.

She and Mac were the feet on the street.

"I fully understand if you'd rather not partner with me on this one," she told him. As badly as she wanted him with her, a part of her didn't want him there at all.

Not after that morning's episode. He'd saved her life.

And could so easily have lost his right along with her.

"When it was just me he was after, that was one thing. But if he's escalating, not caring who gets hurt in the process of taking me down, then—"

"You need law enforcement to help you stop him," Mac said, cutting her off, his tone stern. He was watching all mirrors, almost frantically, as though they were in a war zone.

And while most of the vehicles sharing the rush hour road with them were driven by good citizens on their way to living another normal day, there was an enemy out there.

A war of one.

"I don't want to lose you." As soon as the words were out, she wanted to pull them back. Held her breath.

Until he said, "I don't want to lose you, either."

His words seemed to settle something in her, put them on equal footing, and she let her lapse into personal emotions fade off into the ether. They had much bigger problems at the moment.

"We need to minimize his target area," she said then, suddenly finding a sense of power. A way to be in charge. "He's coming after me, Mac. We don't have to chase him."

The morning's drone, in addition to the methane and the midazolam, made it clear that Manning was smart—and had access to pretty much anything he wanted. With his fame, it was possible that he had people who'd help him with whatever he asked, without needing to know why he'd asked.

There was no way of predicting what he'd come up with next.

Or protecting against it.

But... "We choose where it goes down, Mac," she said. "We limit his access to us and have eyes all around us. On the ground and in the air. We set the parameters of where he gets to try and come after me. And when he does, we have our own traps set and get him."

It was all kind of esoteric now...

"Good. Okay. We've got the plan. Let me focus on getting us back to the station in one piece and then we'll work on it."

It wasn't a smiling morning. Or even a happy moment.

But as she kept watch on their backs, sides and fronts, right along with Mac, Stacy felt a little bit like smiling.

In spite of everything, she and Mac, as a working partnership, were still going strong.

Mac had a bad feeling in his gut. Infiltrating a cop's garage, a perfect injection of prescription medication, the getaway. Methane in a septic tank. And a drone? All accomplished like clockwork without leaving any traceable clue.

As he took the highway exit to cross the patch of desert that led into Saguaro, thoughts of the case infiltrated his focus on his surroundings. Theirs was the only vehicle on the road. No others to protect against any potential attempt to kill.

And wide open desert was much easier to surveil than building after building, possibly hiding or camouflaging who knew what attack.

He had no doubt that Stacy's help would bring the agonizing hours or days before them to a close sooner.

And no doubt that knowingly walking her into further danger, exposing her in any way to a perpetrator whose only goal was to kill her, was going against his every instinct.

His only comfort was that if he kept her close, he could exchange his life for hers if need be. He'd have the chance to jump in front of whatever death knell came ringing in her direction.

"We've got a problem," he told Stacy.

Keeping her head below the top of the headrest, she was leaning back, studying side mirrors.

"I don't see anything," she said after long seconds.

"Not imminent," he told her, realizing how ominous his words had sounded. "Overall."

"What?"

"We've got a guy who's escalating his attempts to see you dead, and crimes that are executed in minute detail with extreme precision."

She nodded, as though she'd been silently traveling in the same direction. "Doesn't fit, does it?"

"Manning's here. Or he's been here, we know that. But what if he's not who we're chasing? He could have gone to some mountain retreat for the week, as his wife intimated, to wait to hear that the job is done. This guy, he somehow knew where we were, and was prepared to drop the bomb no matter where it was."

"He hired a professional."

"Or a team of them. This is all happening so quickly. There were backup plans already in place before they began. The methane, in case the garage heist had to be forfeited. The drone...you don't just go buy one and fly it that perfectly. With Manning having been in prison for the past several years, I'm guessing he's not up on that technology enough to pull off something like that."

"Troy Duncan could be the drone guy."

Mac allowed the possibility. "Still, this is all clearly thought out, planned."

Stacy didn't take her eyes off the area around them as she said, "Manning could have been working on it for years. Who knows how many plan Bs he has stacked up, ready to go into action? He could be escalating and just executing preplanned, even preprepared, actions."

"This guy's got money. And plenty of connections to criminals, after living with them for years. He'd know who to hire."

Jaw tight, Stacy's expression was grim as she continued to keep watch. He'd been doing what they did, discussing the case aloud. He hadn't been out to scare her.

But if it worked...and she'd agree to go into hiding...

"Whoever is executing the plan clearly knows your truck, Mac. It was a given, eventually. We'll need different transportation."

They were staying-to-fight words.

And Mac accepted the inevitable.

Stacy was going to be by his side until the end.

"I'll ask the chief to figure that out while we get to work on building our fort," he told her.

And hoped her case wasn't the last one they worked together.

"Get down!" Stacy's scream rent the truck and she braced herself. Mac turned the wheel to get them off the road, slamming on the brake and throwing the truck in park, then ducked.

Stacy, her head between the seat and metal frame of the

truck, kept her view on the paloverde tree. She'd seen a tell-tale glint.

The kind that came from the front end of a gun when the sun hit it. Almost blinding.

She'd been up against them enough to know.

As soon as she had the shot, she pushed the button to lower her window and pulled her trigger.

Mac, who'd positioned himself with dash protection without losing visibility said, "No body fell."

"Or jumped down," she told him. She'd aimed for the trunk. There'd been no shots fired in their direction. And no way to verify if a loaded gun was pointed at them.

Could have been a hunter, out for illegal game.

She knew it wasn't.

She wanted to get out of the truck. To take on the demon haunting her and get it done. To find footprints at the base of that tree, anything to prove that someone had been up in those branches.

But if he was still up there, no matter how much bravado she mustered, he'd shoot her dead before she took her first step toward him.

Mac was on the phone, asking someone to approach the area on foot, from the opposite side. They were on the lookout for a possible shooter as, keeping low, he shifted the truck into drive and sped down the road.

"If Manning's doing this all himself, he had time to get from the east valley back out here and set up in the tree," she said.

"And if he isn't, positioning someone on the only road into town was a smart, calculated move just the same," Mac told her.

She looked over at him for the first time since they'd

left the gated airstrip community. "You believe I saw what I saw."

"I believe you saw something and took appropriate action."

Or had she overreacted?

Again?

If so, he wasn't calling her on it.

She didn't want to be mollycoddled. And didn't want to make any bigger deal of the incident, either way, so took him at face value.

And told herself, even if she hadn't seen the glint—which she was still certain she'd seen—she hadn't endangered anyone with her zealousness.

Unless, coupled with her sighting of the white van that morning, she was slowly losing Mac's confidence.

If that happened, then whether Manning killed her or not, he'd win.

Mac had to consider the possibility that Stacy was not capable of doing her job. He didn't blame her. Didn't even think less of her.

He just had to determine what he was going to do about it.

If, indeed, that was the case.

Twice in one morning, she'd called out danger with few results.

But then, she'd done so the morning before as well, with the methane, and that had saved her life, and possibly Martha's as well.

If anyone had lit a match, the whole place could have gone up.

The van that morning…she'd recognized a sticker.

A good lead.

And a way to weed out thousands of other white vans rolling around the Phoenix valley.

One shot to a tree in the middle of acres of uninhabited desert…it couldn't hurt.

While she might be a bit quick to jump, her police work was still on track. She'd followed protocol.

His deciding factor, though, was that if he didn't keep her with him, he wasn't going to get her to stop hunting Manning. She'd just do it without help.

Without any kind of protection other than what she could offer herself.

That last realization gave him some doubt to his own culpability in the overreaction zone. Or nonprofessional arena, at least.

As a cop, he never let emotion rule his choices.

And yet, he'd just done so.

His emotional need to keep Stacy safe at all costs had made a critical decision for him.

It was up to him to make certain that neither one of them paid for that with their life.

Back at the station, he had Stacy fill the chief in on their new battle plan. He called Sierra's Web to ask for the experts' input on possible locations for him and Stacy to set up to draw out Manning, and best practice, unseen safety measures that would protect them while they brought the man down.

Alive, if at all possible.

Mac and Stacy each shared their theory that they might be dealing with a professional, or even a group of them, which would highly impact any safety measures put in place.

And then they got to work. Bouncing ideas off each other. Listening to input from others as it came in.

Wherever they ended up, they needed Manning to be

able to find them. To know where they were. Without being too overt about doing so.

"Clearly he's got tracking measures in place," Stacy pointed out to a table of officers, as well as the chief, Lieutenant Stahl and Hudson Warner. "He found us in the east valley within an hour of us arriving. Maybe we just get to wherever we're going, as carefully as we would if we didn't want him finding us, and trust that he'll get there, too. If he doesn't, we find a way to lead him to us."

Pride in Stacy got in Mac's way for a second as he watched everyone at the table nod. She had a way of getting to the inside of a situation and working her way out that generally led to great police work. He'd seen it again and again over the years. Her ability to evaluate all sides and come up with something that made sense.

She was still on.

He wanted to celebrate that victory with her. Not in a condescending manner, not like wow, she wasn't losing it, but in a you-are-one-hell-of-a-person-and-I'm-honored-to-know-you kind of way.

Instead, he focused on the professionals around the table, there to work the case, Stacy included.

Chapter 14

"If we're going to proceed as expected, we get you two to a safe house," Chief Benson said, looking between Stacy and Mac who were seated together on one side of the table. "You can work your magic from there."

Stacy saw Mac's nod. Clearly, he liked the idea.

It would put her where he'd wanted her from the beginning, but sending him in with her, to work with her when Manning hit. It still let her get her man.

And in the controlled environment she'd suggested.

Except that her gut told her Manning wouldn't breach police boundaries. The man knew what would happen to him if he got caught.

Which was why all his attempts to kill her had been so carefully planned.

"We could use a county safe house instead of a city one," Stahl offered.

Hudson Warner, the Sierra's Web expert, wasn't nodding. Neither was Stacy. They were the only two.

"What do you think?" she asked the one non-law enforcement body in the room.

"I think outside the box," the dark-haired man said, his brown eyes meeting up with all those around the table.

"Which is what I think we need here," Stacy said. "We believe his plans have all been put in place already. They're just awaiting execution. He won't be prepared to breach drawn police lines. Even at my place, he didn't come near when Mac and I were inside and we had patrols outside. We need him to think we're out looking for my intended killer. Landon Manning knows me. He'd likely see through any safe house attempt. He might still try to get to me. More likely, he'd head back to Colorado, and as his failure feeds his burning anger and frustration, he'd hurt someone else. Could be his wife. Or, God forbid, his little girl. He knows I don't give in to bullying and that I don't give up. Which is what ended up getting him into prison for second-degree murder. Without my refusal to quit fighting my fight, he'd have had a manslaughter charge at best, but most likely would have walked away with no charges at all."

She glanced Mac's way, and he didn't make any attempt to discourage her conversation. He met her gaze openly.

Five years of trusting in "them" didn't just evaporate.

She wondered if he knew how badly she'd needed that validation.

"Manning needs to believe that I'm hunting him down," she continued, "while I'm in whatever kind of controlled environment we can create."

"I agree." Mac didn't sound happy about that. But she took a lot of strength from his honesty.

"Warner?" Heath Benson didn't look happy as he turned to the expert.

"We had a case not long ago. A schoolteacher who'd happened upon a crime, talked to the police and ended up on the wrong side of some powerfully bad people. Her father had trained her in outdoor survival skills, and she got herself to a small cave. She wasn't there long. We were able to ping her phone and help our client get to her while we did what he'd hired us to do, but what's key here is what she did in the meantime." The man's delivery was compelling. Mac found himself open to considering possibilities, even while he wanted Stacy in the safe house. With perimeters already set and protocols ready to go.

"The woman used all natural items to build a booby trap around herself. Digging a trench around the cave for instance, filling it with twigs, and then covering the entire thing with desert dirt and pebbles so that anyone approaching would walk through it. At which time, she'd hear a loud crunch and know that her perimeter had been breached."

Mac seemed impressed, though she got no sense at all that he was buying into being a part of such a plan. He'd be giving his own input if he was onboard.

"I like it," Stacy said anyway, glancing at Mac again, quickly, but then right back to Hudson Warner. "It makes perfect sense. We just have to find the right cave—it's not like we have a shortage of them here at the base of the Clair-voyants—then get our traps set. And figure out a reason for Mac and I to be trapped out there. Maybe we're hiking and I twist my ankle and can't walk. We try to radio for help, but there's no service…"

"I'd simply pick you up and carry you out." Mac's words stopped her.

He wasn't on her side.

Which meant she had a choice to make.

Try to push through what looked to be an entire department of negativity or give in and do it their way.

"So we figure out a different reason," she said. She'd just told them all…she didn't give in. "Or I go in by myself."

In a million years she'd never have seen herself for the person laying a gauntlet down to the chief.

Or to Mac.

"Hold on a second here." Chief Benson sat forward, his tone commanding.

And Mac rapped his thumb on the table. "Stacy's making a good point here," he said. "A valid one that could mean the difference between getting this guy or getting someone else hurt."

She had to blink. Fast. More than once.

No way in hell she could sit at that table and let her eyes fill with tears.

"I agree," Benson said. "The point is valid. But, hear me out. I saw Tom Brandon, your neighbor—" the chief nodded toward Stacy "—at Rich's this morning. He wanted to know if we were any closer to getting this guy. The old man is clearly worried about you. He couldn't understand why we weren't getting you to a safe house, in spite of how hardheaded—his words not mine—you could be at times. He said your grandad must be turning over in his grave."

Stacy felt every eye at the table on her. Withstood the contact without getting the least bit warm under her skin.

Chief Benson continued to hold court. "Listening to everything here, it's made me think…since Manning is proving to be as astute as he is, and has backup plans to prove it, he'd have one for a safe house. Because if someone like Tom Brandon can't believe you aren't in one, most everyone else would expect it as well. Including Manning. If his first plan failed, and you lived, he'd expect you to be in a safe house."

"Right, and doing it now, after this morning's attempt, plays into what you were saying, too, Stacy," Mac said, his tone growing in ownership of the discussion as he sat forward. "You've refused to go, you think you can get him, and he's showing you, you can't. He's winning, which will fuel his need to succeed even more. He'd have to figure that no one would send you out alone to take on this guy," Mac continued. "He knows you'd be outvoted if you still, in his opinion, were lacking in intelligence enough to take him on, and he would probably take pleasure in having made that, the outvoting, happen."

Mac was making too much sense, dammit. Thinking like a man of Manning's caliber might, in terms of underestimating her intelligence.

"We just need to be predictable," Mac continued. "Shift changes have to be at regular hours, protocol has to be exactly as it's already set. He needs to feel confident that he's got us figured out and will show us just how stupid we were to think Stacy would be protected in a safe house."

"Which means we have to be prepared for an abnormal breach," Stacy said, not happy, but not altogether against the plan.

It was better than heading out on the case of her life— literally—without Mac. She might be hardheaded, but she wasn't a fool.

"I'll get my team on a nationwide search of ways safe houses have been breached in the past," Hudson said. "A smart man would do the same research."

From there a house was chosen. Set out in the desert down the road from an old church. Martha went out to Stacy's house to collect a list of her things. Miguel set out for Mac's place to do the same.

And all that was left was for Mac and Stacy to learn all the ways the house could be breached and be prepared to counteract every one of them.

Oddly enough, she wasn't very worried about that. When it came to the job, she and Mac always found a way.

What was giving her the jitters was knowing that until Manning was caught or a week had passed, she and Mac would be holed up alone in a tiny two-bedroom stone building, with a very small kitchen and only one bathroom. She'd been picturing less intimate quarters.

She could hold her own against Manning. Now that she knew he was out there gunning for her.

She wasn't nearly as confident that she could control her new and wholly inappropriate awareness of Mac. The man.

Mac and Stacy were in the safe house by late afternoon. They'd driven a department-owned unmarked tan sedan with a private vehicle escort in front of and behind them.

Mac took the front bedroom, wanting to be between the only entrance and Stacy. He tested all four of the window locks, making certain that, if necessary, he and Stacy could exit through them. And tested the electric wire around the casings that would alert them if anyone tried to breach the openings, making sure all of them were on and working properly.

He didn't unpack.

Stacy had set up a portable whiteboard. Was filling it in based on a picture of the original she'd shot with her phone before leaving the conference room.

Right after they'd had confirmation that there were signs of someone having been up in the paloverde tree Stacy had shot at late that morning. Not only had officers found her bullet wedged lower in the trunk, there'd also been broken twigs right where she'd said she'd seen the glint. And a partial toe print in a clod of loose dirt on the hard, rock-strewn desert ground at the base of the tree.

Didn't mean it was Manning, or anyone working for him. But it did validate her response.

They'd heard on the drive out to the house that the white van had been pulled up the mountain. The entire front end had been smashed like a pancake to the back seat, making any kind of sticker discovery in the strewn shards of glass like looking for a needle in a haystack. There'd been no sign of a body inside. No blood. And no discernible fingerprints. It was being sent to the Sierra's Web lab for further testing.

The drone hadn't been caught on any radar, or security cameras—which wasn't a surprise. But Mac had hoped they'd be able to at least figure out its launch site. Something to give them a starting place. He wasn't about to just sit around and wait for Manning to come to them—though he agreed that it was a good backup plan.

The Sierra's Web forensics team had been able to narrow down the methane canisters to having been sold in two-packs by a chain of national stores. Sierra's Web was in the process of contacting the store's East Coast headquarters to get hundreds of stores with surveillance footage.

Baby steps. He needed leaps and bounds.

As he came out to join Stacy in what they'd set up as their conference room—by moving the kitchen table into the middle of the living space and shoving couch and chairs up against walls—he noticed her cupping her forearm as she brought it down from the board.

"You should have let them stitch you up," he told her. Other than the first glimpse, he hadn't seen the wound she'd sustained that morning. She'd been tended to by paramedics called to the scene of the drone-induced explosion, and by the time she'd been back in the vehicle with him, she'd had her stained uniform sleeve back down to her wrist.

"It's butterflied," she told him. "I wasn't going all the way to the hospital for two stitches."

The gash wasn't deep, he'd been told by the paramedic. Just enough loose skin that it would have been better suited tied together for less scarring.

She'd switched out her uniform shirt since then.

"Let me know if you need help changing the bandage," he said then, knowing he had to let it go. She wasn't his to worry over. Not if it wasn't life or death.

Dropping his legal pad to the table, along with his phone, Mac grabbed a bottle of water, wishing it was beer, and pulled out one of the two wooden chairs just as his phone rang.

Stacy turned, glancing at the screen: *Sierra's Web Hudson Warner.*

They were waiting on the safe house breach report.

He answered on speakerphone.

"I'm sending over what we have so far of the breach report," the technical expert said. "Our preliminary assessment shows the biggest threat to be by air. You're in a brick building with a tile roof so there's no burn threat, but there could, of course, be an explosion."

"Thank goodness for Arizona's tile roofs," Stacy said, half beneath her breath. But Mac heard. And smiled. For no explainable reason.

"We're setting up aerial surveillance," Hudson continued. "Will have someone watching the airspace within three acres of you twenty-four seven. If a drone enters the airspace, it will be brought down."

He didn't ask how. Didn't need to know what he didn't need to know.

"Of more interest to you, and concern to me, is what my team found. You're both going to want to hear this," Hudson said then. Mac saw Stacy stiffen across from him, and he sat forward.

"Stacy and I are sitting right here."

"We've found a motherlode of posts on private sites on the dark web. Various screen names, but they all eventually lead back to various servers in Colorado. All of which have also been frequently used by the verified Landon Manning accounts on popular social media sites."

Mac automatically glanced at Stacy, met her gaze and nodded. Finally. They could be getting somewhere.

"Millions of people use the same servers," Stacy pointed out.

"Yes, but these posts all coincide, within minutes, of the public Manning posts. Always right after them. And from the same server with the same sign in."

"He was in a minimum-security prison," Stacy said. "But he wasn't supposed to have internet access." Mac glanced at her again. Noticing an almost auburn light in her brown eyes.

Finding it familiar.

And completely brand-new.

At a time when her life was at stake?

At any time?

Being locked in with her in such a small space was already getting to him. Why had he ever thought the safe house a good idea?

"Clearly he had a publicity campaign going to keep his name out there. We know he had email access to approved addresses..." Hudson's voice filled the room.

Mac shook his head. "He's Landon Manning, serving in a prison in his home state." He heard the frustration in his tone. Felt it even more fiercely. "It's likely that he got special privileges—even if they weren't officially granted. I'm guessing he had whatever computer access he wanted. Routed however it had to be routed to not come back on him. Let's hear the posts." Pent-up energy raced through him. He needed to work. Not sit.

"They're all rants, and I mean rants—as in they go and

on, but never really get anyplace—about women in the police force, in general. Women who don't know their place and think they need to get involved in their husband's business. Women who can't leave well enough alone. And then about wives who like coming to their husband's defense so much that they decide to be cops and beat up on men for the rest of their lives. Ruining the lives of great men. In several of them he mentions brown hair and brown eyes. Saying the brown hair needs to burn."

Mac froze. Tuned in. All senses on high alert.

Brown hair burning.

A small, relatively harmless explosion—meant for Stacy's head. It would likely have killed her. Or at least left her with permanent injuries.

And it would have set her hair on fire, too.

Glancing at Stacy, seeing the realization dawn in her eyes—and the there-and-gone flash of raw fear—Mac knew he was going to do everything in his power, no matter how much it angered her, to keep her in his sight, to trade his life for hers if that's what it took. To bring Landon Manning down for good.

Chapter 15

"The biggest problem is the unpredictability." Stacy paced the small living area, stopping in front of the whiteboard. "If we had any idea where he was…"

She stared at the board, feeling like bugs were crawling under her skin. Nerves on edge, ready to start popping.

Until Mac came walking in from the kitchen, handing her a cup of the herbal tea she loved. "I asked Martha to pick some up," he told her.

And then she just wanted to cry.

She sipped tea instead. "I asked for it, too," she told him. And had told their fellow officer to make sure that the coffee was dark roast and strong.

Because that was how Mac had to have it.

"Which explains why there's so much of it," he said, standing there with his own cup. He glanced at her over the top of it. "There's an ample supply of coffee, too."

She nodded. Didn't admit aloud what they both knew. They'd put in orders for each other.

It didn't mean anything.

Only that with all the meals they'd shared on shift, all the times they'd heard each other order, they knew preferences.

"This case sucks," she said then, feeling like it had been forever since she and Mac had been coming off a normal shift.

She'd thought that their last night as just two cops working their jobs—the three shootings—had been tough.

Seemed like a cakewalk at the moment.

And she couldn't find her footing. She wanted to. Swore she would. Was doing all she could. Had no intention whatsoever of stopping until Manning was either captured, or he got her. She couldn't stop. Not and live with herself.

But... "I'm not myself." She had to be as honest with Mac as she was being with herself. He was putting his life on the line, and while she had to accept that she might die, she couldn't be responsible for him losing his life.

Not ever.

She'd put herself in front of the bullet first. Every time.

Frowning, Mac set his coffee cup on the table and moved closer to her.

A move that made her situation worse. Plopping down on the wooden chair she'd deemed hers for the duration, she glanced up at him. Took a deep breath. And said, "I'm... unusually emotional."

Truth. Just not explicit.

Did it need to be to save his life?

Pulling his seat around the table next to hers, Mac sat, rested his elbows on his knees as he leaned toward her, and met her gaze. "Do you need to pull off the case?" he asked. And then said, "I'll understand completely, Stace, and no one, no one," he reiterated with a strong nod of his head, "will blame you. In fact, I think everyone would prefer it."

She withstood his stare. And returned a stronger one of her own. "I'm not going to sit back and wait while others put their lives on the line for me, Mac. How could you even think that I would?"

Mac, of all people.

Didn't he know her at all?

The swell of hurt that swamped her for a second was testimony to her earlier statement. But it was no reason for her to run and hide.

To the contrary.

"Wishful thinking is more like it." He sat back with a bit of a wry grin. "Because to be honest with you, I'm finding a bit of…unusual emotion…showing up in some of my reactions as well."

Another swell. More tamping down inappropriate feelings. "You want me to partner with someone else?" Why did she keep coming back to that?

Was she really so afraid of the two of them breaking up?

And if so, was that a reason for them to do so?

"No, Stace. I don't want to lose *you*. I can't get the picture out of my head of your red SUV against those boulders, seeing it rock…" He swallowed, his chin wavering.

Something she couldn't ever remember seeing before. Not in five years worth of dealing with hard stuff.

Her hand lifted, on its way to take his, until she got ahold of herself and laid her palm on the table instead. Making a decision she might regret for the rest of her life. But knowing inside that it was the right thing to do.

They couldn't do their jobs if they were hiding from each other.

"I was in and out that whole time," she told him, forcing herself to look back. To remember. It was life and death on the side of that mountain.

But it was still life and death.

"From the time I was dumped in the back of my car… I'd be dreaming about times when I was a kid, and then I was awake, aware, planning my moves in various eventualities. Biding my time. Fading out again…"

She shook her head. Glanced at him. Met an incredibly

potent look in those brown eyes and had to look away. To draw a deep breath.

He didn't move. Didn't speak.

It was just like Mac, to know that he didn't need to push or pull. If he gave her time, she'd get it out.

He never pressured her. She hadn't consciously realized that until just that moment.

She thought about the seconds when she'd known her vehicle was going over the side of the mountain. When she'd been certain death was seconds, a minute or two at most, away.

And the last memory she'd grabbed, held tight, so that her last feeling was a good one…

He didn't need to know that much.

"I was actually out again when my SUV hit the boulders. The impact jerked me awake. And that whole time, it's hard to believe it was only hours…looking back on it, it seems like it was days…"

She was procrastinating. Had to just get it out there.

If he left, it was for the best.

But if he could live with where she'd gone, if they could get past it as the team she knew they were…

"I tried to plan," she said slowly. Her memories of that part vague. "Thought about climbing to the back…but mostly, I…dreamed."

She looked at him then. Had to if she wasn't going to hide. "They were…hugely inappropriate dreams about you, Mac. I swear to you, I've never had them before, or even entertained thoughts of that nature."

He had to know that. To believe it.

He was looking at her. Nodded. But he didn't seem like Mac.

She didn't blame him. But didn't regret telling him, either. She'd been remiss in not telling him before they'd gotten to the point of being locked up alone in a safe house.

"I kept hearing you call out to me," she continued, moving forward. Giving him all the ammunition he needed to feel justified in walking out. "It was so weird," she remembered. "It was always just my name. No other words. But it's like I had you in there with me…"

She swallowed. And hurried with the rest, focusing on the darker ring around his iris, rather than any expression there. "You'd be touching me. Doing all kinds of things that sent me straight to heaven and I clung to you, wanted more… I'd hear your voice say my name and I'd be right back there, feeling you, wanting more."

He didn't need to hear that she'd been riding him. Or he her.

She was done. He still wasn't talking. Nor had he looked away from her.

"It's okay, Mac. I'm prepared for you to get up and walk out." As prepared as she'd ever be. But she knew, with every fiber of her being, that it was what she truly, deep down wanted, if he felt it was best that he go.

The weaker part of herself would take a bit longer to get there, but she would.

"You heard my voice." When he finally spoke, Mac's throat sounded dry.

"Yes," she told him, nodding. Needing to be strong. For him. But for her, too. Was actually surprised how much more capable she suddenly felt for having told him.

For speaking her truth, rather than living with potentially shameful secrets, knowing that, no matter how difficult, she'd be able to live with the consequences.

"No, I'm telling you, Stace. You really did hear my voice."

Frowning, she blinked, and looked right back at him.

"What?" Where was he going with that? Trying to tell her there was some telepathic communication between them?

"For hours. I stood just yards away…unable to get to you. I kept hollering your name. Over and over. Needing you to know that you weren't alone. That you had to hang on because help was coming."

Stacy's mouth fell open. She closed it.

Then she pushed back her chair, jumped up and walked away.

There wasn't anywhere for her to go. But Mac understood Stacy's need to escape. Had such a conversation ever even hinted at something like this between them in the past, it would have been after shift, and she'd simply have exited their shared vehicle, entered her own and headed off to her private life.

At least, that was the way he was seeing her departure as Stacy walked down the hall to her room. She'd shut the door. As effective a move as she could make to leave the workday—including him—and enter her personal life for the night.

Her exit was for the best.

There was no justification for him to ignore the message. To walk down the hall and knock on that firmly closed door.

He did it anyway.

Not to start anything.

To save something.

"Stacy, please. I don't want to lose our partnership. And we will, if we don't work through this together."

He heard movement and backed away from the door. When he heard it open, he turned before he could see her, see inside a room he'd inspected an hour before. Headed back to their shared workspace.

Mac didn't want to sit. Or stand. He didn't want to be still. The house was too small for him by himself, let alone two people.

Just knowing he couldn't head out for a walk, a drive, a beer, made him need those things all the more. He could cook.

Feed them. They had to eat.

Pulling his chair back around to his side of the table, he sat. He'd called the meeting.

"I can't do this, Mac," Stacy said as she sat down across from him. Taking the meeting out of his control before he'd begun. "I can't lose you, lose us. I mean, of course, I can. And I will, if it comes to that, but I don't want to. I love my job. I'll be a cop, no matter what, but I actually get up kind of excited, anticipating the day ahead, when I know we're going to be working together. It's been that way since our first year together and me feeling that way has never screwed us up. So let's not make a big deal of this…little issue…okay? Because give me a break. As far as I knew I was in my last minutes, or maybe even seconds, on earth, and I subconsciously chose to go with pleasure rather than fear. That's all this is…"

She looked him in eye. On and off.

On when she'd been talking about them working together. On when she'd been designating her last minutes. Off, when she'd referred to the issue as little. And off when she'd said, "that's all this is."

"If it's in your subconscious, Stace, it doesn't make it less valid. It just means that you're refusing to acknowledge it."

Why?

Why was he making it worse?

"Yeah, well, why were you standing on a cliff calling my name for hours?"

Her honesty, coupled with his deep respect for her, called for truth. His instincts pushed for a comeback as defensive as hers had been. An attack. A fight.

He might win. Shut it all down.

And...

Be where?

Accomplishing...what?

"Because I couldn't bear the thought of losing you." There'd been no other thought. Just that. For hours.

She nodded. Then said, "Well, I'm sorry I perverted your call, Mac. I swear to you, I've never, ever had a sexual dream about you before. I don't sit around and ogle your body or entertain inappropriate thoughts about you."

Not what a guy really wanted to hear.

And exactly what the cop in him needed.

He wanted to just nod. Accept what she'd said. Let it go.

"I don't *entertain* those thoughts about you, either," he told her. "Anytime they've presented in the past, I simply divert my thoughts and move on." And there was the rub.

A king-size, in his face, disturbing truth.

Her nod seemed...easier. If he wasn't mistaken, he'd seen a flash of relief in her eyes. And a hint of something more...gratification, maybe.

If she made something of it...

"So...since we're both aware of the situation and have proven completely capable of keeping our personal lives out of our professional relationship when we're together, we're good to go."

She'd made a statement. It felt like a question.

Because he had to answer it.

"We've proven capable of keeping our humanness out of things because we didn't acknowledge that it was there.

It wasn't permitted to enter our space. And from the sound of things, your awareness is brand-new."

He wasn't sure how he felt about that. Other than to know he couldn't feel anything long term. Not and keep her in his life forever.

"I've never let myself think about you that way." Stacy's gaze was straightforward. Her expression troubled.

So what was she saying? That she'd been attracted and, like him, had redirected every single thought any time it presented?

Or now that she'd had conscious awareness of her feelings, she was finding him attractive?

Why did it matter? Either way, they had to get a handle on things. Fast.

He was going to get hard, just thinking of her having dreams about him, if he wasn't damned careful. As in having to think of her hanging on those boulders, think of life and death, to keep himself on track.

Because those moments had changed him.

And it couldn't mean anything.

"I don't ever want marriage, or any kind of committed relationship, Stace," he said then. And, when her eyes immediately lit with fire and she opened her mouth, he held up a hand. "I'm not, for one second, assuming you'd ever want one with me. I'm just explaining why it's so critical for us to get this out and done," he told her. "My struggle is twofold."

Again, what was he doing? He, who never admitted personal struggles to anyone…

"Personally, I'm just not that guy. No matter how much I loved a woman, maybe even the more I loved a woman, I'd be adamant against any kind of long-term coupling."

She frowned. "That makes no sense, Mac," she said, her

tone easy. Argumentative as it would have been talking about a case. "If you loved a woman, why on earth would you subject yourself to that kind of heartache?"

"To prevent the worse one."

"Which is?"

"The passage of time. Watching the love erode and turn into hate so gradually you don't even know it has until one day, there it is, staring you in the face."

She could shake her head all she wanted. He'd been there. She hadn't.

"Real love doesn't do that," she told him. "I'm not saying I'm at all in love with you, by the way. Only acknowledging the attraction here. And a deep caring, professionally, for the man with whom I entrust my life every day. But real love, it stands that test of time, Mac."

In that moment, she seemed…young…to him. "How would you know that?" he challenged her.

"My parents were married almost twenty years before they were able to conceive me. And I witnessed that love every day of my life, watching my father live without her." The conviction in her tone grabbed his attention, if not his buy-in. "My dad's a great man. One who suffered huge loss but still brings joy to those who are suffering in any way he can. And he does it through the very real love he holds in his heart. In memory of my mother. My grandfather, the same. And Brett and I… I might not have been head over heels in love with my husband, in a man-woman sense, but I loved him deeply. For almost twenty years, from the time we were kids. Until the night he died. I risked my life to save his, without any training other than the self-defense classes my father had me take in high school. Our love changed. It grew in some ways, faded in others, but at its core, it was there. It's still there. Strengthening me as I head out to get the man who took Brett's life from him."

Like strikes of lightning in a violent storm, her words hit him. He tried to blink them away, close his eyes and ignore the thunder. He didn't want to be in that particular storm. Didn't want to see what the lightning could reflect. He'd chosen to live a life without storms that were out of his area of control.

To live his life fighting the bad that could be stopped.

And there she was, the woman he trusted above all, raining upon him. Not for her own sake. His choice to forgo love didn't affect her personally. But there was a passion there that bothered him, just the same.

He wanted to defend his position. To challenge her. To debate.

He had to step aside from it. At least until they got Manning.

"This is all kind of irrelevant to the topic at hand," he told her. "Right now, we're talking about you and me. This... awareness between us. The way I see it, we have a choice to make. We either give in to it, see where it leads, take what it gives us, or we continue working together."

"Which do you want?" she asked him. And he shook his head.

"No matter what I say, by merely speaking it I could persuade you to feel the same way. As I suspect your choice would persuade me. If I knew you wanted to be working partners more than sexual partners, I'd likely opt that way myself," he said.

"So, what...we just...leave the elephant here between us?"

"No." He pulled his legal pad over, flipped to the blank pages in the back, ripped two out and handed her one.

"Write your answer, and a justification for it. I'll do

the same. And then we switch. Only one caveat," he said. "Total honesty."

Desperation might have driven him. A need to get out of the conversation that was overpowering him. He'd acted like a schoolboy. Passing notes.

To get the question settled.

Mac, decorated cop and grown man that he was, hadn't stopped to think.

Stacy hadn't called him on his ridiculousness.

Her pen moved across the page with confidence.

She wrote several lines. Then put the pen down, folded the page and set it in the middle of the table.

After which she went into the adjoining kitchen, and he heard a pan land on a burner. The refrigerator open and close.

Water running.

Apparently, she was making dinner.

For both of them?

Would they be eating together? Catching Manning together?

Mac sat there with a blank piece of paper, having forced himself into a corner, and started to write.

Chapter 16

Stacy saw the paper land in the middle of the table. She'd started the stir-fry for something to do, not because she was hungry. The sandwiches they'd had at the conference table hours ago were still sitting heavy on her stomach.

More so once the folded yellow square landed on the wood of the table.

She'd tried not to look. Standing at the stove, she had the living area constantly in her peripheral vision. Movement catching her attention couldn't be avoided.

It made it hard for her to breathe.

Was that really going to be it? Her entire life at a crossroads, and a few written lines were going to decide her entire future?

No.

She had to talk to Mac.

Find another way.

Maybe if they just had sex, were really bad at it, or at least unremarkable enough, they could put the whole situation to rest.

And be fired, if anyone found out.

No fraternizing between officers on the job.

No exceptions.

Not even if death was imminent.

Of course, if one was going to die, being fired wouldn't be a huge concern.

She wasn't planning to die.

Putting a lid on the thawing food, she turned the heat down to low and walked to the table. Mac wasn't there.

Both sheets of paper were.

His bedroom door was open. The bathroom one wasn't.

Sitting down, she waited for him to return. Took deep breaths. One after another. Deep in. Slow out. In through the nose, out through the mouth.

Whatever would be would be.

Their fates were sealed.

They'd each spoken their truths.

And no matter what they were, if they didn't mesh, she and Mac would be breaking up. If their truths didn't mesh, she *wanted* to break up with him. Anything less would be a sacrilege.

She did not want their truths to be at odds. She didn't want to die, either, but with possible—and according to the day's theory, likely—professional killers after her, she might.

She heard the bathroom door. Watched the six-foot tall, gorgeously fit, blond shaggy-haired man walk down the hall toward her. And held his gaze the entire way.

There was no game playing going on. No hiding. She was, in a very real sense, fighting for her life in those seconds, as much as she had been the night she'd been kidnapped.

With much the same helplessness.

Mac pulled out his chair. Sat. Glanced at her, and looking her in the eye, nodded toward the two folded sheets between them.

They reached at the same time.

And all eye contact ceased.

With shaking fingers, Stacy opened the page. Recognized Mac's handwriting straight off. Had the inane thought that he'd written less than she had. Felt a slice of worry, of fear, that his lack of verbosity meant they were through.

And then, as if pulled magnetically, her gaze went to the words he'd penned for her.

Working together. Sexual attraction can be found elsewhere. You cannot. Five years together proves we fit. I would rather spend most of my days with you, than risk trying something else, having it fail, and being left with no you.

She'd written a bit more.

It was a good thing he hadn't.

With the tears blurring her eyes, she'd never have made it to the end.

I choose to continue being your work partner. Whatever I'm feeling, whether it's a form of love, grows into love, was always love, will never be love, will be. It will be. And I will be happy as long as you are in my life. The only guarantee of that, for as long as we live and choose our employment, is for us to remain partners. As your partner, I do my best work. We hear over and over, from departments all over the state, about the lives we help save. As your partner I get to spend hours with you every day—more hours than I spend with anyone else—making the world a safer place. Doing meaningful work. As your partner, I look forward to every day.

As to the rest... I hope we can continue to be hon-

est with each other. To talk if necessary. To find so-
lutions. Just as we do with every single challenge
we face at work and do better than most. Maybe, at
some point, we end up with a one-nighter. Off duty
and apart from work. We see, as I did with Brett,
that the actual event is nice, but nothing to lose sleep
over. Maybe, after we retire, or a promotion comes
that can't be passed up, we want to reassess. Maybe
we're both happily married by then. Maybe at some
point...is the point. The future will be waiting for us
when we get there.

For now, I choose us just as we are. Flaws and all.

She'd written a damned book. The closest thing to a love
letter he'd ever had.

And all Mac could home in on was *the actual event*
is nice, but nothing to lose sleep over. He had to bite his
tongue not to debate with her on that.

Before his mouth talked her into letting him show her
just how much sleep they'd both want to lose if they got
started with the *actual event.*

Instead, he gave himself time to calm down by reading the note a second time. And allowing that part of his
adrenaline surge, sexual as it was, came from the fact that
they'd made the same choice.

And he had no next step. It felt like a celebratory moment. Did you tip a glass of champagne when you decided
not to pursue a personal relationship?

If you had champagne.

A hug felt in order.

Which would be like taking a starving man to food and
telling him not to eat.

He heard her restlessness across from him. A sigh. Her

pen bouncing lightly against the tabletop, and he knew his time was up.

"We need tomorrow's plan," Stacy said.

Calling his attention right where he'd not been ready to take it. Her face. Her body. Only to find that she was staring at the whiteboard.

Not him.

"Obviously, we aren't just going to sit inside this house. Waiting."

He'd hoped they would. But knew they wouldn't. It wasn't Stacy's way. Or his either.

"It's not that I don't very much want to sleep with you, Stace," he told her. "Because I do."

She swallowed. Looked over at him. And smiled. The sexiest, nonsexy grin he'd ever seen. "Yeah, it's kind of a relief, knowing that I'm not the only one. Now I can lust after you all I want and not feel guilty."

Right. They couldn't act on it.

"It's a get out of jail free card," she added. "No impropriety because we aren't acting on it, and no harassment because we've talked about it, both know the other has the wants, and, in full disclosure, have decided we still want to be work partners."

Yeah. Because she had no idea what she was missing. What they were missing.

He might not ever want a full-time woman in his personal life, but he liked sex enough to lose sleep for it. As did the women he had it with.

Who would not be Stacy. But maybe, at some point, he could encourage her to try again, with someone else.

At some point, her letter had said. *At some point...*

Their futures would be waiting for them.

In the moment, they'd removed their so-called elephant.

And had the most important job of their careers to complete.

"What would we do if this was any other case?" Mac came at Stacy with an energy she hadn't seen in him since the day of her kidnapping—when they'd been taking down shooters.

She welcomed its return with a surge of relief. Of gratitude.

And affection, too.

A feeling she didn't have to fight. That in itself was a load off.

"We'd be out there looking for Manning. Physically drawing him out," she repeated what she'd already fought for at the conference table.

He nodded. "So how do we do that from here?"

His gaze was head-on. Open. Drawing her response. "What matters to him right now? In his current situation? He's angry to the point of probable irrationality due to his lost reputation, his lost career. So that's where we hit him. He's all over social media. We can sit right here and attack him there."

Mac picked up his phone. Dialed and set it on the table. In seconds she heard Hudson Warner pick up. And within twenty minutes, she and Mac had their own secure, untraceable accounts on several of the social media sites where Manning had the most active followers and posted regularly. Both dark web and not.

They spent the next several hours posting from their phones. Checking back at each site every fifteen minutes, in between eating, doing dishes and scheduling future posts.

At shift change, the officers joining them came in to say

hello, to go over protocols, followed by the officers leaving coming in to report no suspicious activity and wish them a good night.

No one seemed to blink at the idea of her and Mac sharing the little cabin by themselves all night. Not even Chief Benson.

A week ago, she wouldn't have either.

She couldn't give it any more thought. She was lusting after the man. Could go ahead and dream about him all night if that's what came to be.

Without breaking any rules or risking the end of a life that she loved.

Without guilt.

As she yawned and stood up, excusing herself to bed, she realized their talk that night had made things much better. Because now she knew that Mac found her attractive, too, and she didn't feel so pathetic coming to terms with her newfound subconscious truths.

All was good until she got to the door of her room, opened it and heard Mac's voice come at her from the living room.

"Sweet dreams!" he called.

And she shut her door with a decidedly unamused click.

By noon the next day, Mac could almost convince himself that the job was going to go like clockwork. He and Stacy would continue to ramp up the tension on social media, which would inflame Manning. He'd charge out to kill Stacy himself, making a mistake, doing something foolish or just plain getting caught by those who were trained to catch men like him.

Or the kidnapper and murderer would send professionals to do it for him.

Either way, they were all ready. Chief of police. County sheriff. Sierra's Web. Officers and deputies pulled from surrounding areas as needed. And him and Stacy, the proven partnership.

"There's been zero response," Stacy said, as they sat at the table, both surfing their phones and eating peanut butter and jelly sandwiches. "Even on the dark web."

"He's beyond being able to get any satisfaction vicariously," Mac told her. "The internet isn't doing it for him anymore. He's here somewhere, getting ready to issue a planned response."

She bit. Chewed. Swallowed. Nodded.

And his mouth watered.

But only for a second.

The lack of attack from Manning had him on edge. He was hoping the tension was just because it left them with little to do, and he and Stacy were just not the sit and wait type of officers.

Unless they were sitting on a house. Then they could be still, shoot the breeze, for hours. To be ready for two minutes of action on a second's notice.

She took another bite.

The man in him noticed.

He had no doubt Stacy would be cover model material in a swimsuit with that long dark hair arranged around her.

And he'd rather have her in uniform with her hair in a ponytail. He got to spend his days with the real woman.

She put down her phone. "We've been here almost twenty-four hours and there hasn't been so much as a pack of coyotes getting our attention, let alone a real threat. What if he's already back in Colorado?"

"Sierra's Web checked in with his wife this morning.

She hasn't seen or heard from him." Which Stacy already knew. "And they're watching all airports," he reminded her.

Officers were also watching Stacy's house and property.

Mac wasn't comfortable with the lack of action, either. Something big was coming. He could feel it. And would take it on. He didn't like being a sitting duck not knowing what was coming.

"We're usually the ones on the offensive," Stacy said then. "We're the hunters."

He met her gaze. Nodded.

"We need to get back out there, Mac. Do what we do best."

His gut agreed.

His emotions greatly overwhelmed his response. Rendering him…immobile. Even while he knew that Stacy wasn't going to just sit at a table for much longer. Not without a specific job to do. Without a plan of action.

So they had to find one. Getting lost in fear for her life was exactly what a cop couldn't do. That was the sort of thing that could ultimately have Mac costing Stacy her life.

The realization hit home hard. "You still think Warner's mountain cave suggestion has merit?" he asked her.

And with a long glance, Stacy handed him her phone. She had it all there. The area. The natural traps—a ditch similar to what Hudson had described. Filled with twigs and just enough ground cover to conceal them. One step and they'd be alerted to anyone encroaching on their space. Tree limb camouflages over their enclosure. Mouse traps barely covered with dirt. The list went on and on.

"Take your pick of them," she told him. "We aren't out to kill him, unless he attacks first. We want our chance to bring him in alive. Personally, I don't want him put out of his misery."

On the surface, the idea had merit. But he had questions. "How do you propose getting safely to this cave? Getting it set up? Getting him to follow you? How is being trapped in a cave any different than being trapped here?"

"First, I was thinking Sierra's Web would scope out the exact cave. And set the traps, whatever we choose. Second, we quit hiding. He had no trouble finding us when we were out doing our job. We head back to the station, and then, later in the day, as if we're on a call, we drive out to the base of the mountain. And we have each other's back as we get to the cave. Just like we always do. The cave will need to be accessible and close, and we'll have predetermined natural shields, a route through tall brush, for instance, to get us there. Or maybe Hudson Warner watching a drone camera to alert us to any danger. Third, no patrol around us. We do this you and me. Like always. As long as we stay in the cave until he appears, we're safer than we are here. And the key is, we need a reason for being there. We can radio in that we've got something, that we're checking it out, one of us could even shoot a bullet to make it seem as though we're under attack, and I can slide down a ravine and appear as though I hurt myself. You get me to the cave. You can jump in any time here, Mac. I'm open to any tweaks this idea needs."

He nodded. Cop to cop, she had every angle covered. And while the idea was a wild one, under the circumstances, the overall plan made sense.

"It's either we take a chance to bring him to us, or I live my life as a prisoner, live in constant fear of attack. He could go underground for weeks, or months. Sometimes fugitives manage to elude the law for decades. How do I have any kind of life, knowing that at any time he could strike out at me. Or worse, at those I love?"

Love. There was that word again.

She'd used it in her note.

Mac shook his head against a thought that didn't serve the moment, and said, "I'll call Sierra's Web." And in the meantime, he could hope to all the fates that be, that Manning made a move, was in custody, before the mountain plan became action.

Chapter 17

The plan made Stacy nervous, but not as much as sitting around with nothing happening. They could be giving Manning, or his professionals, time to wipe out the safe house somehow. Considering the small explosive dropped by a drone meant for her scalp, methane gas released into her home's plumbing system, being kidnapped in her own garage and being shoved over a mountain... Manning wasn't fighting in any ways they were used to.

His only signature seemed to be expertly planned unpredictability.

From what she'd seen of the man during her times in court, fighting him, he'd be enjoying the cat and mouse game he was playing with her. Not as much as he'd have enjoyed having her simply disappear off the face of the earth as originally planned...but the man seemed to get off on showing her he was the superior one of the two after all.

If she let him make her cower, she'd risk being a mouse for the rest of her life. And not just with Manning. He'd have won a mental battle inflicting wounds from which she might not ever recover.

She would be strong for those she loved. As her father had been. Her grandfather. Brett. And Mac, too.

Just admitting that her partner mattered, being able to

think about him with her heart and not feel guilty, gave her strength. Fantasizing about his body to get through tough moments…well, that was a delightful bonus.

Did she want more? Of course. But then, she'd have liked to have grown up with a mother. To have a father who found his life's calling a little closer to home. And not to have buried Brett, too.

She was almost excited when, a couple of hours after lunch, Mac's phone rang. With an entire mountain at their backs, she and Mac had the best chance of bringing the case of her life to a successful conclusion.

Expecting the caller to be Sierra's Web, she was surprised to see the chief's 911 come up on Mac's screen as he tapped for speaker call and set the phone between them.

"Mac, Stacy, we've got a missing and endangered. Jimmy Southerland's four-year-old daughter."

"Mariah?" Mac stood abruptly. "Where? How long ago?"

"He called it in five minutes ago. We need all hands on deck. You guys stay there, but I need to pull your protection detail…"

"No way we're staying here." Stacy stood, too, watching Mac. He'd gone to high school with Jimmy. Sometimes stopped at the pub after shift to have a beer with him.

With a quick glance at her, he nodded.

"Jimmy was walking with her out to his car. He got hit from behind. When he came to, the car and the girl were gone. We've since found it broken down out on Granada Road."

A road that led to a popular tourist hiking trail. Stacy's stomach sank.

"Give us a grid," Mac said then, as she reached for her clutch and gear.

He'd already grabbed his and picked up his phone as

they headed out the door. They'd both been ready to run in an instant from the moment they got up.

She'd just never thought...little Mariah. Stacy didn't know Jimmy and his wife, or their only child, personally. But she'd seen the parents around town her entire life.

"It could be a good thing, him taking her to the mountain," she said, after a glance at Mac's tight chin. "He's keeping her close. With Jimmy's money, there should be a ransom call coming..."

"He doesn't have money," Mac told her, topping their car with a bubble and speeding through the first red light they'd come to. They'd been in the desert, but Granada Road felt like it was on the other side of time. "He inherited his folk's mansion, but the money went to charity. His old man wanted Jimmy to have to work, to earn. Said giving him everything would make him lazy."

As shocked as Stacy was to hear that the Southerlands weren't rich as she'd always thought, she was way more focused on the next hour. "I've lived here my whole life and I didn't know that. I'm guessing the kidnapper doesn't, either."

So there'd be a ransom call. "We'll come up with the money," she told Mac. "Saguaro takes care of her own."

"Let's just hope we get that chance..."

With a sharp turn, he squealed out in front of a car that had slowed for them and took backroads through town at a faster clip than she'd have done.

"As soon as we're out of the car, you head up the mountain," Mac told her as they quickly neared the site they'd been given. "I'm right behind you. Every step of the way."

They'd have to split up to cover their territory. But with him behind her, even just to the west of her, they'd be within hearing distance of each other the entire time. Five years of working together, they had their search protocols down pat.

For a split second, as Mac turned the last corner, Stacy was consumed by a stab of fear so sharp it took her breath. "What if this is some ruse to get us out here?" She asked the question aloud, on the verge of paranoia.

Glancing her way, Mac said, "I had the same thought. I put it down to being cooped up in that damned house for twenty-four hours," he told her. "Manning's a master manipulator, coming at us in ways we'd least suspect, making us paranoid, but taking a four-year-old child? It doesn't fit. He's got a young daughter of his own. From what his wife said, he's a great father."

Mac pulled into a turnout, concealing the car as best he could. Her fear gone, Stacy checked her weapon and went to work. Filled with the drive that got her out of bed every morning. To do her best to rid the world around her of any evil that lurked within their midst.

She had one goal. Find Mariah alive.

Every sense, every nerve ending on high alert, Mac watched Stacy head up the mountain, and then took off in his own direction. Combing the ground for any sign of human inhabitation. Listening for the slightest sniffle.

He assumed whoever took the child had her mouth covered, but he'd have to leave her nose free for her to breathe. And scared kids cried.

Before he'd gone far, he put in a call to Jimmy, Mariah's father, just to reassure the man that the entire department was on the case and would find his daughter. And to get any pointers in terms of where she might hide if she got free.

Jimmy had been so distraught he'd barely responded. So

Mac had promised him they'd find her alive. Something he knew better than to do.

But he believed it—assuming they found her soon.

The guy wasn't going to kill Mariah. Not right off, at any rate. He'd need to give proof of life to get any ransom money. And if he'd taken the girl for any other reason, he'd have headed out of town. Not to the mountain.

Until he'd been told differently, Mac wasn't allowing any other scenario to enter his mind. His job was to find the girl, and visualizing finding her alive was the way to do his best work. To have every ounce of his adrenaline focused on a good outcome.

And while he listened for any minute sound a child might make, he'd pick up any other unusual sound as well. Including all signals his partner might send.

Beyond that, he had to trust Stacy to do her job. She was the best cop he'd ever worked with. Partially because while she was aggressive in all her pursuits, she had an eye on all risks always.

But neither of them would put their own safety above that of a four-year-old child.

He grew more and more uneasy as he slowly traveled farther up the mountain, noticing all the little caverns and boulder formations that could hide a person being silenced while searchers walked right by.

It wasn't his first mountain search, by far. Nor his first child abduction.

But it was the first time in his career the two had coincided with each other.

He was sweating in his long sleeves as he pushed through some brush to look around and pulled back as he sustained a sharp prick from a cactus needle on the other side. Cactus needles had been on Stacy's list of a weaponized nature for their upcoming cave maneuver.

The plan had been to give them an excuse to be alone in the mountains…

Mac rubbed his arm and pressed on. He couldn't allow himself to be slowed down by thoughts of his partner's own danger. While the midday January sunshine was warming the valley, it would be cold farther up in the mountain. And when darkness fell…

They had to find Mariah before that happened. Searchers would be called back in for the night.

An hour into the search, Mac heard the muffled tones of the recall siren. Like the town's tornado warning, the sound meant the child had been found.

Thank God. Sending good thoughts for her well-being and unharmed condition, his thoughts immediately went to getting his partner back under protection.

Turning, he gave a whistle that used to get him in trouble when he was a kid. The sound was shrill and carried long distances.

It was a call to his partner for a location check. Stacy's response wouldn't be nearly as piercing as his, but as close as their designated paths had been, he'd be able to hear her.

He'd turned as soon as he'd heard the siren. Was heading toward Stacy's assigned east-west coordinates, and, thinking she might have been checking out any of the innumerable caves in the Arizona mountains, he whistled a second time.

Heard nothing in return.

And, heart pounding, started to run. Downhill. Sliding. Righting himself. Heading east. And calling for all he was worth.

"Stacy!"

Over and over.

A sickening replay.

Had Manning actually been behind the kidnapping after all? An elaborate ruse to get Stacy alone? He and Stace had both had the thought.

Stacy. She had feelings for him.

And he'd finally admitted his for her. To himself. To her.

Did Manning have her? Or maybe she was just out of earshot…maybe she was already heading down to join their peers in celebration of a quick and successful rescue.

But Stacy wouldn't vacate their grid without him. Not ever. They didn't leave each other behind.

And she wasn't answering, dammit. He slid. Reached out with his hand. Took a palmful of cactus needles, and just kept going. If Manning had her…

Mariah's speedy rescue gave weight to his fears. The kidnapper had only held the child long enough to…

It couldn't be. His imagination was in overdrive.

He ran. He slid and scraped.

He called.

With no response.

And for the first time in his adult life, Mac knew what a shattering heart felt like.

She heard the siren.

And Mac's whistle.

Heard him calling her name.

Heard the sound grow more distant.

Heard it all with a growing panic that she fought to contain. Tears squeezed through lids shut to contain them. Even as prey to her captor, she wouldn't let him see the extent of his victory.

He could hurt her body. End her life.

But he wasn't going to take her heart and soul away from her.

She hoped.

Eyeing her gun on a patch of open dirt, yards in front of her, she listened as Manning came down the mountain. She had no way of knowing if she was in his sights.

Could have a bullet in the head at any second.

But as long as there was the possibility of saving herself, of taking him down, she'd be there. Fighting.

She'd seen him behind her shortly after she'd set out on her own. Had hoped if he didn't realize she knew he was there, she could lead him to a cave, duck inside, distract him until searchers could find Mariah. Or she could get a shot off before he noticed, if that was the only way.

Instead, from just feet behind her, he'd called out to her. Telling her to stop. She couldn't see the gun pointing at her back, but she felt it's excruciating weight in the middle of her spine.

So she'd ducked and run. Planning to circle around, to get behind him. Had managed to lose him for a while. Only to see that he'd climbed straight up. With a vantage point that would allow him to see her farther down the mountain. That's when she'd seen the ledge. The drop-off.

Five feet or so.

A jump and roll had happened automatically. Training taking over when thought threatened to freeze her.

It wasn't until she was safely under an overhang of the mountainside that she'd realized her gun, which she'd shoved into her holster for the jump, had come loose during the roll. And she'd been holding her breath, almost literally, ever since.

Waiting for the demon to appear.

Or her life to end.

Her Taser, her Mace…none of it was going to help her against a man with revenge in his veins and a gun in his hand.

She didn't dare move. Or make a sound.

Instead, she listened to Mac calling her name. Taking comfort even as his fading voice told her he was getting farther away. With Manning's superior vantage point, chances were he'd see Mac, take him down, before Mac even knew he was there.

She couldn't let the fiend take down another man she loved.

The thought trickled through her panic. Heightening her senses. Making her aware of the sounds coming from above her and the small rocks trickling over the ledge. Manning was directly above her. Approaching the ledge from which she'd jumped. If she was calculating right, as soon as he left the drop-off, to wind around the mountain to the side of it, she could have a small window of chance to roll for her gun and get back without him seeing her.

A millisecond…

And…go!

She rolled, grabbed, rolled back.

Held her breath.

And heard, "Drop the gun."

Chapter 18

Not finding Stacy, Mac raced far enough out of the interior of the mountain for his radio to have range. Calling into the chief on a private channel, he heard, first, that Mariah was back with Jimmy and her mother, unharmed.

Relief flooded him, even while he stood in a pool of fear. Knowing the four-year-old was okay lightened his load some. If she'd been part of an elaborate ruse, at least whoever had taken her, Manning or a hired man, had some humanity.

"Is Stacy back?" he bit the words out.

"No."

The expected response put him right back in hell. Asking for any available officers to move toward Stacy's assigned coordinates, he turned and ran, clipping his radio back in place as he took rocks and hills at top speed.

It was a bold move, taking a child to get a veteran officer out of hiding. An even bolder one to attack her with officers combing the area. Manning had to know that they'd get to her quickly.

Unless he figured on everyone being out of radio range. And looking for Mariah much longer than it took to find her.

His mind sped as he slid down an incline and clawed his

way right back up again. He'd managed to pull the cactus needles out of his hand as he'd headed down the mountain, but one had broken. Was embedded.

He welcomed the pain. It kept him grounded in the moment. Aware. Distracted him from the agony exploding deep inside him.

He'd known.

And he'd told himself he was overreacting because of his newly admitted feelings for Stacy. Afraid of being overprotective to the point of unprofessional, he'd erred in the other direction. He'd failed to listen to the instincts that made him a decorated cop.

No way he should have agreed to stay partnered with Stacy. Not even for an hour. Not after she'd made her revelation.

And he'd been honest with himself, and Stacy, regarding his own attraction to her. While he'd been under the impression that she just saw him as an older guy, a veteran cop and partner, he'd been able to keep himself under wraps.

But once he'd known that she wanted him, too...

The department's no fraternization rule was in place for solid reasons. In their jobs, conflict of interest, conflict of emotion, of split-second choice, got people killed.

With sweat dripping down his face, soaking the T-shirt covering his back beneath his uniform, Mac kept up his pace, watching his compass to keep him on Stacy's coordinates.

If Manning had her, he could have taken her anywhere.

And he had to believe his partner would have left some sign for him. Given him some way to find her. She wouldn't just leave him.

Not if she could help it.

He wasn't leaving her, either. If he was out on the mountain all night, in the dark alone with the animals, then he'd be there. He didn't go home without her.

Period.

The thoughts continued to tumble as he climbed. Others would be covering the mountain as well. Helicopters had already been on their way to look for Mariah. Mac figured the chief would have radioed to have them keep on coming.

But with all the interior hills and valleys, cliffs and deep gullies, any of them could be right on top of her and not find her.

The chief would call Sierra's Web. Bring Luke Dennison back. With search and rescue dogs. He knew the ropes.

And knew, too, that in all likelihood, if it got to that point, Stacy would already be gone.

They weren't going to get lucky boulders a second time.

He should never have left her.

He'd known...

Was that a voice? Or the wind in a gulley? Playing with his mind.

Stopping, Mac listened. Was certain he heard voices.

Went toward them.

And jerked back, his gut slamming, as the unmistakable sound of a gunshot rang out. Echoing all around him.

Stacy jerked, her body feeling the pushback impact as the warning gunshot rang out. With her head still protected by the overhang, and her back to a mountain wall, she stood, gun in hand, facing Landon Manning for the second time in her life. He'd lowered his gun. She had not.

Because he hadn't dropped the weapon as she'd told him to.

He'd just stood there talking.

A man who looked like Manning, but not one she recognized as anything like the egotistical excuse for a man who'd killed her husband.

"I'm telling you," he said, repeating himself for at least the eighth time. "There's someone out there, gunning for you. It's not me."

She didn't believe him. Wasn't going to be played the fool and have his fiendish smile, his laughter, be the last thing she saw and heard.

She had to outsmart him. Outlast him.

There was no doubt in her mind that if she fired her gun at him, rather than up in the air, the gunslinging rodeo rider would have seen her finger pressure on the trigger and have his own gun up and fired before he went down.

He'd take her with him.

She'd rather that than have him get away.

But if she just hung on, they could get him.

"You're out here all alone," he was saying. "The search has been called off. Everyone's gone. It's a perfect scenario for whoever is after you. He kills you, dumps you in some ravine out here where the animals will get you and they'll never find the evidence."

She swallowed, chin up. He was telling her his plan. She got that. Wasn't going to give him the satisfaction of showing fear.

When she didn't show up down below, the chief would send people back up. Mac would be back, but with help. All she had to do was hang on.

There'd likely be a helicopter at some point. They flew anytime anyone was reported missing in the mountains. She knew the ropes.

Just had to keep herself focused. And show no fear.

She wasn't going to leave the earth without giving Mac

a chance to do his job. Wasn't taking any chances on missing seeing his face one more time.

And if she got out of her current situation alive, if she survived this one, she was going to beg the man to kiss her. To devour her.

She didn't want to die without knowing him completely. She wanted reality to take with her, not to die on a fantasy.

Her arms, her shoulders, ached. Her fingers had mostly lost feeling. They still worked, though. She'd pushed flesh against metal enough to know that much.

"I don't know what else to do to convince you I'm telling the truth."

"Put your gun down."

"And have you shoot me? And throw *me* over the cliff? You think I don't know that's what you'd love to do? Like I said, I get it. I don't blame you. I also don't want to die. I have a wife and daughter who've stood by me, who, for whatever reason, still love me…"

Love. He'd told her all about being a changed man. About having gotten sober in prison. And realizing that he'd been given a second chance. With his wife. His little girl. How he'd come to Arizona to see her. To apologize to her. He'd realized that until he could do so, he wasn't the man he needed to be. He'd chickened out the first time he'd seen her in uniform. Naming the date of the private flight into the east valley. Half afraid she'd arrest him for some bogus infraction. But he'd come back because he needed her to know that, while he couldn't give back the husband he'd taken from her, he was going to live the rest of his days honoring Brett's life. When he came back, he'd heard on the news about the attempt on her life. Had figured in some weird way fate had given him a chance to redeem himself. He could keep an eye on her. Maybe even help save her.

Not in exchange for the life he'd taken. But to do what Brett would have done had he been alive.

She'd heard it all. More than once. Including him saying that he'd been tuned into the local police band radio for the couple of days he'd been there. Had heard the all-points bulletin go out regarding Mariah Southerland. Had figured she'd respond. And had waited for her to arrive. Intending to have her back.

She just didn't believe any of it. She'd heard the man spin his tales in court, too.

Was he so full of himself that he didn't know to change the black hoodie he'd worn on his trip to the city building to look her up? She'd recognized it the second she'd seen him.

He'd lowered his gun the second she'd told him to. And though she'd been waiting, hadn't raised it again.

She could kill him. There wouldn't likely be anyone who'd blame her or make trouble over it. But it wouldn't be a good shot.

And she didn't want to die a bad cop.

Didn't want to leave Mac with doubts about her...

"Drop the gun or I put a bullet in your head."

She heard the voice. Saw the face behind the man she'd held at standoff until her entire body ached.

And though his words hadn't been directed at her, she dropped her gun to her side.

Then, her chin trembling, she watched Jesse Macdonald take Landon Manning into custody.

She was free.

They had him. All the way down the mountain, pushing an insistent ex-rodeo star every step of the way, Mac heard all the garbage Manning had been feeding Stacy up on the mountain.

Trying to break her. To get her to trust him, Mac reasoned silently. Making his final victory that much sweeter.

Other than the part where Manning was lying, Mac heard it all from Manning himself. Stacy stayed one step behind them, ready, he knew, in case Manning tried to make a run for it. She hadn't said a word.

While he hadn't done more than a visual check, Mac felt confident that Manning hadn't touched her. She had met his gaze, and at his silent question in a raised eyebrow, had shook her head. And other than sweat and grime from her climb, there were no visible changes to her since he'd last laid eyes on that beautiful form. Her shirt was buttoned and tucked just as she always wore it. Second to the last button above her belt buckle.

So the buttons and buckle didn't rub, he knew, after having teased her about it a few years before.

"I swear to you, man, I've done nothing wrong. I was trying to help her."

Yeah, yeah, yeah.

Mac didn't bother to respond.

He didn't trust himself to follow protocol if he opened his mouth any more than to read the man his rights, and issue directions when necessary.

As soon as they were able to get a radio signal, Stacy called in.

And Mac smiled as the suddenly vibrant device, exploding with cheers from the various law enforcement personnel on the channel. Just from hearing her voice.

He wasn't the only one who valued Stacy Waltz.

When she reported that they had Manning in custody and were bringing him in, the chief responded, saying he was sending backup to escort them the rest of the way down. No one was taking any chances with the man.

Landon Manning would be lucky if he ever experienced a moment of freedom again.

With Sierra's Web gathering evidence, and Mac and Stacy testifying, the man was going away for a very long time.

And Mac was going to be heading out as well. His preoccupation with his own emotions had nearly cost his partner her life.

He'd rather be dead himself.

Stacy had to watch the interrogation. Several people, including the chief, had told her to go home and get some rest. She couldn't be done until it was done.

Mac stood with her, watching through the glass, listening over the speaker, as Manning continued the smooth talk. The man was good. Knew his story so well, he never missed a beat.

"This is exactly how it was five years ago," she told Mac. "If I hadn't been there myself, if I hadn't seen what happened, I'd have believed him. If not for me there, being a witness, he'd have walked away without any charges at all. He'd have gotten away with murder."

"At least now he's admitted to what he did," Mac told her. "He's given you some vindication."

"Only because he's trying to get something for himself," she told him. "If you start to believe he's sincere, you fall prey to his manipulation. I sat with his wife. Saw a bruise to the right of her eye that I know he gave her, and she wouldn't speak up. Not even with me there taking the stand."

Manning had told her that afternoon that he'd only raised a hand to his wife once. The same night he'd hit Brett. The actions had put him in jail, but he'd said that hadn't been his wake-up call. It had been the look on his wife's face after he'd flung out his hand in frustration and caught the side of her face. He hadn't had a sip of alcohol since.

At the time, he'd told the arresting officer that he'd bumped into his wife. And that Brett had come at him, that he'd only been pushing Brett away and that Brett had tripped and hit his head.

Manning had finally fallen silent. And Lieutenant Stahl, sitting across from him, pushed sheets across the table in front of him. Photos of posts from his dark web sites.

"You have a story prepared for these, too?" Stahl asked.

Manning appeared to read, taking his time, going from page to page. Until he suddenly stopped and pushed the whole lot of them back across the table. "I've never seen these before in my life," he said, looking straight at the lieutenant.

"He looks right at you as he lies," Stacy said. "It messes with your head."

It was messing with hers. She saw her kidnapper, the murderer, her stalker in custody, and still didn't feel like it was over.

"He's fighting for his life," Mac said. "People without conscience can say whatever they have to say."

He'd been acting odd, ever since they'd come down the mountain. Distant. And yet…not. He was right there by her side, making sure people gave her space, watching over her. Had already said he'd be the one driving her home.

But he wasn't looking her in the eye. At all.

It had been a rough day. But a hugely successful one. There would be celebration time.

But at the moment, she wasn't feeling at all open to socialization, either. She needed time to process.

"I swear to you, I didn't write any of that…" Manning

was still denying his culpability. And it hit her…the reason she couldn't seem to believe it was actually over.

Because she knew what the man was capable of doing. The weeks and months ahead, the trial…the entire time she'd be worrying that he'd find a way to get away with it all. He'd come so close the first time around…

"…but I think I know who did." Manning's words grabbed her attention. She glanced at Mac. Jaw tight, his eyes seemed to be trying to bore holes into the glass in front of him.

"This kid, Troy Duncan. He's the kid brother of one of my cellmates. Grew up idolizing me. He wanted to help me out, so I told him to run my social media accounts. Who better to keep my memory alive? Since I've been out, I've been watching out for him some. Seemed like a good guy. Has a job. Does good at it." Manning flicked a hand at the pages again, throwing a disgusted glance in their direction. "This stuff… I had no idea. But he's the only one who'd have had access to my accounts…"

Stacy's heart dropped another notch. "See I told you, he has an answer, an explanation, for everything you throw at him."

With knots in her stomach, she glanced up at Mac. Tugged on his shirtsleeve until he looked at her. Really saw her. "I swear to you," she said, holding his gaze. "I saw him kill my husband."

In the end, it had been her word against his. She'd been believed.

"I know, Stace." Mac's nod, his expression, was completely open. "I've never doubted that for a second. And now we have proof."

Heart pumping harder, from his look, his trust…and his last statement, too. "We do? Where?"

Had she missed something big while she'd been up on that mountain?

"You weren't a cop back then. Didn't have access to records. But they're here now, if you want to see them. Manning had apparently filed for an appeal. The DA hired a pathologist to go over all the evidence one more time. The report proves, medically, that Brett was hit in the head with an object that matches, exactly, an imprint from Manning's fist."

Staring, hearing roaring in her ears, she stepped back. "Why wasn't I ever told?"

"That's the question I asked an hour ago. Because the appeal was denied, there was no reason to notify family. You were young, grieving. You knew the truth because you'd been there…"

She got it. One of the hardest parts of being a cop was dealing with family members. Knowing how best to serve them. What to say, or show, what to spare them of.

"We need that kind of proof now, Mac," she said, staring at the man. Vowing to herself that the truth would win again.

She was going to be free of Landon Manning once and for all.

Physically, but mentally, too.

They had him in custody. The rest would come.

So why was she still afraid? Feeling hunted?

Why wasn't she feeling like celebrating?

Chapter 19

Mac felt more uneasy than he'd have liked as he and Stacy left the station after dark that night. Manning had denied seeing Troy Duncan in Arizona. He knew nothing about a stolen van. Had never owned or even played with a drone. He'd admitted to being at the east valley airport. Claimed that he'd never been at the city building.

And he'd never been in Stacy's garage or even on her property.

Could Duncan somehow be behind the attacks on Stacy's life? Maybe the man he idolized had changed, seemingly because of Stacy, no longer able to win in the rodeo ring, and dedicating his life to making amends for killing a man. If, by any chance, any of what Manning was saying was true...was it feasible that the younger man had decided to kill the person responsible for bringing down his hero?

The dark web rants made it a possibility.

And even if Manning was just doing as he'd done last time, lying through his teeth, he still would have had to have a getaway driver after putting Stacy's red SUV in neutral and pushing it over the cliff. There had to have been a second perp.

He'd mentioned as much to the chief before he'd left. And had been there when the chief had called Sierra's Web, too, to start a photo recognition search on the younger man, on the internet, in the system, anyplace they could search. Mac had screwed up once trying to keep Stacy safe. He wasn't going to take any chances a second time.

"What were you and Benson talking about back there?" Stacy asked as they turned off Main Street, heading out to her place.

He had to tell her. Knowing Stacy, she was already entertaining her own thoughts on the matter. He just wanted her to have some time to breathe.

And that wasn't his call. For the moment, they were still partners. And when they no longer were, it still would never be his right to do her thinking for her. Or make choices as to what she should or should not know. Not when it came to her life.

"We're looking harder at Troy Duncan. If there's any chance at all that Manning isn't lying about everything..."

"His reaction to the dark web rants," she said then, looking over at him. He saw the movement out of the corner of his eye.

Mac kept his gaze on the road. "It's not quite over yet."

"With Manning down, the biggest part of it is. The midazolam. It's a common drug used by veterinarians. There are plenty of those on the rodeo circuit. You notice he didn't deny having access to it."

Their bosses had mentioned that in the brief meeting they'd had after Manning's interrogation. He hoped they were all right. Figured she was hoping, too.

And then he was pulling into her drive. With no intention of leaving her there alone. Proper cop behavior or not.

Even if it meant hanging out in his truck for the rest of the night.

"I've got the jitters, Mac. Like something's not right.

Maybe it's just residual. Probably the Troy Duncan piece. But it doesn't seem smart for me to stay here alone tonight. Most particularly with no transportation."

There'd been no chance to do car shopping. He mentally added it to the next day's agenda. The chief had told them both to take a couple of days off as they'd left the station that evening.

"I'd already planned on staying," he told her, as honest as always. Maybe, when everything was over, the fear was gone, and he'd moved on to another department, another job, he and Stacy would be friends. "But I was half figuring I'd be sleeping in my truck. This makes it easier. I've got my bag from the safe house, and I already know which room is mine." He grinned at her.

And when she smiled back, he finally let himself soak in the relief of knowing that they'd ended Manning's reign of terror.

There were loose ends to tie up, but Stacy was free from the monster.

The whole Manning thing would slowly sink in. She just had to give it time. Seeing the man again…spending those last moments in a standoff with him on the mountain…was still surreal. A nightmare come to life.

Hearing his voice again had ripped her at her core.

"I don't think I'm going to be able to relax until Manning is sentenced and in prison—hopefully not in this state," she told Mac as they entered her home. Hoping she could find the relief that normally came at the close of a case.

It felt good to be in her own space. And to have him there.

Even if he was acting oddly.

Ordinarily she would have gone in and changed the second she got home. But with him there…

"You want a beer?" she asked as he came back into the great room after dropping his bag in his room. Still in uniform as well. She'd already pulled a bottle of hometown brew out for herself.

And was glad when he took the one she held out to him.

They'd had beers together before. But only in a group. For an office gig. Never just the two of them.

She looked in her refrigerator for something for dinner. After they ate, they'd have to find something else to occupy their time until sleep. The thought of watching some television with Jesse Macdonald just seemed…weird.

She had no idea what kind of shows he liked. And that felt off, too. As much time as they spent together, as close as they were—as much as she cared—she felt bereft, robbed, not knowing such a simple thing about his normal life.

He wasn't talking. Was just standing there. "What's wrong?"

He didn't answer.

"Mac?" she asked, her stomach filling with dread. "What aren't you telling me?"

Manning was going to go free. They didn't have enough solid evidence to hold him. She'd known it. They could hold him for forty-eight hours, and then he'd be out. Able to strike again.

Unless Sierra's Web, or their own detectives, or she and Mac, were able to find irrefutable proof that he'd been the man in her garage the night of the kidnapping. That he'd taken her. Or had hired someone else to do so. Troy Duncan could be found, might turn on him for a deal.

She couldn't rely on that.

But with Manning in custody, law enforcement could

get access to his finances. Sierra's Web had already offered their finance expert to do a deep dive on them.

Something that could happen in less than forty-eight hours, she reminded herself. Took a sip of beer. And looked at Mac.

He'd emptied half his bottle. Was looking down at it. Her chest tightened.

"Mac? You're scaring me." He wasn't looking at her, but she couldn't look away.

"When this is through… I'm changing my mind, Stace." She heard the words. They made no sense. Changing his mind about believing what she'd seen Manning do to Brett?

She shook her head. That made no sense, either.

His gaze, when he finally pinned her with it, held something she'd never seen before. Resolution. Like…he was giving up?

She didn't get it. Frowning, she tried to figure out what was going on, to find a way to be a part of the conversation.

Seeing what she thought was a pained expression on his face, her fear rose to panic level. Was Mac sick? Hurting?

When he pulled a chair out from the table, away from her, sat down in it and took a long swig of beer, she wasn't sure she wanted to hear any more.

Not yet. Not until Troy Duncan was found and Landon Manning was charged and locked up.

At the very least…

"We almost lost you out there today because I wasn't doing my job."

Mac's words brought her up short. She shook her head. "What?"

Had she missed something?

"I was so wrapped up in being just a cop so that nothing else got in the way, shutting out all sensation, relying only on thought, that I stifled the instincts that make me good at the job. I knew you weren't safe out there. Not with a killer on the loose."

Oh. Heady with the relief that had been eluding her ever since she'd seen Manning in handcuffs, she almost smiled. "I knew it, too, Mac. I'm sure everyone knew there was a possibility Manning could find me out there, but, in the first place, that was the plan all along, right? To draw him out?"

He glanced up at her from a lowered brow. Tossed up a hand. She wasn't sure if he was acknowledging her point, or just motioning that he had no response.

"Mariah Southerland's life was at stake. What cop wouldn't put their own life on the line in those circumstances?"

He looked at her then. Hard.

Officers had found the child sitting on a boulder not far off the tourist path. She'd been crying, scared, but otherwise unharmed. Detectives and FBI were working the case but had very few answers. All the child had said was that "he" had told her to sit on the rock and not move or she'd be in big trouble. Anytime anyone, including her parents, asked who'd taken her mommy and daddy's car, who'd left her on the rock, she just kept crying for her daddy. The thought was that the trauma of being trapped in her car seat while someone drove her away from her father had been too much for her. And so, for the time being, they'd quit asking.

"Apart from any of that, I'm an adult, Mac. I made my choice. And that was my right. No matter who you are, my partner, my boss, a stranger on the street…you weren't going to stop me."

His eyes glistened. Not with tears. But she saw the emotion there with a strong reminder of their conversation, their notes, the night before.

"You were worried about me," she said softly, her gaze daring him to look away.

He did not. "To the point of not thinking straight."

"Who found me? Who took down my kidnapper?" He pursed his lips, Held his beer in both hands. As though needing to keep them occupied.

"We care," she said then. "As do a lot of partners, most that I know, who've worked together for a long time. Just because I have the hots for your body all of a sudden, and you might have noticed mine—though I find that harder to believe since I'm not your type—doesn't mean we can't do our jobs. If we're doing it in the back seat of the cruiser while a robbery goes down…then we need to worry."

She'd spent a good part of the night thinking it all through. The lines between fraternization and being human.

"We're all human, Mac. Every single cop out there…"

When she saw his face relax, Stacy wanted to reach out and touch it. To touch him. Place a soft kiss against his lips. Instead, she stood and asked him if he wanted homemade vegetable soup for dinner. She had some in the freezer.

And when he answered in the affirmative, helping himself to a second beer, and searching out saltine crackers and bowls, she went to work with a smile.

Mariah had been found. Landon Manning was in custody. And Mac was there.

All in all, a very good day.

She didn't believe she turned him on. In all that had gone down that day—a little girl's abduction, the capture of a murderer turned kidnapper—the one thought that completely dominated his thoughts as he lay in bed down the hall from his partner was that one. She didn't believe she turned him on.

She wasn't his type.

Showed how little she knew. Problem was, a strong confident woman, a woman who knew exactly what she wanted, didn't generally want to waste time on a guy like him. Someone who had no interest of ever being more than a casual date.

Lying there in desperate need of a cold shower, not wanting to wake her by having one—or to risk her figuring out why he was taking one—Mac almost laughed at the irony in his pain.

Perhaps some of the lighter heart he was feeling that night had to do with the fact that he'd been lucky enough to be given the perfect partner. For him, at any rate.

He and Stacy hadn't had to have some long, drawn-out agonizing heart-to-heart talk to deal with what had, at the time, seemed to him to be an irreparable problem with devastating results. With the awareness between them of personal feelings, those feelings seemed to procreate by leaps and bounds, which had made it seem impossible for them to continue as partners.

With a few simple words, she'd made the impossible possible again.

All cops are human. They all feel. And as long as he and Stacy weren't hooking up—in the back of the car or otherwise—they'd be fine.

Thankful that he hadn't had a chance to call the sheriff yet, to accept the position he'd been offered—something he'd thought he'd had to do as soon as he got Stacy to safety—Mac rolled over. Closed his eyes.

And smelled...smoke?

Flying out of bed, Mac screamed Stacy's name as he pulled on the clean uniform and skivvies he'd laid out the night before—a habit he'd formed after his first emergency call—and rushed out his door. Just as Stacy, also in uniform, though not fully buttoned up, raced toward him.

As they ran through the living area, he saw the brightness of flames out front, and, hearing a telltale rumble, rushed toward the house door leading to the garage. Smoke was already billowing up beneath the automatic garage door.

"There's no flame out back yet," Stacy yelled through a cloth she'd grabbed from the kitchen. The back wall of the garage had no exit. Holding the towel she'd thrown to him, he nodded toward the truck and she ran. Before either of them were fully inside, he pushed the button on the ignition. Yelled at her to buckle up, and, throwing the truck into gear, pushed the accelerator all the way to the floor.

Cracking wood, splintering glass, the sounds of crashing all around them hurt her ears as they burst through the garage wall and out into the night. He spared a quick glance at his partner. Saw her eyes open, no visible blood anywhere, and sped with bumps that sent their heads to the ceiling, as they crossed her desert property and out to an access road to neighboring land.

He couldn't slow down. Tried to think, to assess. Knew only that they had to get out of there, get away, as quickly as possible. He was pretty sure he'd broken a chassis on the truck. But didn't smell gas. The windshield was intact. The broken glass had to have been something in her garage. Maybe head light glass, too.

"You okay?" he hollered as he sped out the service road to the long stretch of highway that would take them farther north. Toward a secluded mountain community for people far richer than he was.

"I got a text," she told him, her voice raised to be heard

over the rumble of noise his truck was making against rough road.

A text? Had he heard her right? Couldn't take his eyes away from his driving that second. Was almost at the road when it hit him that if anyone was watching for an escape, they'd have the road covered. Switching course, keeping his headlights off, he threw the truck into four-wheel drive and careened them toward miles of desert land.

"From Sierra's Web," Stacy said. "It woke me up. It told me to get a burner phone and call a number. Not the one we've been using. It told me not to trust anyone."

Her voice was shaking. His breathing was rickety, too. But he kept his shoulders straight and his head up as he acknowledged what she'd said.

An explosion sounded in the distance. With lead in his gut and pain in his heart, he knew Stacy had just lost her home and everything inside it.

Figured, by the tears in her eyes, that she knew, too.

"We're alive," he told her.

And vowed that one way or another he was going to keep her that way.

Chapter 20

She didn't want to keep traveling across the desert. She had no idea what they were driving into. What lay ahead.

And she didn't want to stop, either, to be a helpless body lying in wait to have a trap sprung upon her.

So when Mac pulled over in the desert behind an eight-foot retaining wall surrounding Golden Gulley, the upscale community built at the base of the Clairvoyant Mountains almost twenty miles west of Saguaro, she looked at him slightly wild-eyed.

"What are we doing?"

"Talking at the moment," he told her. And she nodded. Good. Talking was necessary. They had decisions to make.

"I left my phone at the house," she told him, nervous as hell as she glanced around them. Coming up against a pitch-black darkness that comforted her in the cover it gave them,, and scared her to death, too. Who was out there?

Were they being watched?

Glancing frantically around, she did her best to have their backs. To protect Mac, if she could, from whatever nightmare she couldn't seem to get out of.

"No one followed us." His words were soft. Kind.

Her glance shot back to him, wide-eyed and seeking. "How can you be sure?"

"It's me, Stace."

Just those words. Right. Mac knew how to detect a tail—and how to lose one—better than anyone she'd ever known. Even better than her.

And she jumped back to what she'd wanted to tell him. "I figured, since Hudson told me to get a burner phone, that mine had been compromised."

Mac had pulled out his phone while she was talking, and she stared at it as though it was loaded. And aimed right at her.

"You need to get rid of that. They'll find us." She heard the panic in her tone. And just…couldn't step away from the fear. The godawful paralyzing sense that she just was not going to win.

Or ever be safe again.

"I have a text from Warner, too," he told her. Relief flooded her. She wasn't alone. They'd included Mac. A fresh flood of mind-numbing fright followed right behind. "Turn off your phone! Crush it. Something."

He turned it off. His expression grim as he looked at her. "My text only said that they'd found Troy Duncan. He's been in jail in northern Colorado. Was picked up for drunk driving. He'd been using a fake ID, so wasn't there under his own name. Sierra's Web tracked him down with photo recognition software, running it against Arizona and Colorado mug shots for the past week."

But…she shook her head. That didn't make sense. If Troy hadn't just started the fire at her house and Manning…

"He got out of jail?" That didn't make sense either. *Nothing* was making any sense. Unless. "That's why Sierra's Web told me not to trust anyone? They're trying to tell me someone, one of *us*, is dirty and let Manning go?"

That didn't add up, either.

"I don't know what they're saying, but, Stace, I'm one of them."

He was looking her in the eye, like he was imparting some serious message. She couldn't slow down enough to get it.

"They texted you not to trust anyone. They did not text me the same message, and I'm the lead on the case. Think, Stace."

She nodded. Got where he was going. And couldn't believe he'd even…

"If you want to go, do it," she said to him. And then just kept spewing. "But if you think, for one second, I'm going to let anyone make me doubt you, then you can just stick it where the sun don't shine, buster." The phrase she'd heard her grandfather say growing up just came up out of her.

Slowing down, she met his gaze, the glints of his eyes, in the darkness. "If I can't trust you, Mac, then I just don't care anymore. About running. Or even dying. If I can't trust you, I can't trust me, either, because my heart and soul tell me that you're true blue."

He touched her face. Palm to cheek. Something he'd never done before. And she cradled his palm between her cheek and shoulder. Took a breath.

And began to find her strength.

They had to get down to business. Agreeing with Stacy that it was best to ditch his cell phone, Mac ran it over with the truck several times, and then buried it in the desert.

"We need to lose the truck, too," he told her. "And get to some kind of hiding place before it gets light outside."

"We have to get a burner phone, Mac. To call Sierra's Web and find out what we're up against."

He agreed. And taking the cash he kept in the truck's

glove box, along with the registration and license plate, he grabbed his emergency bag out of the back, which had extra bullets among other things, and started to walk. They both had their guns. Stacy had what cash she'd had in her bedroom. And her Taser and Mace.

"We're both in fresh uniforms. We have our badges," he said, thinking out loud. "I think we need to risk stopping in Golden Gulley for a phone and a few supplies, and then head up into the mountain. At least until we have more information. It'll give us time to come up with a plan."

She kept pace with him easily. Pushed by the devil at her back. And energized by a strange gratitude to be alive with Mac.

"From now on, we don't split up," he told her. "Not even in a separate room in the same building. Not until this is done."

She nodded. Wasn't sure she could pee in front of him, but wasn't going to worry about it, either.

It wasn't likely that they'd have the convenience of a bathroom in any event.

"You think Manning is out?" she asked as they walked. As much to shut up the thoughts in her head as to get an answer. Anything he said at that point would be the same as her—only a guess.

"I think that I hope he's out," he told her, bringing her mind back into clearer focus. He hadn't just guessed. She might be keeping pace physically, but he was steps ahead of her mentally.

And she quickly caught up. "Because with Duncan in jail, if it isn't Manning, and anyone he would have hired would have hightailed it upon his arrest, we have a much bigger problem."

"And not one single suspect." He delivered the grim

news she'd just arrived at herself. As her mind slowed, she heard a replay of the loud bang they'd heard while driving.

Could hardly begin to contemplate the fact that her home was likely the source. That there'd been an explosion. And focused on what she could process. "If we're lucky, everyone will think we blew up with the house," she said.

"I'm guessing that was the plan," Mac agreed, his voice soft on the cool night air. She shivered and he moved closer to her. Put an arm around her shoulders.

Like a pal. Or a parent, she told herself.

But let herself lean on him, anyway. Just for a minute or two.

"They made a mistake then," she said next, as though she and Mac had walked with their bodies tucked together... ever. "Because just like there'd be no evidence left behind, they also have no proof that we died."

His chuckle, so...out of place...had her looking up at him. "What?"

"So you, Stace, to find the bright side. Even in this."

She might have elbowed him—if she'd wanted to lose contact with his side against hers long enough to do so. And if she hadn't heard the admiration in his tone.

"We're going to get through this," she said instead. Conviction lacing her tone. Born of hope, or some natural instinct, she didn't know. Didn't care.

She just had to keep believing.

Until a time came that she couldn't.

The sun was coming up as they neared the town. While most of the thousand or so homes were in gated communities, the main strip was open to public traffic. Mac had been to the area a few times, and could never get over how completely different Golden Gulley looked, just feet away from rough barren desert and succulent mountain that housed mountain lions, rattlesnakes, brown recluse spiders and numerous other potentially deadly prey.

But once you left the dirt road leading up to the small municipality and entered the walls surrounding it, roads were perfectly paved blacktop, with garden dividers separating the lanes. Even at dawn, the overabundance of color from the plethora of flowers hit him. And the fruit trees lining the sidewalk sides of the road were all perfectly groomed, all the same size, sporting luscious looking fruit. Lemons, grapefruit, oranges.

It was the type of place where Stacy deserved to live. Her spirit should be surrounded by beauty.

But even as he had the thought, he knew better. Stacy would shrivel and die if she wasn't charging out to do good.

And she'd suffocate without her open space.

The thought brought him upright as, silently, they headed toward the only place that looked open for business. The first business heading into town. A gas station and store combination.

Stacy had lost her home. But… "I know it's too early to be thinking ahead, but…you've got the big house, Stace. Insurance will probably help rebuild, and there could be other funds once this all gets solved, but in the meantime, you still have your property. And a home."

She nodded. Then said, "I can't really think about that right now."

And he wished he'd kept his mouth shut. But figured he'd made the right choice to remain a working partner, rather than risking anything more. If he hadn't, he wouldn't be there with her. Wouldn't have been at her place when the fire started.

Until she said, "I could always stay with you, if need be."

And then, when he stumbled, she elbowed his side, stepped away and reached for the handle to open the store's front door.

Had she been serious?

Did he want her to have been?

While the thoughts were a distraction they couldn't afford, at the same time, they kept him focused on a future where the danger in front of them had been conquered.

And it dawned on him that's what she'd been doing all along. Holding on to something that felt good, even if only in fantasy, to keep her from giving up.

He was an intelligent man. Knew a lot. Sometimes Stacy knew more.

They made a great team.

He moved quickly through the store, grabbing what he thought they'd need, while she did her own shopping. Mac allowed the possibility that they'd find a way, at the end of the current ordeal, to continue partnering with each other. The thought lifted him.

Gave him a surge of the optimism Stacy generally seemed to have in abundance.

They both bought phones. The clerk didn't ask why two uniformed officers needed them. Just rang them up, bagged them and handed them over with the other supplies, mostly food, they'd picked up. He'd grabbed some extra batteries to add to the one in his emergency bag.

She'd picked up an extra first aid kit. And some pain relievers.

If not for the fact that they'd almost been burned to death in their sleep, and had no transportation, they could have been heading out on an adventure. A part of him chose to pretend for a few seconds that that was the case.

Right until someone else came in the door, and he was

all cop. Ready to defend with his life. The woman was middle-aged. Picking up premade breakfast sandwiches and juice boxes.

He still kept his eye on her. And the small blue sedan she'd parked out front.

Until they were out of the store, and the parking lot was no longer in sight. They immediately headed back out of town, into the desert, toward the mountain. Finding a cove to huddle in together while they activated their phones, taking turns keeping watch.

And then, gun in hand, he crouched, hidden behind shrubbery, and watched the desert, glistening with a near blinding morning sun, while Stacy called the number she'd memorized.

"Thank God you called."

Mac recognized Hudson Warner's voice on speaker-phone, even with the volume down so low. It had occurred to him, the cop, that he'd never seen the text. Had only Stacy's word that it had come at all, let alone that it had been from the verified number. And while he hadn't doubted her, at all, at the moment his mind was all over the planet in terms of foul play. The kidnapper could have sent the text.

"Where are you?"

"In hiding," was all Stacy said. They'd talked about hearing Warner out before giving away any personal information or asking for possible assistance.

The text she'd received had told her not to trust anyone. They had to know why. Had to know if Manning was still in custody.

"When Benson called to say there was a fire at your place, I was afraid we hadn't been in time…"

"I got out." She didn't say how. But described the blast. She got out because Sierra's Web's text had woken her.

Mac didn't like the coincidence of that. Every attack against Stacy had been so carefully planned. So perfectly timed.

And yet, if they'd texted to warn her...

"Landon Manning isn't your guy." Every instinct Mac had went on high alert. Keeping his back to Stacy, standing up right in front of her, his head barely visible above the desert plants, he listened carefully.

"We've had a team on his financials since he was arrested. Everything adds up to a T. The man is an IRS dream. We've got his phone, too. Everything is clean. His phone's location is kept on. I can see where he's been, see money spent. I see funds in and funds out. We've already been deep diving for foreign accounts and made a thorough pass last evening. There's nothing."

As he listened, Mac watched a bobcat slink along slowly in the distance, hunting. He'd never have known it was there if not for the movement. And the sun shining on the golden coat.

The fact that it was still hunting past dawn was a bit odd. Could be rabid.

Hudson's voice continued. "His wife moved out of their big house when he was sent to prison. She's been working, too. He's still getting sponsorship monies and they're all accounted for. In addition, we used his phone to trace him to a ranch in Colorado during the time we saw the black hoodie at the city building. There was no surveillance footage at the ranch, but we caught him on a traffic cam in the area. Following his phone's location, he was here when we saw him on camera in the east valley. We also have him in Arizona this week, but at a campsite an hour south of here. Security cameras show him on-site. Credit card usage supports this as well. He ate at the same diner every meal, including breakfast and lunch the day of the drone strike. Hard as it is to accept, we believe he's telling the truth."

"Is he still in custody?" Stacy asked. He'd left it up to her to tell Sierra's Web that Mac was with her. Until she indicated that she wanted to do so, he was remaining silent.

"Yes. I'm reporting only to you at least until later this morning. It's a corporate decision. I've run it by my partners. If need be, we'll sever our employment with the Saguaro Police Department and take you on pro bono."

Mac turned, met the look of fright in Stacy's wide-eyed glance up at him, and put his finger to his lips.

Something was definitely off. Way off. Life-ending off.

Until they knew what, they had to gain information, not give it.

And in the meantime, he had to be better at everything he did.

He had a feeling he was about to enter a battle that would mean more to him than anything he'd ever done. Or ever would do.

He was not going to let Stacy Waltz die.

His heart would die with her.

Chapter 21

Stacy didn't like hiding at Mac's feet.

She didn't want to cower in front of anyone.

Wished she could bury her head in her knees, close her eyes and sleep. She wasn't so much physically tired as her heart and soul just needed respite.

With each word that Hudson Warner spoke, she felt her chance of inner peace slipping further away. If Mac hadn't been standing there, exuding his warmth all over her, she'd have had to dig impossibly deep to find the strength to hold the phone.

Manning wasn't their guy?

If Warner had talked to him, was making his assertions based on anything Landon Manning had told him, she'd have been able to refute his words. But with the hard proof they'd been seeking for long days and nights right there, she couldn't argue.

As much as her heart needed her to be able to do so.

Weighing her down even more was where that proof led them next.

If not Manning, then who? She didn't even want to think the question, let alone ask it.

But if she wanted to stay alive, she had to know. She couldn't take down a mystery man. Or fight a mirage. And now that Mac was with her...

He'd almost died in her home that night. Because of her. No one else knew he'd been there.

The case had seemingly been over. He'd been going to drop her off—the chief had offered her department transportation of her own for the night, but since he'd told them to take a few days off in the next breath she hadn't wanted to have to return the vehicle in the morning—and then head home.

Two off-duty officers shacking up together would raise eyebrows, if nothing else.

Her thoughts weaved in and out of Warner's proof that Troy Duncan also hadn't been involved in any part of the attempts on Stacy's life. Once they'd found the younger man sitting in a jail cell, and had access to his phone and financials, they were quickly able to rule him out.

"He's still being held," Warner said. "He made the dark web rants under Manning's name, but that's for the FBI to sort out." Rants that Sierra's Web had uncovered. And would be reporting.

Warner had been speaking quickly. Like a machine, clicking off each pertinent piece of evidence.

"I spent precious time filling you in on Manning so that you don't get yourself killed still thinking it's him."

Stacy stood. She couldn't keep hiding. "Who's after me?"

"We don't know yet," Warner said. "But we know he's local. And he could be in your department."

No. Oh, God, no. She felt the blood drain from her face. Her fingers went cold. Mac was the lead on the case, and Warner had only texted him about Duncan's whereabouts.

If Warner was about to tell her Mac wanted her dead, he'd lose all credibility with her. And then what? How were she and Mac, on the lam, going to find out anything?

They would. They had to.

"I'll make this as quick as I can, but you need to know details to understand. And maybe fill in some pieces. The city building access of your files. We've checked every single signature sign in against the surveillance photos in and out of that building during the time your file was accessed. They all check out except for one. We have an illegible signature—a straight line—and a Saguaro Police Department general key card going through the restricted access lane. There are no cameras there.

"There are a couple of those cards," Stacy said. "They're generally kept with reception."

"Fine, we'll check on that. Next. We got parking sticker records from Parker Lake and ran it against owners of white vans in the area. Two names came up. One is a college student who's had his van in Tucson with him since he went back to college after Christmas. The second is owned by the grandson of your chief of police."

Her stomach lurched and her hands started to shake. "The white van that crashed over the mountain...the stolen van...wasn't the one I almost hit."

Stacy glanced up at Mac who just shook his head. But the look in his eyes, he was all there with her. Ready to go to work.

He wasn't leaving her.

She might run from him. Maim him a little if she had to, to get away. He'd almost died in her home. She was not going to let him get himself killed for her.

The chief? She just couldn't believe it.

It made no sense.

And just because the van had been on the road she'd taken home that night didn't mean that it was at all involved in her kidnapping. It had just been something she'd seen minutes before. Something worth checking out. Most particularly since one like it had been stolen and ditched the very next day.

It was as though Mac's voice was in her head talking to her. Giving her facts. Keeping her on track.

She'd been a little off-kilter that night. Had almost run into the van. Could have been her fault.

It had been heading from a pullout.

The kid could have been parking with his girlfriend.

"The four-wheeler at the end of Stacy's drive, and at the crime scene…your description matches department four-wheelers. As well any number ones owned privately by members of the force. And who better to know your schedule. And one of our techies was able to enhance security camera footage to determine the brand of drone used by the airstrip." Warner just kept talking. "It's the same kind the Saguaro Police Department just requisitioned and received."

Her glance met Mac's and held. She hadn't even known the department was looking at drones. Had he?

His eyes didn't talk to her. Didn't tell her either way.

Even if the drones were the same brand, it didn't mean they were the same make or model. Or that one was missing.

"I intended to get the drone information to Jesse Macdonald, as soon as it was reported to me, but you all were already out on the Amber Alert."

Wait. He'd still been reporting to Mac before Mariah's disappearance, but hadn't texted him that night…

She was still having the thought, not even beginning to process yet, when Hudson Warner said, "As to yesterday's supposed kidnapping…"

Supposed?

"Kelly Chase, our expert psychiatrist and a child specialist, did an interview with Mariah Southerland late yesterday afternoon. Her mother asked Chief Benson to have her interviewed by a child specialist. He called me and I set it up. I wasn't in the interview, but I've heard tapes from it, and have been in consultation with Kelly. She's convinced that the child wasn't kidnapped. She was left on that boulder by her father. He threatened her that if she moved, she'd be in big trouble. The reason the little girl just cried for her daddy every time anyone asked anything was because she was answering their question. Who took you? Daddy. Who left you there? Daddy."

"So what are you telling me?" Jimmy Southerland had made up a kidnapping to get the entire police force out looking for her? Made no sense.

"Did you know that Jesse Macdonald called Southerland once the two of you were split up on the mountain yesterday, looking for the child?"

Stacy's skin crawled. Her throat clogged. Her chest so tight she couldn't draw air.

She shook her head.

Dropped down to the ground, the phone still clutched in her fingers. The entire world had gone mad.

She gasped for air and a question came out. "Why?" She wasn't sure who she was talking to. God, maybe.

"We don't know yet." Warner's voice just kept coming. She needed to hang up. Couldn't move enough to make it happen. "We have no motive. Not for any of the people involved."

"It makes no sense," she said then. Talking because when she did, her body did the natural thing and took a breath. "What good did it do to get us all out on the mountain? If it wasn't something Manning had done to occupy every member of the force and get me alone?"

Mac had already had her alone. That one was a no-brainer.

But if someone was trying to frame him?

Or just plain kill her one heartbeat at a time…

Making her think Mac had betrayed her.

It still made no sense. Drawing them all out to the mountain.

Except that Manning had said he'd seen someone, hadn't he? That he'd been there to keep her safe?

Or was she just imagining things?

"Talk to Landon Manning," she said then. "He rambled so much yesterday and I had to tune it all out. I knew he was trying to manipulate me. But I think he said something about coming to town to talk to me. Heard the fuss, came out to the mountain, knowing I would be there. He wanted to help search since, you know, he's living the rest of his life in honor of Brett…" Her voice broke. She made herself breathe and started again. "He said that he thought someone was following me…"

Mac would be the logical suspect on that one. He'd waited for her to set off and then had headed to his own coordinates.

She couldn't help what conclusions others might draw. She knew it wasn't him.

As the shock filtered from her brain, the sense that someone was trying to make her doubt her own heart, was trying to manipulate her into giving up control of her mind took hold, and she shook her head.

Started to think. To talk. "The kidnapper could have seen Manning, knew he'd been seen, cut bait, put Mariah on that boulder, told her to always just answer 'Daddy' to any question and no one would hurt her family..."

"Great. We'll talk to Manning..."

"And Mr. Warner, please don't waste any time or resources looking into Mac. I can vouch for him over and over...he's the one who saved me from the drone. And found me over the mountain, who called for help and saved my life."

"Have you ever heard of the hero complex?"

Of course she had. She was a cop. Had a degree in criminal justice. "You think Mac is deliberately causing all these near deaths just so he can save me?"

He'd met her in the hallway of her home that morning, before she'd been able to get to him, to wake him to warn him. Had rushed her out of the home. Known where to drive to keep them away from the flames.

He'd ended her standoff with Landon Manning the day before.

Everything inside Stacy stilled. Just her and stillness.

She'd recently told Jesse Macdonald that she had the hots for him. Had intimated that she loved him in her note that night at the safe house.

What more could he possibly want?

It took every ounce of self-control Mac had to just stand there. To hear what was being said about him, from a source he'd been trusting with Stacy's life, and do...nothing.

He needed to grab the phone and crush it beneath his shoe. To hit a rock so hard with his fist he'd know nothing but the physical pain.

He *knew* he wasn't the one who'd been trying to kill Stacy Waltz. But if everyone thought he was...the real killer would get her. He couldn't just walk away.

No matter what she thought. What she believed.

You think Mac is deliberately causing all these near deaths just so he can save me?

He heard her words again, and while a logical voice in his brain could see how she'd been so thoroughly played she couldn't be blamed for doubting him, another part, a very small, barely acknowledged part, shriveled up and died.

Or started to, until she said, "Every second you spend looking at Mac, you're giving my intended killer the chance to succeed." He heard the words. The strength behind them.

And went weak. Every sinew. Every muscle. Defensive energy drained out of him.

A surge of warmth hit him, one he'd never ever felt with such impact in his life, and in the next second, he started to fill up again. With the cold anger it was going to take to kill a killer. If that's what it took.

"Jesse Macdonald is standing right here, Mr. Warner," she said then, with no warning to Mac. "He was with me in my home last night when the fire started. Asleep in bed. I'm thinking even someone with a major hero complex wouldn't kill himself in the process of trying to look good."

My home. Asleep in bed. Hearing her say the words, admitting something that could hurt her reputation with the department, brought another surge of warmth. He let the distraction pass through him. Focused on finding whoever was after Stacy.

The other end of the line had fallen completely silent. "We need a motive," Mac said then. "Why would someone from the department want her dead? What does Stacy have that anyone would want? Or anyone in town for that matter? We've been over her life, you've been over her life. What did we miss?"

He shot the questions like the professional he was. With a good dose of personal fire beneath them. No one was going to hurt the woman who'd just heard evidence against him, and had chosen to listen to her heart, to believe in him, instead.

He'd never personally witnessed such a show of...the love she'd talked about. The kind that lasted through anything. Even death.

"Ms. Waltz, please take me off speakerphone."

Stacy glanced at Mac. He nodded. She pressed to end the open call.

After a few seconds Mac heard her say, "Elizabeth." Verifying her middle name? Or had Warner told her to say her middle name if she was in trouble?

She'd turned so he couldn't see her expression. But he heard the conviction in her, "Yes... With my life, yes... I'm positive. I've been riding with Jesse Macdonald for five years. Look at our cases. There's no sign of hero complex. If anything, he's unassuming. Doesn't take the credit he's offered. He just turned down a major job offer with the sheriff's department that would have made him look like a real savior. And I've got one more piece of information for you. I just this past week told Mac that I'm interested in him, personally, and he chose for us to remain work partners. That's not a guy trying to impress me. If you want to assign someone to verify everything, all but that last, which you'll have to take on my word, you do that. Go verify. But we need help out here, and since it's us against the world at the moment, we're trusting you to be it."

She was silent for another moment, and then Mac heard her say, "Yes, I will."

At which time, she tapped her phone and said, "Go ahead."

Hudson Warner came back on the line. The man didn't apologize. There was no need. He'd been doing the job Mac had been asking him to do.

They discussed, the three of them, Sierra's Web coming to get them. To meet them somewhere. But they determined that if they could stay gone for at least a few hours, it would give Warner and his teams, including forensic experts, the chance to spend the time at the latest crime scene. And not draw any attention to the Golden Gulch area.

At the moment, whoever wanted Stacy dead could assume she'd burned up in the fire. An official report might say there were no signs of human remains in the debris. But not yet. Not with the explosion. There'd be too much to comb through to know for certain.

And Mac was expected to be taking a few days off. No one would be looking for him.

Not unless they wanted him involved in the investigation now that it looked to be closer to home. He expected "they" wouldn't. Sierra's Web would be watching for calls to his line, and have someone watching his home, just in case.

His truck abandoned in the desert was a concern. He and Stacy gave as much of a description of its location as they could. Hudson Warner said he'd take care of getting it out of there and into a scrapyard as soon as possible.

And he and Stacy agreed to call in to the same secure number every two hours until further notice.

In the meantime, they had to climb. To find a cave.

And to set their boundaries.

Just like Stacy had wanted to do two days before.

Mac was beginning to realize that his partner was far wiser than he'd even thought. Scales ahead of him. In matters of life, as well as work.

What he did with the information, he had no idea.

And couldn't think about it, either. Until he knew they had her someplace safe.

Chapter 22

They hiked for a couple of hours. Up, and over, too. Circling around a mountain range that was so large it would take days to get to the other side. And yet, they'd already made it to the top of two small peaks.

They didn't stand there long. From the first peak, she'd made a call to Sierra's Web. The two-hour check in. As far as Sierra's Web could tell, it was believed that Stacy had perished with her house. The department appeared to be in a state of shock and grief. Warner reported that Benson had told him Mac had a few days off and he wasn't planning to call him back. There was nothing Mac could do to help Stacy, and he needed the time. Benson swore that the department would pay Sierra's Web whatever it took to help their detectives find whoever had done this to her. Then Warner had told Benson about the van registration with the lake sticker. Heard that Benson's eighteen-year-old grandson was not at home and his phone appeared to be off. No one knew where he was. Or they were denying knowing, at any rate.

It was feasible that Benson didn't know that—the young man, who was well known and liked around the station, had driven to the lake, and possible that the young man had gotten ahold of a courthouse secure access card, used it and returned it. But why?

Same with finding a way to access the department drones. He'd likely have heard his grandfather speak of them. Had known they were there. Not yet in service. His grandfather trusted him. She could see it happening.

What on earth would the kid have against Stacy?

"He has to be working for someone," Stacy told Mac after they'd hung up. And then, at his instruction, had destroyed her new phone.

He was already scoping out the landscape. "It's a burner. They can't trace the number, but..."

"...he department could put a trace on all towers from which a phone call had come, giving them our approximate location," Stacy finished his statement for him.

Mac started back down the peak. Something they'd already determined they were going to do after the call. The trek up had been for phone service only. "Assuming that the killer has the number to the secure line Warner gave you," he said, lifting a hand up to her.

Without thinking, she took it, held on and jumped down to level ground next to him, before they half slid down the next patch directly in front of them.

It was only when he'd let go of her hand that she realized what they'd done. Holding hands. Him offering to help. Her accepting.

A definite variation from their protocol. More like a couple, than partners.

Working partners. Police partners.

Shaking off the tingling of warmth his grip had left behind, she continued the rest of the way down to the small gulley they were planning to follow west, keeping enough distance between them that neither made any other natural moves that included them touching.

And staying close enough that they could both duck behind the same rock face if necessary. Two hours later, planning to use Mac's burner to make the second call to Sierra's Web, they stood at the top of the peak they'd just climbed, but were so far into the mountain range that they had no service.

Stacy looked at Mac. "Our job is to stay hidden," she told him, hardly believing that she was saying the words.

From the beginning she'd refused to let the fiend force her into hiding. Had been fighting what had turned out to be the inevitable ever since. She'd been so certain she wouldn't hide, and yet there they were, further into the Clairvoyants than she'd ever thought she'd be, than she'd ever wanted to be. Hiding.

Was her death inevitable, too?

"Right," Mac said, frowning at her as they stood looking out over lower peaks and valleys, and up at higher ones. "Where are you going with that?"

"I think it's time to make the choice to stay out here for the night. We've got the provisions. We definitely know how to prepare safe lodging. The ditch perimeter, all the things Hudson talked about, those warnings of someone getting close will work for mountain lions and anything or anyone else who might happen upon us. But we need time to prepare. We can't just keep hiking farther into nowhere, waiting to make a call in the hopes of getting the all-clear to come home. Darkness will fall and we'll be unprepared to meet it…"

She was rambling. Heard the panic starting to taint her tone. But stood completely by what she said. She was afraid. And still thinking clearly. Whatever game anyone was trying to play with her mind…she wasn't going to let them win that one.

Life or death.

Mac looked around them. "I agree," he said, but didn't

seem at all happy about the plan. He seemed to be studying the entire Clairvoyant landscape. And then pointed. "There."

It took her a few tries, him pointing out landmarks that she could find to get to what he'd seen. And once her gaze arrived, she knew he'd found the perfect spot. A cave set back far enough from the edge of a cliff to be private—and to give ample warning if anyone got at all close.

They could live there for years and never be invaded.

The idea—her and Mac staying lost for years—wasn't nearly as unwelcome as she'd have thought, even a day earlier. Another couple of hours passed as they made their way to the cave he'd spotted, keeping an eye on their coordinates so they'd know how to get back out again. They spent another few hours getting the place set up for the night, and Stacy continued to entertain herself with the fantasy. She and Mac, alone in the wilderness, like the settlers of old, or the Native Americans who really had lived for centuries in those very mountains. Setting up house.

Securing the cave, first, with a flashlight check of even the smallest crannies, they used the branch of a pine tree as a broom. And then stripping paloverde branches of their leaves, mixing them with other small brush to make sleeping pallets. From there they concentrated on their perimeter.

It was good to be working toward something other than running. The only conversation they had pertained to the tasks at hand. Ideas for making them safest. Which plants and desert ground cover to use to make the loudest sound if stepped upon. They tested some out.

Laughed a little.

And all the while, they were watching over their shoulders. Making certain that if they got close to the cliff edge, they were down low so they wouldn't be seen.

On constant look out for drones—though as far in as they were, the chances of one finding them were minimal. Unless their want-to-be captor was close.

Which was possible.

So they remained on constant vigil.

They'd eaten semicold breakfast sandwiches purchased from the convenience store, followed by the banana and orange Stacy had picked up. Had consumed four granola bars. Peanut butter on bread was on the docket for dinner. They had one loaf. And then a box of crackers to put the high protein spread on as well.

Mac had had a wearable water pack in his emergency bag. She'd been lucky enough to find a second in the store. They'd filled them and had been wearing them, drinking from the straws that were always accessible with a turn of their heads, throughout the day. He'd packed a couple of gallons more water at the base of the emergency bag he'd strapped to his back with elastic cords as they'd set out. He'd strapped his go-duffel to her back, and it had smaller water bottles in it as well as other supplies.

Thank God for Mac's truck, and the preparedness their daily grind had instilled in them.

If they hadn't been on the run, hiding for their lives, she might have found the adventure fun. Because it was with Mac.

One thing she knew for sure—if they survived, she was going to remember the experience for the rest of her life.

Keeping a handle on her imagination, fighting the panic, was easier when she was physically exerting herself. But then they were done.

Dusk was falling.

Mac did a last check of their area, keeping the beam of

his flashlight low to the ground so it couldn't be seen from above or below them, making them potential sitting ducks.

Then, turning off the big light, he ducked his tall, athletic body into the cave and sat down on his roughly hewn mat. Right beside hers.

They'd been up since before dawn. Needed to sleep. It had been a physically grueling day.

She handed him a peanut butter sandwich.

"How long do you think it will be before Sierra's Web sends someone looking for us?" she asked him. They'd failed to find cell service to make any other calls.

He shrugged. "If they've got the killer, I'd think they're already looking. If not…" He took another bite, chewed, swallowed as though he didn't have a care in the world.

The peanut butter was sticking in her throat. She didn't want to waste water washing down every bite.

Mac spoke again. "Knowing our plan, I'm counting on them figuring that we're out of service. If they want to find us, chances are they will. They've got Luke Dennison, his team, and search and rescue dogs at their disposal. If you're still considered dead, they're not going to want to do anything to make anyone think otherwise. Instead, their investigation will be just what Warner described from his call with Benson—instead of finding the killer to save a life, they're finding him so he can be prosecuted for murder."

And another option, one he didn't mention… Sierra's Web could have a mole.

Fear struck anew.

She'd been trying not to doubt Hudson Warner or any of the Sierra's Web team members. She'd certainly done nothing to make any of them want her dead. But she'd have trusted her child's life to Chief Benson, too. If she'd had a child.

"We're screwed, aren't we?" The words were so unlike her, even she was shocked by them. Mac's snap of the head in her direction made his reaction clear. She couldn't read his expression, but she knew him well enough to fill in the blanks.

"Anything could or might find us, Stace, but we're well armed and we have the mountain at our back. Our odds are good."

"As long as no one gets close enough to throw something in here…"

The cave had already begun closing in on her. She'd been gassed and burned out of her home. Had an explosive drop out of the sky and nearly hit her head. What was next, a fireball from a mountainside perch? Landing on their pallets made out of flammable brush?

Mac's shoulder rammed into hers. "You aren't going to quit on me now, are you?" he asked, his tone teasing.

But with a note she didn't recognize.

"You're worried, too." She said the words out loud. Because of the surreal circumstances. The darkness.

They had no ability to run through a mountain range in the dark. No transportation. No way to make a phone call, even.

"I don't like not knowing," he told her then.

She shivered. The night's cold would come. They had shelter, but no blankets. Just the long, leaf-filled branches they'd brought in to cover themselves.

And many hours to get through before the light came again.

Mac would have liked to try a night hike. Or sit out under the stars. Both would be preferable to being caged in. And it would be poor police work. Putting them at risk. Not only from whatever human or humans were out to get Stacy, but from all the other predators that hunted for dinner every night.

Stacy talked about television, of all things. Wanting to know what shows he watched.

Not many. He wasn't a big sitter.

What shows he'd watched as a kid.

He'd been more interested in the gaming console hooked up to the television in one house and forced to listen to kiddie shows in the other.

When that conversation soon petered out, she dragged him into a conversation about cop shows. Those he'd seen. Both in the past, and more recently as well.

Eventually, Stacy produced a small pack of disposable disinfecting hand wipes, taking one for herself, giving him one and they took turns heading to a pre-dug hole to relieve themselves, him last so he could fill the hole with dirt. And they laid back.

He waited for the deep, even breathing that should tell him she was asleep. After long minutes of feeling her restlessness, he began to pray for that breathing.

For her. And himself, too.

Instead, he lay there and listened. Catching every coyote howl. Every owl hoot. And myriad other sounds he didn't recognize.

Feeling Stacy's body heat, even as the night's chill seeped into his bones. She was smaller, so she had to be feeling the cold even more than he was. But hadn't yet pulled her branches over herself for cover.

Should he do it for her? In case she was asleep and just restless about it? For all he knew, she fidgeted and sighed every night when she was out.

In the cave the temperature shouldn't drop as low as freezing. Was a bit of chill worth risking waking her?

Her hand moved, ever so slightly. He wasn't sure if it was a sleeping twitch or deliberate movement, but the appendage was moving again. Touching the back of his fingers.

Then…nothing.

Did she need the comfort of human touch?

Closing his eyes again, trying to will himself to keep them that way and give his body some chance at sleep, he had to admit the warmth of Stacy's hand resting there was…nice.

He heard another sigh. He was really going to have to look up the possibility of people emitting what sounded like such deliberate gusts of air in their sleep. Opening his eyes, he turned his head to look at her, and thought he saw the glints of opened eyes staring back at him.

For no good reason, Mac turned his hand over. Felt her palm fall against his. Gave her time to snatch it away. When she didn't, he threaded his fingers through hers. Holding on.

When her fingers gave an answering grip, pleasure shot through him, pooling in his groin.

"I can't help thinking…" Her voice sounded thick in the darkness. Could just be that the air in the cave lacked circulation. He didn't think so. But he wanted that to be the reason for the odd tone as he laid there, failing to respond. To draw her out.

"What if this is the last night of my life?"

No. He wasn't going to let her give up. How he'd prevent it, he had no idea. But he had to keep her alive. No matter what the morning brought to them.

Or, at the very least, give up his life for her, trying to save her. Die before her. Because he sure as hell didn't want to live without her.

The thought stuck there. Stunning him into complete silence.

"I don't want to spend my last hours on earth lying in fear." She just wasn't stopping. He held tight to her hand.

He knew what she wanted.

He just couldn't give it to her.

Well…technically he could. The bulge beneath the zipper in his uniform pants was proof of that. It wasn't something she could see in the dark.

He had to be the strong one of the two of them. Because they were going to get out of there alive. The reign of terror would end, with guilty parties locked up for the rest of their lives. Or damned close to it.

And he and Stacy would need to be able to continue on.

He couldn't lose her.

Agonizing minutes passed. Her hand slowly left his.

And Mac swallowed a lump of regret that nearly choked him.

Chapter 23

Stacy had one clear thought.

He wasn't telling her no.

Mac wouldn't roll over and kiss her. He'd never initiate anything between them. If she knew him at all, she knew that much.

And she did know him. Sometimes better than he knew himself.

Just like he did with her.

It was the type of knowing that came from complete trust.

And for her, true love. The kind that, once there never died.

That existed without condition.

Maybe she was living in fantasyland. Creating a fairy tale in her mind as a result of experiencing more trauma than she could bear.

She didn't really care.

Not anymore.

Truth was, life could end at any moment, for anyone.

And she didn't want to go out lying in a bed of panic.

Moving her freed hand slowly downward, she heard his low hungry moan and lifted her palm against the side of Mac's upper thigh. Lightly grazing its entire length. After scaling to the top, she just kept going. Across the plain of flat stomach he'd risen to meet her and on to the next peak.

She knew it would be there.

Didn't take a partner who knew you well to figure that one out. The way his body had stiffened the second her hand had touched his had clued her in on that one.

Her knuckles got there first, but her palm was right behind them, sliding over the jutting mountain on Mac's belly. And resting there.

Not moving. Just cupping him.

Giving him a chance to roll over. A long chance.

Had his interest started to abate, she'd have rolled over. Instead, she felt the manly muscle moving against her palm. A jerk. A spasm. Nothing overt. Just Mac's desire letting her know it was there.

She laid there, on fire, pools of sweetness swirling in her lower body, her nipples tingling. And…laid there.

Unsure of what to do next.

She was a great cop. A great friend. She was sure some great other things, too. She was no femme fatale.

"I've…uh…actually never initiated…things before," she told the walls of the cave. Hoping Mac would hear.

"You're doing a fine job of it." The voice…it was Mac's… and something completely new, too. A depth, a timbre that ignited her all over again. With more force than ever before. Even in her wildest dream of him.

Still, he laid there. Mostly still beneath her.

Figuring she'd had all the permission she needed, Stacy forgot about where she was, or why. Her mind filled with Mac.

All Mac.

Rolling, sliding one of her legs between his, she rested her breasts over his upper arm and chest, letting her nipples feel the pressure of her weight against him, and dropped her mouth to his.

* * *

Mac gave her all the time he could to change her mind. To figure out that she didn't really want what her imagination had conjured up to keep her alive during her time on the boulders, waiting to be rescued.

Even after those sweet lips—the most delicious ever—touched his, he held back. Letting her experiment.

Problem was, she didn't quit. Her lips explored his, causing his penis to feel like it was coming out of his skin. He opened his mouth just enough to make it easier for her to see what was there and be done, and then she was moaning. Pushing her tongue into his mouth.

"You sure you want this?" he practically growled then.

Her eyes were open, pointed right at him. He yearned to see into them. Didn't dare turn on the flashlight. "Positive." He heard the hunger in her voice.

Reminded himself she'd been married for nearly five years—she knew what she was starting—he rolled her over, grinding his aching penis into her thigh just long enough to give him a second of relief, and then kissed her fully. His lips devouring hers. His tongue dueling and dancing with his partner's. Treating her to things he never should have shared with her.

Things he'd been wanting to show her ever since she'd admitted that sex wasn't all it was cracked up to be.

And once he'd broken all the rules, there was no holding him back. Sitting up, he started in on her buttons. "I need to see beneath the uniform," he told her. "I want the woman."

He'd admitted it. He wanted her.

Real bad.

And got the shock of his life. For all her strength and lack of girliness, his partner liked extremely...girly...underthings.

"Stacy Waltz, please tell me you haven't been wearing these to work every day for the past five years."

"Can't," she said breathlessly, squirming and pushing sheer, lace covered breasts into his hands. "I've always had a thing for underwear that makes me feel like a woman…"

Undies. He could hardly stop himself from heading straight down there. Ripping the pants off her and seeing what the bottom half of her intimate decor did for her.

The thought of how quickly things would end stopped him.

They had a good ten hours until dawn.

And he was going to fill as many of them as he could with ecstasy.

Him and Stace.

How had he not known it would be that mind-blowingly incredible?

And he hadn't even been inside of her yet.

If she was going to die, she wanted it to be right there in that cave. With Jesse Macdonald's body inside of hers.

Thirty years of living and she finally knew that sex really could elevate you to another planet. One where only sensation and the highest joys existed. There were no thoughts other than finding more pleasure. No awareness of anything around them. Just a need for as much as she could get as long as she could get it.

Mac traveled with condoms in his wallet, of course. And the wallet always went to bed in the next day's uniform pants, so he was ready to jump and go at a moments' notice.

She'd once teased him about that, when she'd asked how he'd gotten ready so quickly on one of their out-of-town emergencies, but that night, she was overjoyed to have them there.

Though, she wasn't the one who'd thought of them. She'd been whirling on ahead without any thought of precaution.

When the last condom was used, he stayed inside her as long as he could. And then held her until she slept.

It was a good sleep. Deep. Peaceful. The best she'd had in…she didn't know when.

So much so that when she awoke, just as dawn was breaking, she didn't want to. She just wanted to stay right there in her Stacy-in-wonderland cave forever.

Opening her eyes, she glanced toward Mac…only to find empty space where he should have been.

Sitting up, she quickly dressed, was just pulling up her pants when he burst into the cave. "Grab everything you can," he said, his voice almost harsh. "We have to go."

Heart thudding, her brain still yearning for the land of foggy happiness, Stacy shoved her feet into her shoes as she stuffed the couple of things she'd left out of her bag back in and turned for Mac to strap it to her body. While he fixed his own pack, she strapped on the rest of her gear, helped him clip his pack, and they were out.

"Grab your pallet," Mac said as she exited, bending to get his own. "Throw it over the cliff."

He wanted no sign of them having spent the night there.

Which could only mean one thing. Something had spooked him into thinking that someone was after them.

"It's not Sierra's Web?" she asked, as soon as they were heading around the side of the mountain to go…somewhere.

"I don't know." His words were sharp. "There are two of them. Together. About the same height. Maybe half an hour's climb down, across the gulley. I saw the sun glint off binocular lenses, I think. I'm not sure if they caught me or not."

But the lenses had been pointed in their direction. She got that much.

And just because someone was in the mountains with a pair of binoculars didn't mean they'd been searching for Stacy.

She and Mac weren't going to wait around to find out.

"Give me your phone," she told Mac. Took it from him when he immediately pulled it out of his pocket and handed it over. "I'll keep an eye on it to see when we get service," she told him. Turning it on, and then, as soon as no bars showed, back off again. "We can figure out between now and then whether or not we call in."

It had to be all business. She got that. Wanted it.

If they were being hunted, an unforeseen bullet could come flying at any moment.

But she missed him.

Missed *them*.

And had a feeling that they were never going to be *them* again.

Mac hadn't even looked at her when he'd come into the cave. Nor when they'd headed back outside again.

The harshness in his voice—it was as new as the passion had been the night before.

And she figured she knew why.

She'd pushed him into a corner—Jesse Macdonald didn't believe in forever, and never kept his lovers in his life for long. She'd left him no choice.

And she had to pay the price.

She'd had the night she wanted.

But in the process, she'd lost the man she loved.

Mac had one thought. Keep Stacy safe. He didn't give a damn if she was a cop and fully trained and capable of protecting herself in her own right. If Stacy's kidnapper was in the mountains, death could come any second.

All the little caves and indentures, the overhangs, boulders and natural growth that he used to keep them unseen, would also hide a killer.

Stacy was staying close, watching for phone service. He was purposely guiding them to a high point of the mountain to get just that.

She'd provided granola bars. An energy bar. He wondered, but didn't ask, if the food was sticking in her throat as it was his.

They'd split their last banana.

While he led the way.

The interior was safest, but they had to know their enemy. If Stacy's kidnapper had been caught, and Sierra's Web was out there looking for them, there was no need to take risks climbing deeper into a world where they had little chance of survival once their supplies ran out.

If Sierra's Web was in the mountains to find whoever was after her, he had to know that, too. To have some indication of who might be friendly. To get Stacy to a safe place and guard her while the others found the wanted man.

"I'm scared to death that we'll come upon one of our own," Stacy said, walking closely beside him as they slowed to flatten their stomachs against a cliffside and sidestep to what he believed was a ledge that would give them service. "Do we shoot first, so we aren't killed? Or trust that they're out here to help us?"

He didn't have an answer to that, so said nothing. He couldn't borrow trouble. He had enough of it in every step he was taking.

Stacy turned on the phone as soon as they were on more solid ground. Full battery. No service. For the next hour, it was more of the same. They'd seen no sign of another human out there with them. Which worried him. If the two people he'd seen were on their side, they'd be trying to be visible to them.

And his quest for phone service was sending them farther and farther out of the mountain range. He didn't like that, either.

"Got it!" Stacy's low cry of victory came just as they reached the top of the peak on the outer edge of the mountain. Standing in the middle of a patch of six-foot plant growth, they could see, but not be seen.

He hoped.

She dialed. He gritted his teeth together as he kept watch. And listened.

One ring...

"Warner here, are you okay?"

"Yes," Stacy answered. "Someone's out here."

"We know. We're there, too. Dennison and his team headed out at first light. They're all in beige pants and orange shirts. They'll have on orange wristbands with Dennison's unit number on them. Trust no one else."

The words were delivered ominously. Every syllable succinct.

"We can't stay on here long enough to be traced," Warner continued. "We've closed in on your kidnappers. There are least three of them. Can't verify if police are involved or not. Benson's grandson is. No time for a full report. Just watch your backs. Every second. And watch for the orange wristbands."

With Dennison's unit number. Mac noticed that the tech expert didn't designate the number. Warner knew that Mac and Stacy knew it. Authorities had used it to designate the Dennison case the previous year.

"We need another cave, Mac. We've got to let the mountain have our backs."

"But if we're seen, they could shoot from another mountaintop and obliterate us. They could shoot an explosive in…" She knew it as well as he did.

Was she giving up? Just wanting to curl up in his arms so that if she went, she died feeling good? She'd said something similar the night before. Speaking again of the dreams she'd had while her SUV had been balanced on the edge of death.

"Our best bet is to keep moving. It's hardest to hit a moving target." He wasn't letting her plan her death. They weren't giving up.

He got it. So many days of being strong against constant fear. Existing with death on her shoulder every second. It would wear on anyone.

And blurted the one thing he believed would keep her looking toward the future. "You know, Stacy, all those times last night, and not pulling out right away. There's a chance something slipped through. You could be in the process, right now of…well…you know."

He couldn't say it. Couldn't even think the words that would complete that sentence.

But she obviously did. He saw the most beautiful expression flash over her face…

Then the sharp blast of a gunshot in the canyon obliterated the moment.

He dove. Fell to the ground on top of her, his body gouged by the various things in the duffel he'd strapped to her back. No way a bullet would make it through his pack, his body and her stuff to her heart. Slowly, he scooted them up to the wall of a small peak.

Another shot fired. Echoing through the small valley to the left of them.

"It's not coming in our direction." He felt Stacy's body move beneath him as she spoke, and slowly rolled himself off her.

She was right. One shot had come from the north. The other from the south.

Just one of each.

"Could be Dennison's team found them," she continued.

Or "they" found Dennison's team, Mac knew, but didn't say out loud. He was trying to keep her positive.

He owed it to her after five years of her optimism keeping his head above water.

Keeping Stacy believing in a future was the purpose he clung to as they started to slowly climb again, moving back to the interior of the mountain, toward a smaller, higher peak, where, hopefully, they'd have a view of those looking for them down below.

They'd had a head start.

And, other than scrapes and bruises, were in great physical condition.

They had plenty of ammunition and were both steady shots. Both hit the bull's-eye every time they went to the shooting range.

Besides…if there was the slightest chance that something *had* slipped through the night before, a chance that Stacy could have what she most wanted, a child of her own, a little family in her big house, then he had even more reason to make sure she stayed alive.

For her. And for any possible new life that might be forming.

He didn't let himself figure into the picture.

He clung to the vision for her.

And pressed onward.

Chapter 24

She knew there was no baby. Nothing had leaked. Mac had been overly careful about that. But the fact that he'd dug so deep to try to give her strength...

Even if he hadn't been able to finish the sentence...

She clung to the thought, a little smile inside, as she quaked with fright. Fearing with every step she took that it could be her last.

Would she hear the bullet before it hit her? Or would she just be there one second, and then not?

Or worse, would she hear the bullet and see Mac fall?

Shaking her head, knowing full well that she had to focus all her mental abilities on keeping watch, looking for any sign of movement, Stacy trekked on.

For hours.

Shots rang out a second time. Closer to them. Heart pounding, she moved up to Mac's side. Ducking with him into a little cavern. Her hand touching his.

He didn't pull away.

"What do you want to do?" she asked him softly. And then continued, "Because I'm tired of being hunted."

"You want to hunt."

"Don't you?"

He didn't answer.

"You do, don't you?"

They were both perusing the entire horizon within view, each with their free hand on their gun, as they spoke.

"It's our way," he finally said, sounding more like the man she'd been trusting with her life for the past five years.

"Then let's get to it," she told him, finding her own core steady as they finally came face-to-face with what could be their last major choice as partners. Their last one on earth.

"We don't know our enemy," he said, his tone firm, though almost at a whisper.

Reminding her that their hunters, their prey, could be moving closer to them. Could already have them in their sights.

Maybe not their physical bodies—shots would have fired at them already if that was the case—but the killers could be closing in on their location.

"We know Benson's grandson," she shot back, just as softly. And fiercely. Linking her fingers with his. "We have to assume we're equally matched," she added. The kid had long expressed the desire to become a cop. Had been training at the shooting range since he turned eighteen. And he had others working with him. Possibly cops. Possibly Jimmy Southerland.

"We can't hope to reason with them," Mac said then. "If we had any idea of a motive, or how high up this goes, then maybe, but right now...we'd come off as desperate."

She agreed. "Which means we have to take them down before they get us."

As he wrapped his grip around the fingers touching his, Mac's other hand pulled his gun out of its holster. "We're outnumbered. Warner said there were at least three of them."

Looking her in the eye, he continued. "If we have to shoot first, we do."

She nodded. Understood what he was telling her. They weren't going to play this one according to protocol.

She jerked, her heart pounding.

"What?" Mac's whisper was right in her ear.

More with her eyes than her head, she nodded to the right. And then down. Several yards below, heading up toward the cavern in which they hid, were two men. Wearing jeans. No orange shirts. No wristbands. Neither of them Benson's grandson. Nor were they Saguaro cops. She'd seen them before, though.

"They're miners," she whispered back. "They work for Tom Brandon."

Mac's elbow pushed against hers. "I've seen Jimmy at the bar, playing pool with one of them."

Her heart sank, and for a split second, she and Mac held gazes. Sierra's Web had told them the kidnapping had been faked...

The men split up. Veered off on either side of them.

As though they knew exactly where they were.

And it hit her.

They weren't going to get the chance to hunt.

They'd already been prey in a trap before they'd started the conversation.

Mac's gut was speaking to him. Urgently. "We have to jump them." He made the pronouncement. Didn't allow another thought. "It's our only shot."

When Stacy nodded, the walls around his heart shored up.

He squeezed her hand. Felt her fingers on his, as though saying goodbye.

And maybe they were.

But they'd go out fighting for their lives.

Not die as sitting ducks holding hands.

He'd promised himself he'd save her. His mouth filled with bitter bile as he nodded for her to head off to the right while he broke left. She knew how to keep herself covered.

As did he.

The next minutes needed his full focus. If he got to one attacker soon enough he could…

Hearing a branch crack directly below him, he had no more thought.

Holstering his gun, he jumped. Landed on heavy flesh. Rolled.

Heard the gun go off. Felt the blow against him. Blood pooling against his hand.

And landed a fist in the face inches away from his— one that was staring at him with blank eyes, wide open.

What the hell?

Jumping up, watching the rugged, bearded man flop to the ground, Mac still felt no pain. Saw the blood on his hands.

Saw the blood pooling on the ground from beneath the other man's body.

And, pulling his gun from his holster, backed to the mountainside, pointed in a circular direction all around him.

Where had the shot come from?

And why hadn't another followed it, killing him?

Without waiting to find out, Mac scaled around the edge of the drop-off, and, keeping behind boulders, made his way higher up on the mountain.

Listening.

Looking for Stacy.

Had she shot his man?

Made no sense.

That would have left her back open to the guy's accomplice…

Stark cold fear struck him.

If she'd given her life to save his…

He slid, he clawed and he ran. Stepping as silently as possible, going from boulder to boulder up the mountain, taking it on an angle, bringing him closer to his partner's direction.

At least the one she'd started off in.

I might need to call in a dead body. He threw the thought away. Along with the fact that he had no way to contact anyone. No matter the state in which he might find Stacy's body.

He'd long since passed the cavern where he'd last touched his partner. Squeezed her hand. Was sweating, feeling the blood pounding through his veins.

Stopped behind a boulder to assess his location.

And heard, "Mac!" A harsh whisper.

One he knew.

Turning, he saw Stacy, fully intact, crawling down an incline toward him.

Throat tight, he ran toward her, hauling her behind the boulder with him. Pulling her into his arms and squeezing with every ounce of energy in him.

She was alive.

"Mac… I can't breathe." Stacy whispered the words against her lover's neck. She was holding on as tightly as he was. Didn't ever want to let go…

Or to feel his arms drop away from her.

Which they did.

"My man's dead," he said then, studying her gaze intently. And she nodded. Blinking away tears that she refused to let fall.

He was there. Standing in front of her.

Perfectly okay.

"I know."

"You do it?" The three words were all that came, like he could barely get them out. He thought she'd shot the man? As soon as she'd seen him, she'd assumed he had.

She shook her head. "I don't know who," she said. "I had my guy in sight. Was ready to jump when I heard the shot. The guy I was after stopped, and then took off in the opposite direction."

"In my direction?"

"No, that's what was so weird. He took off down the mountain. Was out of sight before I could get a good shot off."

"So who shot Jimmy's friend?" he asked, nodding toward the ground he'd left behind him.

"No idea." But… "Sierra's Web?" She desperately wanted to think so.

Mac didn't seem convinced either way. He just kept perusing the landscape visible from both sides of their boulder. "Whoever it was, either they are an excellent marksman, or they missed their guy," he said. "I'd already jumped him. We were rolling on the ground when the bullet hit." He showed her his hands. Small streaks of smeared blood were left, and it looked like he'd tried to wipe off a whole lot of it.

Reaching into her pack, she pulled out her wipes. She couldn't help it. She had to do something. Had to get the stain of a killer's blood off Mac's hands.

She didn't know what it said to her that he let her do so.

He was as freaked out as she was? Nearing the end of a tether that felt as though it was tightening around her throat, too?

She'd find her strength, and then, in a low moment, or when the adrenaline dropped off, the fear would be there. Waiting insidiously, an accomplice to those who wanted her dead. A product of their campaign to kill her.

But Mac…he'd always been so calm. So…not looking at her as though she was a pot of gold. Which he currently seemed to be doing. She tried to hold the gaze, to soak in it, but his head just kept on moving. Taking in their surroundings.

"We have to keep going," he said. "We risk being seen, but if we just sit, we have less chance of finding these guys. And more chance of being ambushed."

He wanted to stay on the interior of the mountain for another hour or so, and then move up and outward before nightfall. At least to make a phone call.

She agreed. Was ready to get moving. To try to wipe her mind of the fact that they were leaving a dead body behind them.

Incredibly thankful that it wasn't Mac's.

When she'd heard that gunshot…in the direction she knew he'd gone…

"I love you, Mac."

He'd stepped around the edge of the mountain wall behind their boulder. Stopped. Didn't turn around. And then started out again.

She was right behind him. Watching one side of them while he watched the other, the mountain hugging their sides.

"When I heard that last shot…"

He climbed up a boulder. She followed. "I can't die without telling you."

"You aren't going to die." His voice was gruff. He kept moving.

And she kept up with him every step of the way.

Chapter 25

Mac had a real bad feeling about that shot. If it had been meant for him, because he was reaching for his gun, why wasn't he dead?

His first thought—that he'd been shot, since he knew he hadn't fired his own gun—had slowed him down. There'd been a couple of opportunities for the shooter to get off another round. To get Mac on the second try.

And he hadn't done so.

If it was Sierra's Web, they'd have come to get him.

Unless they'd seen imminent danger in the area.

Which meant he and Stacy could be walking into a minefield at any second.

Stacy.

Loved him.

Had put it right out there.

He couldn't deal with it.

Had to stay focused.

"We need to go up and out now," he said, changing course as he spoke. "They know we're here. Climbing out puts us in more danger of being seen, which is what makes it something they won't expect us to do."

"You think it's possible these guys are turning on each other?" Stacy asked from behind him, indicating to him that she was once again on the same mental path he'd been taking.

His partner.

"I don't know. Either that or someone knows why they want you dead, and they want to be the one to kill you."

He didn't mince words.

They were fighting demons they didn't know, trying to avoid bullets from areas they couldn't possibly pinpoint. They couldn't predict their killer because they didn't have any idea what drove him. Had no inkling of a motive.

He was no longer certain he could keep her alive.

Their time was running out.

They were halfway up the tallest peak inside the mountain range. They planned to get over it and start heading down as they worked their way out over smaller peaks to the edge of the range. They'd be exiting on the Saguaro side of the Clairvoyants—if they made it that far.

They'd eaten more bread and peanut butter. Had had to refill their water packs. Stopping only long enough to prepare and pour, consuming as they traveled.

She was growing slowly numb inside. Figured it was partially a product of fatigue. Physical, yeah, but more psychological.

Who hated her so much?

A dead man lay over the mountain peaks behind them. A life lost because of that hate.

It made no sense to her.

Mac's abrupt stop in front of her shocked her out of her thoughts. He held up a hand, pointing over the cliff they'd been traveling along because of the taller, fuller trees that gave them cover.

Reaching his side, she tucked up against him, to see

what he had to show her, and felt his arm come down out of the point and rest around her.

It took a moment to see what had caught his attention. The movement was slight. There and then gone. But as her gaze adjusted, she predicted the next move. And the next.

A man was moving stealthily among the cacti, desert trees and brush that grew lower on the mountain. Every few steps he stopped, gazing upward. She had him about one hundred yards below them. But one thing was clear. There was no way they could head over the mountain as planned without him seeing them.

And worse… "He's got an assault rifle," she whispered.

And no orange or beige at all.

Where was Sierra's Web? Why weren't they on the trail of those following Mac and Stacy?

Doubts crept in again. Was anyone on their side?

How could an entire police force and nationally renowned firm of experts all be against her? Want her dead?

They'd come far enough out of the mountain, were high enough above other peaks, that she had cell service. Had had it for the past twenty minutes.

Still wasn't sure she wanted to tell Mac.

Maybe they shouldn't call out.

They couldn't live in the mountain for much longer.

She had to trust someone.

Starting with her partner.

"We've got cell service. You want to call out?" she asked him.

He shook his head. Just as she saw another body move. Tall, but slighter, not far behind the rifleman.

"Could just be a couple of guys out doing some illegal hunting," she said then. The disgusting problem wasn't uncommon. Sportsman wanting mountain lions to stuff and hang.

"You might be right, but we can't take the chance," Mac told her.

That's when she heard a tumble of small rocks behind them. Turning, she caught the top of a head before it disappeared. Drawing her gun, she saw Mac do the same, and he motioned for her to move slowly along the mountain wall to a fairly large gouge in the rock face that would have to serve as cover. If the head continued up and around the mountain, they'd have a chance to take the guy down before he could get them.

Unless…before there'd been two of them. One on each side…

She turned, gun in front of her, and saw Mac lunge at the man who'd just rounded a corner, gun pointed. Mac landed before the gun went off. Deflected the bullet. She kept her gun aimed and ready looking for a shot as the men scuffled. And kept an eye behind her, too. Preparing to rapidly fire two shots in opposite directions.

Mac had knocked his assailant's gun away, but the man was fighting hard. Landing blows. Moving Mac and himself toward the fallen weapon, while pounding her partner's gun hand against the ground. Mac kneed the guy, maintained hold of the gun, until…

She swung around as she heard a foreign sound from behind her. A scuffle.

And saw Benson's grandson round the curve of the mountain, a pistol pointed right at her. She'd been a second too late.

"NO!" Mac heard Stacy's scream. Saw her fly through the air as he wrestled for control of his gun. He was filled with an inhuman anger, propelling his arm upward, going for the jugular. He let his gun go, using both arms to pull tight against his assailant's neck, just as he heard a shot.

"Stacy!" he called out automatically. Calling to her as she might lay dying. He felt his prey go limp in his arms and jumped up, grabbing his gun. Running over to the bodies in the dirt. Stacy on top of Benson's grandson, her knee shoved up between the young man's legs and her forearm across his throat.

He didn't see blood. But he heard a sound behind him. Turned to see the man he'd strangled, eyes open, still lying on the ground, but reaching for his own gun.

"Stacy!" he hollered again, his voice filled with agony, and warning, throwing himself on top of her. And felt blood splatter hit him on the cheek.

"Mac!" Stacy screamed.

He glanced behind him, saw the shooter dead on the ground, his gun still clutched in his hand.

"Tell him…" His gaze swung to the body on the ground, seeing the wound just below the left collarbone. Blood pouring out of it.

He shoved his fist on it, applying pressure as hard as he could. Was aware of Stacy throwing off her bag. Heard a zipper.

"Hold on," he said then. Only starting to realize what had just taken place.

Benson's grandson had shot the man Mac had already subdued. And that man had come back enough to shoot him back?

Or had he been aiming at Stacy?

The young man groaned, and Mac pressed harder, fearing, from the amount of blood, that a major artery had been hit. "Hold on," he said again. "We've got you."

"Tell him I took them down," Scott Benson said. "I didn't know. I swear I didn't know."

Stacy was back, kneeling down with gauze and her supply of wet cloths. "Shh," she said, helping Mac get the gauze packed into the wound, as he continued to apply pressure. "You can tell him yourself as soon as we get you down from here."

"I didn't know," Scott said again, his look urgent as, with wide open eyes, he held Mac's gaze. "He said I was helping him to protect his land. To guard it. They'd found gold, and I was going to get a percent for guarding the land..."

Half thinking that the kid was hallucinating, Mac nodded anyway. "I'll tell him," he said.

"I didn't know."

"Know what?" Stacy asked.

"That I was...keeping...watch...so they could kill you."

Mac saw her hand shake as she wiped at Scott's face, and reached for the phone. He heard her swear, assumed there was no service.

"I took the drone." Scott's eyes were clear again as they focused on Mac. "From the station." His story came in patches. Scott's voice growing weaker with every one. "Wanted to check it out... Broke it... Bruce said he'd fix it... They used it... I found it... Said I was already in too deep." Scott lifted his head, as though he was trying to sit up. With pressure still hard on the young man's chest, Mac held him down. Held his head while it lay back against the hard dirt.

"Said I'd take the fall for all of them." Scott's words were disjointed. His eyes closed. "My grandpa too, if I talked..." Scott's voice drifted off. His eyes closed.

Mac almost hoped they stayed that way. That the young man could remain unconscious until they got a helicopter up to rescue him, but a part of him knew that wasn't likely to happen. So when Scott's eyes popped open again, Mac said, "Is there anything else you want me to tell him?"

Getting his last words to his grandfather seemed to be keeping the guy alive. He'd dig deep for any words he could think of to pull from him.

"I'm going farther up," Stacy said. "I have to get service."

"No!" Mac couldn't risk it. Not again.

Scott's mouth moved. He gurgled a little. Then said, "Two more."

"There are two more out here?" Mac asked. Scott didn't respond.

Then, very softly, eyes closed, mouth hardly moving, Scott said, "Tell him I got him." His head fell to the right.

"He's still got a pulse," Mac told Stacy. "Let's get some branches, make a stretcher," but even as he said the words, he knew his plans were hopeless. He and Stacy couldn't carry a stretcher out between them. The terrain was too rough.

They not only risked doing further damage to Scott Benson, they risked getting themselves killed as well.

Grabbing a heavy enough rock to suffice, he placed it over the gauze, using it to keep pressure on the wound in place of his hand. "Let's get to cell service," he said.

And was glad when Stacy took his hand as they headed around the mountain wall once again.

They were alive. Stacy couldn't let herself think about anything else for the first minutes after she and Mac set off. They were both on guard, watching, careful as always, fully aware that though she'd survived once again, she was still not out of danger.

Maybe she never would be.

"I don't get it," she told Mac. "They found more gold? That's what's behind all of this? So what? My grandfather was the one who complained about the mining, the trucks, the noise, the pollution, destroying the earth. He filed complaints, but nothing ever came of them. Tom Brandon owns the land. He's allowed to harvest his own minerals. My grandfather built the other house, moved, and the two of them tolerated each other just fine after that."

A whirring sound interrupted whatever response he might have made. Both of them looked up at the same time. Saw the helicopter. Waved their hands and ran back toward Scott Benson.

She worried that the chopper wouldn't have enough room to land, but the pilot had a much better view than she did and found a flat piece of ground just over a small hill from the ledge where they'd almost lost their lives yet again.

In minutes a paramedic was tending to Scott. But she knew, even before she saw the woman shake her head, that the young man was gone.

All he'd ever wanted to be was a cop. He'd been too young to attend the academy. To join up. So he'd been offering private protection service to a friend.

And then had gone full metal in the mountain to try to prevent his consorts from killing Stacy. That was how Chief Benson was going to hear the story.

Scott might have let greed get the better of him. He shouldn't have stolen the drone from the department. They'd probably never know what else he'd done, knowingly or not, to help those who were after Stacy. But in the end, he'd risked his life to protect Stacy and Mac.

He'd gotten himself killed attempting to save them.

"I wonder if he was the one who shot Jimmy's friend?" Stacy said to Mac as they stood together, as partners, with a foot of desert ground between them, and watched paramedics load Scott's body onto a stretcher. Strapping it down for a secure ride.

"I'm going to say yes," Mac told her, his face grim.

"We still have two more out there," she said then. Did they stay to get them? Or ride back in the helicopter and hide out somewhere else?

She had no home. No possessions, other than the uniform on her back.

Mac met her gaze. Held on. Looked like he was about to say something when the helicopter pilot approached from over the hill. Heading straight to them.

"I'm supposed to tell you both to climb aboard," he said. "Sierra's Web took down the remaining suspects. It's all done. We're here to take you home."

Stacy took a step back. Didn't want to go.

She didn't know the guy. How did she know if he was telling her the truth?

It was done?

The horror was over?

"Hudson Warner and Chief Benson are waiting for you at the hospital," the man told them. Stacy still didn't move.

The pilot pulled out his phone, showed them a photo of the chief and Warner. Sent as proof. Just in case.

And she stood immobile. Couldn't make her muscles work.

Not until she felt Mac's hand in the middle of her back. A light touch. The touch of a stranger. Guiding her over the hill.

It was over.

Mac saw Stacy to a seat right behind the pilot. She strapped in, expecting him to sit across from her, but he moved to a seat in the back. On one side of the stretcher.

It was truly over.

All of it.

For a second there, as tears filled her eyes, she wished she and Mac were back in their cave.

Thought of the night before.

And prayed that the memory would be enough to help her start her life over one more time.

Chapter 26

Stacy was safe. His job was done. Mac kept repeating the words to himself as he was checked over in the emergency room, and was just as quickly released.

Benson and Warner were both talking to Stacy, who'd also been checked, as he came out. Even in her dirty, well-used uniform, ponytail awry, she looked beautiful to him.

And more than he'd ever be able to handle.

She was safe. His job was done. He heard the words as a rhythm, right along with the tires of the chief's unmarked, high end police sedan on the highway as they headed back out to Saguaro Bend. Stacy was up front with the boss, Warner in the back with him. Mac figured it worked well that way. His partner hadn't looked him in the eye since they'd been brought down from the mountain.

Not that he'd given her much of a chance.

Back at the station, they were met with a line of cheers as he and Stacy walked down the hallway together to the conference room for their debriefing.

From there, he'd be free to head home.

He'd need transportation.

Stacy needed that plus a home.

Random thoughts hit him as he walked along the floor of the station that had been more of a home to him than any other he'd ever known. He accepted a couple of pats on the back. Nodded. But held back, too, letting Stacy collect most of the love from their pseudo family. She'd go far in the Saguaro Police Department. He'd be shocked if she wasn't offered a promotion. Lieutenant at least. Maybe assistant chief. The woman had a way with people that many cops lacked.

Lieutenant Stahl was a great cop. A great leader of cops. But he didn't deal with the public in any way that could be deemed a success.

Cheers and voices faded as they entered the conference room. Leaving a deafening silence as Warner and Benson came in behind them, closing the door.

Stacy sat in the chair she'd been using throughout the case.

He took his next to her because it was about the case.

Benson started in, stopped, teared up and started in again. He thanked them for trying to save his grandson. For making his last moments as comfortable as possible.

Then he apologized to them. "I knew he was heading for trouble," Heath Benson said. "His parents didn't marry and he never really knew his dad. He got in with some bad kids in the east valley. Older guys. I tried to tell my daughter, but she just kept saying she could handle things…and I stepped too far back. The van… I didn't put that together. When the one showed up at the bottom of the mountain… it seemed so obvious that it was connected. I blame myself fully on that one. The van that went over is now evidence for the Denver police in a case involving a ring of vehicle thefts. But back to us…when I heard that the drone used in the east valley was the same as the ones we'd requisitioned… I knew."

The man looked down. Shook his head.

"You should be proud of him, sir." Mac spoke with heart. With soul. He'd watched a young man die. Had heard his last words. And spent the next five minutes repeating them, verbatim, to his grieving boss.

When his voice faded, Stacy's picked up. "He died with honor, sir. Doing the job of a cop even without a badge. He saved Mac's life out there."

The dead man they'd left on the bluff. Jimmy Souther-land's friend.

"About that," Warner said, looking at the chief, who nodded. "Southerland was in on it all along," he told the two of them. "It was his four-wheeler at Stacy's house that night. And that she saw just before she went over the mountainside."

"Tom Brandon is in custody as well," Benson said, with a shake of his head. "His wife's agreed to testify against him. He was the ringleader of it all."

"And are we ever going to hear just what *it* was?" Stacy's voice sounded odd. Fed up. Angry. And lost.

It was the lost part that Mac had to fight off. But just until Hudson Warner started talking. Then Mac just sat in shock.

"Brandon and his son Bruce hit a new vein of gold where they've been mining for years. It led to what turned out to be a much larger, much less polluted vein that covered enough land to turn them all into millionaires."

"On their land?" Mac asked.

"Yes," Benson said. "But not originally. It was on the land he bought from Stacy's grandfather."

Then Warner started to talk again. "We kept coming back to those records of Stacy's being messed with. Why would someone be looking at her property records? If it wasn't Manning…everyone else in the area either knows the history of the land or could ask dozens of others who knew. So we did a deeper dive."

"What kind of deeper dive do you do on land ownership?" Stacy asked, frowning,

But Mac had a strong idea he knew what was coming. And said, "Mineral rights." He should have guessed.

And when Warner nodded, Mac sat back. Way back. Scooting his chair away from the table. So much for Stacy getting a promotion.

Chances were, she wouldn't be working another day in her life.

"Mineral rights?" She sounded confused. "They go with the land."

Hudson Warner shook his head, looking straight at Stacy. "Your grandfather sold Brandon that land decades ago, but, because he knew Brandon was a miner, and hated the mining, he kept the mineral rights, which automatically pass on to any heir he has left, before they can revert to the land owner."

Mac seemed to feel Stacy's intake of breath, as much as he heard it. She stood up, glaring at Hudson Warner, as though the man could somehow take back what he'd said. "Are you telling me I almost died, Mac almost died for some damned rights? Why didn't he just ask me for them? Or offer to share them with me?"

Mac could answer that one. "He couldn't risk you holding your grandfather's views and shutting off any possibility of him getting that gold."

Nodding abruptly, over and over, she stood there. And then said, "I own a gold mine worth millions?" as though that part was just sinking in.

Warner's face was deadpan as he nodded.

Until Stacy fell back into her chair. Then, the technical expert smiled and said, "Congratulations."

At which time Stacy broke into tears.

Floods of them.

And Mac quietly let himself out to find a change of clothes.

She was a millionaire? Owned a gold mine? Stacy could hardly comprehend the information. She'd had a shower at the station, leaving the conference room almost as soon as Mac had. She'd called her father, who hadn't picked up, and left a message for him to call her. She had a new burner phone, given to her until she could get herself a new cell of her own.

She'd been told she was being put up by the department at a lovely hotel not far from Saguaro, at least for a night or two. Longer if she wanted.

And they were providing her with an unmarked department vehicle until she could purchase a new one of her own.

Mac had been given the same—the car portion, that was.

They'd walked out to the parking lot together. She'd felt nothing at all like herself as she'd told everyone she'd be fine and headed out as soon as she'd seen Mac getting ready to go.

"It's wild, huh?" she said, to break the unbearably awkward silence between them.

She'd known she'd lost him. That once they returned home, if they did, nothing would be the same between them.

A pile of money wasn't going to help that.

"No one deserves it more than you do, Stace." His tone was... Mac from the mountain. And for a second her heart soared. Could miracles happen?

And make fairy tales come to life?

Complete with a happy-ever-after?

No sooner had she had the thought than Mac nodded at her, pulling out his keys, said, "Take care," and headed across to the car he'd been assigned.

Hers was right in front of her. He'd walked her to her car.

And then left.

Take care?

For a second Stacy started after him. Angry. Filled with fight.

And just as quickly as the will to go after him had come, it dwindled. Jesse Macdonald had written it all down for her.

At her request.

He'd told her what he did and didn't want. What he could and couldn't do.

He'd made his choices.

And they were right for him.

With that thought, she got into her car, pulled behind Mac into traffic, and as soon as she could, turned to head to the closest box store.

She had some shopping to do.

Possessions to replace.

Before she could check into a hotel where she knew no one, to eat by herself, and try to figure out what she was going to do with the rest of her life.

Mac drove around Saguaro, every street, past his parents' houses, the people he'd known all his life. And eventually ended up at home. He typed in his passcode at the gate of the community. Something he'd have to do until he got a new truck, and then a new bar code sticker for the windshield.

He pulled up to his place.

Stacy was safe.

And while she'd lost memorabilia that she'd never be able to replace, she had the means to go wherever she wanted.

Buy whatever she desired.

Be whomever she chose.

He couldn't have scripted a better ending.

For her.

And for him, too.

He was getting exactly what he wanted.

Stacy was safe.

And he was home. Alone. Just as he'd ordained.

Exactly what he wanted.

Except that…he didn't.

His house, the thought of a new truck, the flattering offer from the sheriff's office that he'd just called to accept… none of it gave him any pleasure at all.

The things that he used to value most didn't matter to him.

He drove around the block. Looked at his house again. Thought of another long shower, some sweat shorts and a T-shirt. Ordering delivery from three different places and eating parts of all of them in bed.

Didn't matter.

Second time around, he headed back out the gate. Drove to Stacy's hotel. Took an elevator up to the room he'd heard the chief mention when he'd given her the key.

And knocked.

He heard her approach the door. Waited for the pause as she checked the peephole. Stacy was Stacy. She'd always check the peephole.

Even before…

When she opened the door, still wearing her uniform, a glorious smile on her face, he shook his head.

"How do you do it?" he asked.

Still grinning from ear to ear she replied, "Do what?"

"I just broke your heart and you're still glad to see me."

"I will always be glad to see you, Jesse Macdonald. I love you. The person you are. Not who I need you to be for me."

He didn't walk into the room.

Didn't trust himself to be alone in there with her and a bed and nobody looking for either one of them.

"I'm not sure I'd be good at...any of what you want. Having kids...the idea isn't horrible. But then we're both stressed and tired. Our careers are pulling at us. The two-year-old is having fits and the baby is teething and..."

She put a finger to his mouth. Her digit was shaking. "I just poured a glass of wine," she told him, sounding relatively steady. "You mind if we take this inside, because I really need a gulp or two."

When she put it like that...and the residual reaction of her uncertain soft touch still throbbing against his lips...

Hands in his pockets, giving himself a firm command to keep them there, he followed slowly behind her. More of a meander. Like him being there with her was no big deal.

Just partners, coming down from days of running for their lives.

They needed a private debrief, was all.

She uncapped a bottle of beer. Handed it to him.

And one hand came out of his pocket.

He drank an eighth of the bottle. Pulled it away.

"I just... I don't want the love to turn to hate," he said then. "I can't bear the thought of ever hating you. But I figured out something that's even worse."

She'd taken a seat at the dining section of the room. Lifted her black police shoes to the table, crossing her ankles.

"What's that?"

Did she have any idea how sexy she looked?

Was she doing it on purpose?

"Not loving at all."

Her feet fell down to the carpet with enough force to have been heard in the room below.

"Excuse me?" Her chin was wavering. Her eyes shooting warmth, and suddenly moist, too.

"Not feeling a deep love for one person is one thing. But to feel it…and waste it…" He shrugged. Held his beer with one hand. Kept the other trapped.

Just not at all sure what he was hoping to accomplish.

"Are you saying you love me, Mac?"

With a sideways cock of his head, he said, "I'd have thought that much was obvious. The problem is…how do we…"

He didn't get the words out. Stacy flew at him. Knocking the bottle out of his hand to pour out on the carpet, as she wrapped her arms around his neck and covered his mouth.

His arms came around her. No permission. They just did.

When she finally pulled back, he started to talk, and she shook her head. "Just let me…okay?"

He nodded.

"This isn't a case, Mac. The only plan we're going to have going in is to promise to remember this…right now… this minute. How we feel. And the time on the mountain, the best and worst…any time life starts to get the better of us, we come back to what our deepest hearts have learned."

She made it sound so…possible. And the way she'd greeted him at the door…knowing him…happy with whatever he could give her…

Mac gave up. Then and there.

Just quit.

Stopped fighting the one battle he suddenly realized he'd been meant to lose. "I love you, Stacy Waltz."

"And I love you, Jesse Macdonald," she told him. "My Mac," kissing him even as she led him to the bed.

They fell together. Got out of their uniforms with much more finesse than they'd used the night before, fell to the quickly exposed sheets and touched each other in ways they'd already discovered. And in new ways, too.

Right up until Mac hovered above her spread legs, and she closed them. "Condom," she said. "I'm guessing you didn't manage to refill your wallet sometime today?"

He opened her legs again. "You want to fill that big house of yours with babies, right?"

Her eyes glistened. "Yes, but not until you're ready..."

He looked her straight in the eye as he plunged into her. Kept hold of her gaze as they moved together, moaned together.

And came together.

Figuring that if the fates had any more bounty left in store for them, they'd just made their first baby.

Epilogue

Mac took a bite of chocolate-covered strawberry and fed the rest to Stacy. Juice dripped over her chin and down to her chest.

He licked it off.

Then sat back in the limousine, sliding his hand up beneath her slim-fitting, long white dress just a little, enjoying the darkness with her.

"My parents handled themselves well," he said. Purposely bringing up family to calm himself down enough to wait until they were in the honeymoon suite the men and women in the department had rented for them at one of Phoenix's five-star resorts. A wedding present for their new, very lovely and very determined assistant chief.

A position that would have Stacy's brain receiving all information, and giving suggestions as she saw fit, on all major cases, without actually being out on the streets. Unless it was to attend a police or community function.

"I think my dad's actually going to stay in town this time," she said, sounding happier than he'd ever heard her. And in the three months since they'd come down off the mountain, Mac had heard a lot of happiness from her. More than he'd ever thought possible.

He'd expounded a fair amount of his own, too. Something he was growing used to. And liked even more for the fact that the emotion wasn't completely new. He and Stacy had been happy together for five years.

And he'd figured out that as time passed, trust in what lasted grew.

His trust in her as a cop.

A loyal partner.

A lover.

And a lifetime.

"I told him about the baby," she said then.

And Mac smiled. He'd known she would. They'd only found out for sure the day before. Had decided to wait to announce until after the wedding. But... Adam Sorenson was a man you just wanted to share your news with.

"And?"

"He talked about selling his place in town and building a small place on that driveway that's left on our land."

Her driveway.

They'd had the land cleared. Small nubs of new growth were already beginning to show through the ash and dirt.

They'd shopped for all new furniture for the big house, too. She hadn't wanted to live anywhere else, despite her newfound wealth. And he didn't, either. She'd bought the Brandon property. Had the house taken down. The mine closed.

And was in the process of getting the mining operation going where Tom had struck gold. Out of sight and sound of any residence. She was creating much-needed jobs for Saguaro, and was giving the city 50 percent of the profits, too.

The rest, she'd signed over to a company the two of them owned together.

There might be a time when Stacy "got over" the trauma she'd been through. When she quit waking up in the night in cold sweats, reaching for Mac. And falling back asleep in his arms. A day could come when she quit missing the things she'd lost—all the keepsakes from her former years that kept memories of other times alive. The day could come. He didn't think so.

But he understood that she was still going to be okay. That she *was* okay. That they'd always be okay.

Because love didn't burn up in fire or get shot. It didn't die.

It just kept growing.

And building.

As long as those who'd felt its power took care to remember it was there.

* * * * *